ATHENA'S ASHES

I0637538

THE STAR THIEF CHRONICLES
BOOK TWO

JAMIE GREY

Book Layout ©2013 BookDesignTemplates.com
Cover Design: Christa Holland, Paper and Sage

Athena's Ashes / Jamie Grey -- 1st ed.

To my parents.

Thank you for letting me check out a dozen books at the library every week. All that reading has finally paid off!

ONE

For someone who was supposed to be the best thief in the galaxy, Renna had been spending entirely too much time locked up lately.

Not that a high-security hospital room in a secret MYTH base was much of a prison for her, but the IV line snaking from her arm might as well have been a pair of Saltani iron handcuffs. She swung her feet over the edge of the lumpy bed and watched the holoscreen on the far wall. Stats scrolled past, red text on the black background. Her vitals were stable; blood pressure was fine. Looking at her chart, she was the picture of health.

Except for the cybernetic implant taking over her mind.

Renna rubbed the back of her neck where the original incision site had started to throb. It had been doing that a lot lately, thanks to Navang's depraved experiments and the drugs he'd injected her with. Drugs he'd used to create a whole army of human-robot hybrids.

Thana Samil, the MYTH doctor in charge of her case, said it was nothing to worry about, but Renna knew better. In the five days she'd been locked up here in the MYTH facility, the pain in her head had only gotten worse.

And then there were the weird side effects. She hadn't stepped foot outside her room, but she knew a bank of super-servers sat in the northeast corner of the facility, as if she'd drawn the blueprints herself. Communications relays resided on each corner of the roof. She'd even felt the throb of the automated defense cannons guarding the facility.

If the doctor and her team didn't figure out how to slow down the integration between the implant and her nervous system, Renna would be a walking machine before she had the chance to stop the person behind all this.

Pallas.

If Renna's hunch was right, the traitor was close enough to touch. Maybe even inside this facility. But she'd never find him if she was trapped here for the rest of her short life. She slid off the bed to pace the stark room, careful not to disturb the needles in her arm. Six steps to the door. Turn around. Six steps back to the bed.

She'd done this to herself. She'd volunteered to be locked away and dissected, just to keep Myka Aldani safe. To keep *Finn* safe.

Her pacing slowed as a pang of longing shot through her. Captain Nick Finn. Former gang member turned MYTH soldier and her first childhood crush. Now, she suspected that she'd fallen in love with him, which worried her. Renna had spent most of her life making sure that *didn't* happen. Yet somehow his bright blue eyes, square jaw, and straight-laced moral code had slipped through her defenses.

And oh, the way his fingers had tantalizingly stroked her most sensitive places...

Renna felt herself go warm as she remembered the last time she'd been with him. She'd escaped from Navang, but not before he'd started the process of taking over her implant. Finn had spent the night in her room, waiting for her to regain consciousness, and she'd practically begged him to make love to her. She could still feel the heat of his skin. She inhaled, half-expecting to smell his scent—sandalwood, gun grease, and something that was inexplicably him.

She needed to know what was going on between them, and if that meant more bunk-side exploration, she'd totally take one for the team. But until she knew how to stop Pallas and put an end to these experiments, she wasn't going anywhere, despite the urge she had to run back to Finn. She'd stay in this facility and let them poke and prod her, just to protect him and Myka. Even if it made her crazy.

The lock on her door beeped, and high-heeled shoes clacked across the threshold. Speak of the devil.

Renna turned as Dr. Samil entered the room. The young doctor wore a pleasant smile despite the slightly frazzled appearance of her long blonde hair escaping the messy bun she always wore. Renna leaned back against the edge of her bed. "Do you always have to look so happy at the prospect of stabbing me with those instruments of torture?"

Dr. Samil's blue eyes sparkled. "For someone who's done her

share of killing, I can't believe you have a needle phobia."

"We all have our weaknesses," Renna said with a shrug. "Pointy, shiny, metal bloodsuckers just happen to be mine."

Samil set her holopad down on the counter and pressed her thumb to the scanner to unlock the drawer. She pulled out a tray of tools. "I guess it's time for the torture to begin."

The doctor brushed her bangs back off her forehead, and Renna gritted her teeth as she slid back onto the bed, preparing to be poked.

"How'd the last test go? Is the implant fusing normally?" Renna stared pointedly at the far wall as Samil fumbled with the glinting needles on the tray. "Or whatever normal is in this fucked-up situation."

The doctor shook her head, flicking a finger against one of the syringes before pushing the plunger. Pink-tinged liquid squirted from the needle. "I wish I knew. I haven't seen anything like this before. It's fascinating." Her voice was full of that breathless excitement Renna had come to hate. "Whatever Dr. Navang did prompted your ordinarily harmless implant to start fusing directly with your nervous system. If my hunch is right, any other cybernetic implants installed during this time would also fuse to your body. You could even start picking up other electronic signals."

Renna flinched. Not only because of the quick jab of pain as the doctor deftly slid the needle into her arm, but because she was already picking up those electronic signals. Things were progressing faster than the doctor knew.

"Relax. I promise this won't hurt."

"That's what Navang said." Renna tilted her head and fixed

Samil with a frown. "And look how that turned out."

The doctor finished injecting Renna with whatever drug cocktail she was trying today, then smiled. "There. Wasn't so bad, was it? I promise I don't like torturing you any more than you like being tortured. Unfortunately, I need one more sample to check your antibody levels."

"Of course you do." Renna grudgingly let the woman extract a vial of blood and then crossed her arms as Samil slipped the vial into her pocket. "So what did you mean about the other implants?"

Dr. Samil nodded as she tapped some information into her tablet. "Navang wanted to create an army of hybrids he could control, right? Well, the first step was to keep their bodies from rejecting the modified implants he installed. But it didn't work. His technique destroyed some of their own tissue and risked the constant rejection of the implants. Hence the need for a steady infusion of the anti-rejection medications.

"The new formula he tested on you was a different attempt at the same thing. If he could find a way to make your body fuse with the implant, make it think it was part of itself, eventually technology could overtake biology. Even better, when the process was complete, depending on the type of implant, he could have different types of soldiers. He'd be able to control them all using his neural network. They'd be nothing but mindless robots until he gave them orders."

Samil's voice rose as she spoke, her gestures growing even more animated, but a dull ache had started in Renna's stomach. She remembered the expressionless eyes of the minions at Navang's lab as she'd slaughtered them to ensure Finn and Myka's escape. Her heart squeezed as she recalled Viktis's assurance that she would make it. Her skin crawled at the realization that she was nothing more than an experiment to the doctor, a shiny new toy to be studied until the novelty waned.

But this was Renna's life. She wasn't going to sit here helpless while other people tried to save her. "How long do I have?" she interrupted before Samil could get even more excited. The woman positively hummed.

Samil paused, blinking at Renna. "Of course. Right. My assistant has had some success in creating a new drug to slow the fusion. It's not exact, but I'm hopeful it will work." Wispy, flyaway hairs floated around her face like a halo as she shook her head. "I'm confident we'll have a breakthrough soon. I promise we'll figure this out."

"Don't make promises you can't keep, Doctor. The headaches are getting worse every day." Renna rubbed at her sore temples, closing her eyes as a wave of pain started to build. She shored up the walls surrounding her heart and refused to even think about losing the connection she'd made with Finn. "On the plus side, if your drugs don't work and the implant takes over my brain, I hear metal body suits are all the rage this year."

Samil crossed her arms and leaned back against the table, a frown marring her pretty features. "You're awfully calm about this whole situation."

Renna shrugged. She was ten years younger than the doctor, but she suddenly felt like she was a hundred years older. "I've learned to deal with the unexpected in my line of work, doc. If you can't change something, you figure out how to work around it. It's the only way to survive."

"That's a cynical view of life for someone who's only twenty-three."

"You saw my file. I grew up in the Izan tenements on Earth, with a prostitute for a mother and a background in stealing. I've worked hard to move on, but growing up like that leaves a scar. Or two." Renna forced herself not to touch the physical scar on her neck, the daily reminder of that life and everything she'd worked so hard to forget.

Thinking about her mother's attempt to kill her in a drug-induced rage still made Renna flush with shame and hatred. Still made her wary of trusting anyone. Even Finn.

Samil's expression softened. "I know. And for someone with your past, you've come a long way. You're now part of an inter-galactic organization, doing your part to save the universe. You've become something bigger than just a thief. I admire you for that."

"If I had a choice, I would've been long gone by now. I'm no hero, and I certainly am not a team player. I don't need to depend on a galactic organization. I just need myself." Renna settled back against the pillows and crossed her arms. "MYTH can keep its good deeds. I'm just in this for the dental plan." And just maybe to make sure she got a shot at happily ever after.

Samil chuckled, and Renna felt a responding smile twist her lips. Despite the needles and the fact that the doctor viewed Renna as a science experiment, she liked the woman. Samil was whip-smart, and if anyone could solve this puzzle, it would be her.

"What am I going to do with you, dove?" the doctor asked with a shake of her head.

"Save me, I hope." But the doctor could stop using that stupid nickname any time now. Thinking of Renna as a meek little dove was laughable.

"I'm doing my best. I do wish Navang's facility hadn't been destroyed. If I had access to his drugs and research, it would make all of this so much easier. Or even Myka Aldani. At one time, he was the key to all of this."

Renna's pulse jumped, and she dropped her gaze to the stark white tiles on the floor. This was exactly why she'd sent Finn on the run with Myka. Destroying the facility had been the only way to stop the human-robot hybrid army Navang and Pallas were building, but it had also signed Renna's death warrant, and put the kid in even more danger.

Had she made the right choice? Could she have stopped Navang another way?

"Do you know why Captain Finn destroyed the place?" Samil asked. "It doesn't make sense. The captain doesn't disobey orders."

"You know Finn?" She clenched her hands in her lap at the unexpected pang of jealousy. The past seven years had changed Finn into a different person, and those years were wrapped in a protective cloak that seemed to surround his heart. He was different, but that Finn from her childhood still remained. She'd thought they'd have plenty of time to get to know him again, to figure out if there was, in fact, a relationship developing under her nose, but life never worked out the way she planned.

Samil nodded. "I was ship doctor for a year on the *Athena*. He's a good man. It must have been something big for him to turn his back on MYTH." Her blue eyes searched Renna's. "Are you sure he didn't tell you anything?"

A lump formed in her throat, and she had to swallow around it before answering. "Finn and I didn't exactly get along when I came on board." Sticking to half-truths was the safest bet for now, until she figured out who she could trust.

"Right. I'd heard he was angry that Major Dallas wanted him to work with a thief on the last mission. You, I presume?"

"Guilty as charged. He wasn't likely to confide in me either way."

"Probably not. I know how he felt about people like you." Samil's eyes widened. "I mean, people who don't follow the law." She shook her head with an apologetic frown. "I'm sorry, this isn't coming out right. I just mean Finn's a good man. For him to go on the run from MYTH means something is seriously wrong."

Renna nodded. "I get it. I'm a thief. Untrustworthy. But I was hired to do a job and that's what I did."

"I didn't mean anything by it, Renna. I'm sorry." The doctor glanced at the door. "Now that I've put my foot in it, I'm going to go make sure my assistant has your newest sample. Stay positive, Renna, it's going to be fine."

"I hope you're right because it feels like my brain is about to ooze out my ears."

Samil unlocked another drawer with her thumbprint and rummaged inside. She pulled out a small, flesh-colored disk. "Here, put this medipatch on. It should help with the pain."

Renna slapped it on her arm. "Thanks, doc. I'll see you later. Hopefully much, much later."

Samil smiled as she left. The door swished shut behind her, and the sound of the lock re-engaging echoed through the room.

TWO

Renna blinked open her eyes as someone knocked at her door. It slid open before she could respond, but she'd pretty much given up on the concept of privacy. Doctors, nurses, even security staff were in and out of her room at all hours of the day and night. She'd gotten used to sleeping through it in the time she'd been there.

"Good morning, Miss Carrizal." The boy's olive skin was smooth and unlined, his dark hair cropped close to his head. Although he didn't look old enough to carry a gun, a standard MYTH-issued blaster sat in the holster at his waist. She recognized him as one of the MYTH guards permanently stationed outside her room.

"Something I can help you with, Private?" she asked.

"We're here to take you to meet with the admiral."

Renna yawned and sat up on the bed, rubbing her eyes. "Can I use the bathroom first? I'm sure the admiral won't mind, especially if I brush my teeth." She grimaced. "Turning into a cyborg does nothing for the morning breath."

The young soldier frowned, but finally nodded. "You have five minutes."

He retreated from the room, leaving Renna staring at the door. About damn time someone beside the doctor was finally paying attention to her. She'd already been at the facility for five days. Any longer and she would've had to find a way to manipulate them into letting her leave.

After making sure the *Athena* was long gone, she'd sent her distress signal to MYTH. It had only taken a few hours for their team to arrive at Aldani's labs. Based on that, she guessed this facility was on Titus Beta, a nearby planet in the same star system. But wherever they were, MYTH had locked down the comm channels so tightly that she couldn't get a message out, even with her implant's new and improved abilities.

But if the admiral finally wanted to see her, maybe that meant things were moving and she could start putting her plan in place.

Quickly, Renna brushed her hair and tied the dark length back into a neat ponytail. She used the ultraviolet cleaner on her teeth, grinning at her reflection in the mirror to make sure they were clean. She'd like to chug down a cup of coffee before having to face the firing squad, but at least she felt halfway human.

The guard opened her door, gesturing with his gun. "Time's up. Come along, Miss Carrizal."

She bit back a smirk. He was lucky she felt generous this morning. The kid's grip on the blaster was all wrong. What exactly was MYTH teaching their recruits? It would only take her two moves to disarm him. Finn would have read him the riot act if he'd been under his command. He'd been so tough on the new recruits. More than a few of them had burst into tears during his training sessions.

Renna fell into step with the private as they started down the long, brightly lit hallway. Another guard joined them from a nearby room as they passed. The two men flanked her, walking close enough that the scent of starch on their stiff gray uniforms tickled her nose.

"Where we headed?" she asked as they turned right down another corridor. The plain white walls and metal floors were standard pre-fab bunker materials used in most buildings on the Outer Rim. Her surroundings didn't lend much help in figuring out exactly what planet she was on, but maybe she could get one of these rookies to slip up.

The younger guard walked like a marionette beside her, pretending not to hear her question. He wouldn't last long with that stick up his ass. She'd be more than happy to knock him down a peg or two. "Come on. It's not like I'm going anywhere."

"The admiral and her staff are waiting in the large conference room." He snapped out the words with his jaw clenched. "There will also be six MYTH agents and four guards stationed outside. I suggest you stay on your best behavior if you ever want to see the outside of this facility again."

"You sound like you're scared of me, private." Renna smiled slyly. "I'm so honored. But didn't you hear that I've turned over a new leaf? Respectable, that's me."

His whole body was one stiff mass of muscles, and Renna chuckled. Baiting him was too much fun. He was just so...earnest.

They reached the end of the hallway and turned left. Four guards in their gray-and-gold uniforms stood at attention beside a thick glass door, each carrying a modified sonic rifle.

Renna let out a low whistle. "What exactly do you think I'm going to do to the admiral? I don't even have a weapon."

He blinked slowly once, and then his flinty eyes settled on her face. Without moving his stone-hard facial muscles, he pressed his thumb to the scanner on the wall and the door slid open, revealing a large conference room with a round, white table and eight chairs.

"Sit down. The admiral and her staff will join you momentarily."

"Whatever you say, sweetheart." She flashed him an unrepentant grin and threw herself into one of the chairs. A low buffet table sat along the far wall with a pitcher of water and eight glasses, while a giant holoscreen took up the opposite wall. Just another non-descript room, in a non-descript building, on a non-descript planet. Pretty much exactly what she'd expected from MYTH leadership. Everything was neat, orderly, and by the book.

No wonder they had no idea Pallas was running circles around them.

The door opened, and six MYTH special agents marched into the room, taking up stations in each corner, with two on either side of the door. They wore the shiny, black, full-body suits she'd first seen on Finn back on Hesperia.

Another twinge of longing shot through her. Dammit. Why did everything remind her of Finn?

Stop it, Renna. Staying on her game was the only thing that mattered right now because, if she failed, she'd never get the chance to see Finn again.

She crossed her arms and pretended to study her fingernails while she snuck glances at the motionless soldiers. Three men, three women. Two were Ileth, one Delfine, and three humans. None of them had Finn's intimidating presence, just the same cold glare that he'd shot her when they'd first met back on Hesperia. That look had almost turned the blood in her veins to ice.

But this was quite the honor guard for a lowly thief, even if they weren't as scary as Finn. What exactly had they told everyone about her?

The door slid open again, and a tall, muscular woman marched into the room. Her jet-black hair was pulled back into a no-nonsense bun, and wrinkles framed cool gray eyes.

The agents snapped to attention, saluting as she took a seat at the head of the table.

Renna continued to lounge in her chair, legs outstretched. She wasn't MYTH yet and didn't owe anyone a salute.

After the admiral had taken her seat, two more humans with major's stripes on their chests entered the room—one male, one female. Renna's muscles went rigid. Larson. What the hell was he doing here? Her skin crawled with his unexpected presence. One of Navang's last reveals was that Major Larson worked for Pallas. He was a traitor to MYTH and to the Coalition.

He was also apparently part of the admiral's advisory group.

Something surged in her implant, sending a zap of pain through her. Renna sucked in a sharp breath and squeezed her eyes closed. Her mind spun and sputtered as her implant tried to process a new stream of information. Unlike feeling the facility's communications arrays when she'd first arrived, this was sharp and painful, like needles stabbing into the soft tissue of her brain. A slow trickle of data started to download to her implant, easing the pressure enough that she could open her eyes.

The admiral quirked an eyebrow. "Is everything all right, Miss Carrizal?"

Renna forced her voice to stay steady. "I'm fine, ma'am." She'd have to be careful, especially with Dr. Samil. They couldn't know about the changes happening in her head or they'd never let her go.

"Very well then, let's get started. I'm Admiral Kamila Usamov. We've brought you here today to debrief you on the Myka Aldani rescue mission and the destruction of Draven Navang's facility on Vall." The admiral steepled her fingers and watched Renna, letting the silence stretch between them.

As much as she wanted to be stubborn and wait the woman out, Renna needed to make them think they had the upper hand. Engaging the admiral in a battle of wills wasn't part of the plan. After thirty seconds, long enough to make it look like she was putting up a fight, Renna dropped her gaze to the table.

The admiral smiled, but before she could speak, the door slid open again.

Renna's jaw dropped as a dead man stepped into the room.

THREE

M ajor Dallas?" Renna's words were barely a whisper.
The major had been the one who'd recruited her
for the mission to rescue Myka; it was his fault she
was sitting here today. But he was supposed to be dead, killed in
the attack on Hesperia.

"Hello, my dear." His blue eyes crinkled as he smiled and took
the seat beside her.

Renna's thoughts did cartwheels through her head. "We
thought you were killed in the explosion when we left with
Myka." Finn would be so relieved his mentor was still alive. She
couldn't wait to tell him the good news.

Dallas chuckled, shaking his salt-and-pepper head. "Takes
more than a bomb to kill me. Our bunker held, and eventually
another MYTH team was able to get most of the staff out. I'm
glad to see you're doing well."

Her face tightened into a frozen smile. There were a few other words she would have chosen instead of "well," but at least she was alive.

Usamov nodded at him. "Thank you for coming, Major. As the original commanding officer for the Aldani mission, your input is invaluable."

"Of course, Admiral. I'm honored to be included." Dallas squared his shoulders and fixed the other occupants of the table with a cool gaze. "According to my intel, we have a rogue element within our ranks."

Renna felt dismay flicker across her face, and she quickly schooled her features to remain blank. How the hell did he know that? Pallas and Major Larson's betrayal was still secret. Only the crew of the *Athena* knew the truth about what had happened on Vall.

Dallas continued, oblivious to her sudden tension. "I was shocked and dismayed to hear Captain Finn has stolen the *Athena* and is on the run with the Aldani boy. The captain has been completely loyal to our cause since the day I recruited him. There has to be something we don't know about this situation."

Renna's muscles unclenched, and she let out a silent breath. Her secret was still safe. She'd have to make sure it stayed that way. As soon as Pallas knew they were on to him, he'd either go to ground and they'd never find him, or he'd launch his attack and they'd all be dead. Neither option really appealed to her.

Admiral Usamov glanced at Renna. "That's why we've asked Miss Carrizal here. We're hoping she can tell us what happened on the mission. Perhaps there's an explanation for the captain's behavior."

Every eye in the room focused on her, and Renna swallowed thickly. Everything depended on her answer. Finn, Myyka, Viktis. The galaxy.

Nothing like putting a little pressure on a girl.

She let her gaze drift around the table, stopping briefly on each of the majors before speaking. "As I'm sure you all read in my report, after tracking the boy across most of this system, Captain Finn and I broke into the facility on Vall and discovered that Dr. Navang was using Myka's DNA to create a cybernetic army. We rescued him, and Captain Finn took the boy back to the *Athena* for medical treatment. Unfortunately, I was captured by Navang's men. He ran several experiments on me before I was able to escape."

"Do I understand that you had a pirate on board the *Athena* as well?" the admiral asked.

Renna nodded. "Correct. Viktis Korrik. Son of former President Korrik."

"And now a pirate." Usamov's lips thinned in distaste.

"A very good pirate," Renna corrected. "He agreed to help us infiltrate Navang's lab and rescue Myka after his ship was destroyed and his crew murdered by Navang's henchmen."

Dallas raised one of his neatly trimmed eyebrows. "And Finn agreed to this?"

"He didn't have much of a choice. As Major Larson can confirm, we left Lenue in a rush after the attack on that city. Viktis was already on board." Renna paused. "Whatever you may think about him, it was lucky we had him with us. Navang was working on some seriously illegal tech."

Among other things.

The horrors she'd seen there still haunted her at night. Men and women transformed into cyborgs with glowing eyes and metal limbs. The sound of their screams as they died in a shower of sparks and blood. The technology that had taken over their humanity.

Renna noticed her fingers drumming against the tabletop and quickly dropped them to her lap. Tells like that would get her in trouble here.

"Navang was behind the attacks on the various cities in this system," she continued. "He took the injured citizens and experimented on them, implanting them with his cybernetics. He created a drug that melded the implant technology into human physiology." Renna paused, swallowed. "He turned them into hybrids."

Beside her, Dallas inhaled sharply. "Could he control them?"

"Yes. He was creating an army."

Shocked whispers and mutters broke out at the table. Renna sneaked a glance at Major Larson from beneath her lashes. He sat perfectly still, no reaction, no indication he was part of Navang's plan. That would have been too easy, of course.

Finally, Usamov held up her hand. "Silence. Let Miss Carrizal finish."

Nausea burned the back of her throat as she pushed away the images of the stark facility, the blind obedience Navang had forced on his test subjects, the way the hybrids had gone eerily silent as Viktis had dispersed a technological virus through their neural network. Instead, she focused on the people in the room to steady her trembling heartbeat. She couldn't afford to feel guilt or fear.

"Dr. Navang used Myka's genetic material to develop a new drug, which he then injected into me after Viktis and I were captured. According to him, it will force my neural implant to fuse to my nervous system and eventually become part of me. If I survive the process."

"Did he say anything else?" Larson asked. "Any hint as to why he would do this? What he hoped to accomplish?"

Renna watched the major. A trickle of sweat crept along his hairline, but he didn't break her gaze. "I'm afraid not," she said finally, shaking her head.

"But what about Captain Finn, Myka, and the *Athena*?" The admiral sat back in her chair, her gray eyes troubled. "Why would they run? Once you retrieved him from Navang, the boy was safe."

Renna shrugged. "I have no idea. I thought everything was fine until we landed at Aldani's lab. That's when I discovered Finn and Viktis were actually working together. They took the boy and Aldani and fled, leaving me behind."

"But why?" Dallas asked. A frown marked deep lines around his mouth. "Finn would never work with a pirate."

"I wish I knew. Maybe they thought they were protecting the boy?" Renna paused, letting her shoulders sag. "I trusted them." She let her voice hitch on the last word.

"I'm sure there's a perfectly reasonable explanation." Dallas patted Renna's hand. "I know Captain Finn, and he would never do something like this without good reason."

Usamov rose to her feet and paced behind the table, arms clasped behind her ramrod-straight spine. "I don't disagree, Major, but the bigger question is: What did Navang hope to accomplish with this army, and is anyone else involved? It concerns me that we don't have any intel on this. How did we miss it?" Her voice sharpened into icy daggers as she stared at her advisors.

Renna bit back a shiver at the woman's expression. She was suddenly very glad she didn't report to the admiral.

Finally, Major Larson cleared his throat, breaking the uncomfortable silence. "Unfortunately, we can't ask him, since Renna and her crew decided to destroy the facility. All traces of the experiments, hybrids, and tech are gone. We have nothing. The boy is our last clue to what Navang was planning. He *must* be found."

Usamov turned her laser gaze to Renna. "Can you tell us why Finn's team destroyed the facility? He must have known how important that intel was to MYTH."

Renna shook her head. "I don't think the captain was behind it. He and the *Athena* had already left the planet. Maybe Navang rigged it to explode if it was discovered."

"Or perhaps you had something to do with it yourself." Major Larson's gaze bored into hers as if he could somehow read the answers there.

And there it was: casting suspicion on other people to cover his ass. Good thing she needed him to lead her to Pallas or the major might wake up to a knife at his throat the next morning.

Renna forced away the delicious image of him begging for his life and shook her head apologetically. "I think you forget, Major. Navang had been experimenting on me. I was lucky to make it out of the facility before it exploded. I was in no shape to go setting off bombs."

"Renna has done exactly what we asked of her, Larson," Dallas protested. "And at great risk to herself. This situation is not her fault." He turned his gaze to Renna. "I understand Dr. Samil has started to synthesize a version of the drug, and it seems to be helping slow the fusion of your implant?"

She blinked at him. The last thing she'd expected was for Dallas to come to her defense. Maybe the guy wasn't so bad after all. "As far as we can tell." She turned to the admiral. "Ma'am, the lab might be destroyed, but you do have one last example of what Navang was trying to do. Me."

Usamov stood motionless at the head of the room, pinning Renna with her cool gaze. "What exactly are you offering, Miss Carrizal?"

This was it. Everything rode on her convincing them of her sincerity. It might just be the biggest con of her life. "I want to help you. I want to become a part of MYTH. Let me track down Finn and the *Athena* and get to the bottom of this. I might be the only one who can find them."

A nearly inaudible gasp spread around the room, and the MYTH personnel fell into a shocked silence. But Renna ignored them, keeping her expression calm and not breaking the admiral's gaze. Right now, no one else mattered. It was like facing down a man-eating terrorcrest. One heartbeat of fear and it was all over.

Dallas was the first to speak. "I agree. I was the one who brought Renna into this, and I still stand by my decision. With a little discipline, she could be a real asset to MYTH. And she's right. Finn and the pirate have worked with her and they trust her. She knows where mercs go to hide. She can find them."

Admiral Usamov shook her head, her lips barely a slash on

her stern face. "This is highly unusual."

"We can't trust her," Larson protested. "Even more importantly, she's the missing piece to Navang's experiments. We can't just let her go traipsing around the galaxy. What if we could use her to strike back? To uncover his data? This could be the leap ahead MYTH needs to become—"

Usamov held up a hand, cutting Larson off mid-sentence. "I think we have everything we need from you, Miss Carrizal," she said coolly. "You may return to your room. We will need to discuss your proposal further."

Renna stood and let her gaze drift across the group one last time. "Please believe me when I say I'm not proud of my past, but I'm ready to make a change. To do the right thing. I think my skills could be invaluable in your organization, and I would be honored to be part of MYTH. I hope you consider my offer."

The words felt rehearsed in her mouth, but she hoped they came out as sincere. If nothing else, the intent behind them was true. She needed them to agree to this or everything was lost.

Dallas smiled encouragingly at her, but the rest of the staff kept their faces blank. Not a good sign.

Renna straightened her spine and brought her hand up to her forehead in a crisp salute. Then she marched from the room in her best military manner.

Only when she rounded the corner to her room did she let her shoulders sag.

She'd done the best she could. Now it was up to them.

FOUR

S he must have said something right in the debriefing because, two hours later, Dallas stood in her room, taking in
the hospital machinery and stark furnishings, the locks on
every drawer, the sensors monitoring her every move.

"You mean to tell me they put you in a holding cell? For five
days?" A muscle jumped in his jaw. "Unacceptable."

"It's fine, Major. I understand their caution. I am a thief, after
all. And one with an implant that could explode at any moment."
Renna shrugged. "But if you could figure out a way to get them to
at least give me a holovid, I'd appreciate it."

Dallas shook his head and sat stiffly in the hard plastic chair
beside the vitals monitor. "I can do better than that. Admiral
Usamov has agreed to send you after Captain Finn and the *Athena*. Consider this a trial run for your acceptance into MYTH. If
you're successful with this mission, you'll become a full-fledged

member."

Her eyebrows shot up. That had been much easier and faster than she'd expected. Interesting. "Did you have something to do with this, Major?"

He smiled. "I wish I could say yes, but other than vouching for your skills, Admiral Usamov made this decision without my input. However, I believe she made the right one." Dallas leaned forward, elbows on his knees. "What aren't you telling us, Renna?"

Her pulse jumped, but she kept her face expressionless. "I don't know what you mean, sir."

"Renna, I know Finn. I know your history with him. I know he didn't trust you farther than he could throw you. And *he* was the one who turned traitor? I don't buy it."

"Your guess is as good as mine, sir." Renna shook her head. "But you're right. Finn and I didn't get along. I don't know what he was thinking."

Dallas studied her long enough that Renna had to glance away, cursing herself for the action. He continued in a low voice. "I know there's something you're not telling us. And I *will* find out. Finn is one of my best men, and if he's in trouble, I need to help him."

Her fingers twitched, and she twisted them together in her lap. He sounded sincere. But then again, she'd sounded sincere earlier, too. She couldn't risk it. Even if he wasn't the person who'd ordered the hybrid army and planned to destroy MYTH, trusting the wrong person would put more than herself in danger.

She smiled reassuringly at Dallas. "Whatever our differences,

I admire Captain Finn very much. I promise I will do my best to find him and his crew. You'll be the first to know the instant I discover something else, Major."

Dallas frowned, the lines around his eyes deepening with worry. "Very well. That's all I can ask. The admiral is looking into giving you a ship and crew to locate Captain Finn and the boy. I assume you know where to start looking?"

Renna had quite a few ideas, but none of them had to do with finding Finn. The longer he stayed hidden, the safer he'd be. "Actually, sir. If it's possible, I'd like to start here at headquarters."

"What do you mean?"

She leaned against the edge of the bed and tucked her hands into the pockets of her black leggings. At least they'd let her take off the gods-awful hospital gowns after the first day.

"I'd like access to the MYTH personnel files. Knowing more about the crew of the *Athena* may help me figure out where they went or why they ran in the first place."

Dallas shifted in his chair, his expression shuttered. "I'm afraid that's not possible. Only top officials have access to that level of classified information."

She knew that look. He was torn between doing his duty and helping her find his captain. "Come, Major. This is MYTH. Anything is possible. You want to find Finn, don't you? That's the best place to start."

Dallas got to his feet with a heavy sigh. "No promises, Renna, but I'll see what I can do. In the meantime, I'll have them move you to better quarters. There's no reason to keep you in the hospital wing any longer."

"Thank you, sir. I promise you won't regret it."

He shook his head as he left the room. "Make sure I don't, my dear."

Dallas made good on his word, and Renna was moved to another wing of the facility an hour later. The new room was much nicer, with soft rugs and a large, comfortable bed. There was even a large-screen holovid on one wall.

Now if they could just get her some new underwear. These army-issued briefs were killing her.

But at least there were no needles in this room or the constant low hum of the monitors. And no sign of Dr. Samil, either, though that was probably only temporary. Renna's head still pounded and her mind felt fuzzy. Not a good sign. Especially when combined with the strange data download that had happened in the conference room. She still had no idea what that was all about.

When Dallas pushed open her door the next morning instead of Samil, Renna hated the relief that flooded through her. Not another test or jab or examination, just the slightly starched major with the graying hair and kind smile.

"I trust you slept well, my dear?" he asked as he scanned the room. "At least it looks more comfortable than your hospital cell."

"It was lovely. Thank you for getting me moved."

"Of course. The least I could do." He glanced back at the door. "You'll be pleased to know the admiral agreed to give you limited access to the MYTH database to view the *Athena's* personnel files."

Renna whistled between her teeth. "I'm shocked. But you don't sound very happy about it, Major."

"Renna, I believe you have Myka's welfare in mind, but I don't believe you've told me everything. Until you do, I cannot help my crew. Please. Tell me what's going on."

She shook her head. "I'm sorry, sir."

"So am I." Dallas opened the door and gestured to the hallway. "Follow me. I'll take you to the server room."

An uncomfortable pressure built in Renna's chest as they walked through the facility in silence. She risked a glance at the major. Worry had etched lines around his mouth she didn't remember from the first time they'd met. She wanted to tell him the truth, more than anything, but she couldn't risk Pallas finding out what she knew. And if Major Dallas was the traitor...

She shook her head. No sense in thinking like that until she learned more.

The major stopped in front of a thick, metal door and entered a code into the keypad. The door slid open, revealing a bank of flickering holoscreens. "You should be able to access the MYTH servers from here. I'll be back in an hour."

Renna took a seat in one of the high-backed chairs and used the holo keyboard glowing blue above the long, curved desk. She quickly did a cursory search on the *Athena's* crew—Captain Finn, Lieutenant Li Keva, Flight Lieutenant Mark Kojima. Most of the information that came up was the dry, impersonal facts the military had gathered about each of them. She downloaded them to her tablet to skim through later, just in case.

Then she cracked her knuckles. Now that she'd created a paper trail, she could get to the real reason she'd wanted access to the system. Her fingers flew over the keyboard as she built her own temporary firewall. She needed to make sure no one would catch the hack she was about to install to disable the search tracer on the server.

When everything was in place, she grinned at the holomonitor. "Time to play, gorgeous," she muttered. She pulled an optical disk from her pocket and slipped it into one of the drives on the machine. A few more clicks and her hack was installed.

After that, it was easy to open Level Three security information on all MYTH leadership. She might not know exactly where to start, but she did know Major Larson was up to his eyeballs in something sketchy. He was the best chance she had of finding the answers she needed.

Renna quickly skimmed through his file. Major William Larson, forty-three years old. Born on Earth. Joined the Coalition military at age eighteen. Married at twenty-four. Joined MYTH at thirty-two. Exemplary record—no blemishes or suspicious activities. The perfect soldier.

Renna tapped a finger against her chin. The man's file was spotless. A little *too* spotless. She typed in another command, and her hack stripped away the next level of clearance.

That was better. With Level Two access, Major Larson's file didn't look quite so squeaky clean. A reprimand after a mission on Anat where three of his men had been killed suspiciously. A formal complaint lodged by another commanding officer regarding insubordination and excessive violence toward prisoners. A number of written warnings about shirking of duty. A series of tests run by Dr. Samil on his physical state after a mission three years ago.

It looked like he'd had some sort of health problem, but the medical jargon made her head ache, so she quickly copied over the records to a storage disk and backed out of his file. Nothing that pointed directly to Pallas, but if the man was unhappy with MYTH leadership, he might have been an easy mark.

One traitor down, one to go. "Pallas, where are you?" she whispered as she typed in a search command. The only thing she knew was that the name itself was a reference from one of the ancient earth myths. She'd looked it up back on the *Athena*. Pallas had been a Greek Titan. The God of Warcraft. Whoever had picked the name had chosen wisely.

She rubbed the back of her neck, rolling her shoulders to ease the ache that never seemed to go away now. She was running out of time; the MYTH server scanners had to be getting close to finding her hack. But there was one more level to go. Level One clearance. It was a long shot, but she was running out of options. Her fingers flew over the keyboard as she tried to code a back door into the file structure. The server beeped and the light on the front of the box flashed red.

Denied.

Renna frowned and tried again. The server squawked at her a second time. Shit. Why couldn't she get through? She closed her eyes and took a deep breath. She was too keyed up; she needed to relax and let herself feel her way into the hack.

A stab of pain shot through her head, and Renna gasped, the sound echoing through the room. Her eyes flew open, and she felt the same trickle of data seep into her implant as she had in the conference room.

What the hell?

A moment later the light on the server flashed green, and she was in. Like her freaking implant had interfaced with the server and found a workaround to the firewall without her help.

Her pulse raced as she stared at the bank of servers. Gods, the implant was moving so much faster than she'd expected. If this kept up, she'd be a robot in days, not weeks. Cold fingers scraped across her skin, and she swallowed the sudden lump in her throat. She was running out of time. Time to stop Pallas. Time to be with Finn.

With a huge effort, she pushed her panic away. More importantly, she was running out of time right now with these MYTH servers. Renna ran a quick search, and her stomach flipped as the machine brought back a hit.

MYTH had a record of a Titan Industries. Based in the Costa system. Planet Crius Beta.

She grinned at the monitor. Pallas was a Titan. They had to be connected. Someone using that name was too much of a coincidence.

A quick scan of the files proved useless. The company had been created five years ago as a front for MYTH to get a foothold on the planet to manufacture long-range communication components. Strangely, there was no other record of who'd created the business or how it was connected to MYTH now. Like someone had purposefully kept the information vague.

Beep.

Renna jumped in her chair. A red light flashed frantically in one of server banks on the wall, the shrill scream echoing through the room.

"Shit!" Renna quickly pulled her hack from the system and dismantled the firewall, backing out all traces of her presence. She ran a fast scanner through the server, deleting any searches she might have left behind, then shut down the terminal. If MYTH looked, they'd only have records of her viewing the *Athena* crew information and nothing more.

She pulled her data disk from the console. Another beep sounded and she dropped it. It clattered under the desk. "Dammit. Pull yourself together, woman." She crouched to pick up the disk, then slipped it into her pocket.

Her gaze fell to the console. If she'd had more time, she could have pulled a lot of data from MYTH's files, a lot of information she could sell to the highest bidder.

Her fingers twitched, but she twisted them together. She'd made her choice to throw in her lot with MYTH for now, and thinking like that would only get her in trouble. Betraying this organization would mean betraying Finn. Air left her lungs in a rush at the notion of forsaking his trust. Something she wasn't ready to do. She'd made a promise after all.

Renna shook her head and composed herself. Look at her, playing by the rules. Finn would be so proud.

FIVE

Someone knocked at her door, and Renna glanced up from the data she'd pulled from the MYTH computers.

"Come in," she called, shoving her tablet beneath her pillow. At least they'd finally given her a little privacy.

Dr. Samil pushed open the door and smiled at her. "Good morning, Renna." She stepped into the room, a metal-globed med-drone gliding behind her.

Renna bit back a shudder at the tray of sterile tools the drone carried in its spindly arms. "Not a social visit, I take it?"

Samil nodded at the floating machine as it hovered near Renna's head. "Did Monty give it away?"

"That and the instruments of torture he's carrying."

Samil chuckled and unwrapped a syringe. "Nice to see your flair for the melodramatic is still intact."

"Maybe I can start my own robotic acting company once this

implant takes over. Shakespeare in the Park: Cyborg-Style."

The doctor frowned. "Renna..."

She shook her head. "It's fine, Doc. I'm just tired this morning and my brain hurts. Let's get the probing over with."

In silence, Samil drew two vials of blood, checked Renna's vitals, and listened to her heart. Renna stared at a spot of dust on the wall and tried to ignore her racing pulse and the feel of the doctor's cool fingers against her skin.

Finally, the doctor pulled out her ventroscope. "I'm going to examine your vision now, Renna. Hold perfectly still. I promise this won't hurt a bit."

Renna arched an eyebrow. "You know I don't believe you when you say that."

"Would I lie to you?" Samil's lips twitched, but her face stayed serious. "Now don't move. This will only take a second." Samil took the mask-like metal device from the tray and pressed it to Renna's face.

Renna's skin turned icy where it touched, but she only had a moment of wonder before a sharp red light stabbed into her eyes. Searing pain, like someone had taken a scalpel to her eyeballs, shot through her. She curled her hands into fists, nails biting into her palms as the pain subsided.

"Deep breaths, Renna. Are you all right?" Samil removed the device from Renna's face and helped her lean back against the pillows on the bed.

"Damn, Doc. What the hell was that?" Renna asked weakly. She squeezed her eyes shut against the throbbing pain and took a shaky breath.

"A full neural scan. And it should not have been that painful.

I'm worried."

"That makes two of us." Renna wiped a trickle of sweat from her forehead and tried to force her shoulder muscles to unclench. It felt like her whole body had been squeezed through a tiny tube lined with needles.

Samil muttered something under her breath and pulled Renna's digital medical records up on her tablet. "I need to run some calculations," she said, brushing her hair away from her face.

Renna clasped her hands together, resisting the urge to yank the woman's ponytail holder out of her hair and weave a tight braid to contain the rogue tendrils. "Whatever you need, Doc. I'm not going anywhere."

"Actually, that's not true," Samil said with a frown. "Major Dallas wants you to meet him in the debriefing room when we're done here. I'll let him know it'll be a while. You're in no shape to move right now."

No thanks to her. Renna gritted her teeth. What the hell was the doctor doing in the first place? She was supposed to be working on a cure, not playing around with new toys and using Renna as a fucking lab rat.

"What's going on?" Renna asked. "Is the degeneration happening faster now?" She already knew the answer, but she wanted ed to hear it from the doctor's lips.

"I'm afraid so. If we don't figure this out, you're going to run out of time." Samil chewed her bottom lip as she studied the monitor. "The neural integration has slowed thanks to the drugs, and your body is fighting really hard to keep it that way. But even more interesting is how the implant is adapting to these changes. If I'm not mistaken, it's establishing its own pathways, creating external networks instead of the internal ones we'd expect."

External networks. That had to be how Renna had felt the *Athena* or how she'd hacked into the servers. But why did it hurt so much?

"I'm going to adjust the medication we're working on for you. I think we should have something ready by this afternoon. I'm even more hopeful we'll have a breakthrough by the end of the week." Samil tucked her tablet back into her coat pocket. "Get some rest for now. I'll have Major Dallas call for you later when you're feeling better." She patted Renna on the shoulder. "We're going to solve this, Renna. You're too important to lose right now." Dr. Samil smiled and left the room, Monty humming along behind her.

"Too important to lose right now," Renna muttered as she let her eyes drift closed. "What happens when I'm not important anymore?"

A few hours later, Renna rolled over in bed and stretched, feeling her muscles burn and stiffen. Lying around all day wasn't helping her keep in shape. She needed to get the hell out of here.

Especially if Samil was right and she was running out of time. The urge to be with Finn burned like a glowing ember in the middle of her chest.

The flashing blue light on her tablet caught her eye, and she pushed away the sliver of fear and urgency that was her constant companion lately. Switching on her device, she scanned her messages.

There were the usual sale ads—she saved one from the specialty boudoir underwear designer she liked to splurge on. Twenty-five percent off on bras and lingerie. Maybe MYTH would hold a delivery for her.

There were two feeler emails from potential clients that she deleted without even reading. She didn't have time for that sort of thing right now. Saving her own skin, ensuring Finn and Myka's safety, and acting as Renna, Warrior Princess, for the galaxy was a bit more important.

The last message was her weekly subscription to the *Galactic Free News*. Renna's gaze lingered briefly on the article about the arrest of Kitty Cordoza, one of most notorious mob bosses in the galaxy. Good. The woman deserved to spend the rest of her life in prison. She was the one who'd crated Myka Aldani and shipped him all over the system. Too bad Renna hadn't been there to witness her detainment in person.

But what she was really interested in were the classified ads.

Back when she and Viktis were together, they'd used a complicated code to communicate with each other while they were out on jobs. If he and Finn needed her now, that's how they'd get a hold of her. As she read through them, her shoulders slumped. Nothing.

Renna tossed the tablet on the bed and rested her head in her hands. In this situation, no news was good news, no matter how much she missed them. She should be happy they didn't need her. But she ached to know Finn was all right. That he was safe from Pallas. Gods, when had she gotten so obsessed? Finn was a soldier; he could take care of himself. And she'd do no one any good if she worried about him instead of the job at hand.

It had to be all the time on her hands. She had nothing else to think about besides Finn. The sooner she got out of here, the better.

Renna slid off the bed, landing lightly on her feet. The room bobbed like a ship, and she swallowed back a surge of nausea as she clutched the edge of the bed. Evidently, Samil's device had affected her more than she'd thought. Her head still buzzed at a low-level frequency, almost like a mosquito flitting around her head. That could stop any time now.

She crossed gingerly to the washbasin and splashed her face with water. It helped calm the spinning a bit and she took a deep breath. The residual pain from the attack had finally started to fade, but her mind kept coming back to the fact that Samil's device had felt like something crawling through her brain. Her skin erupted in goose bumps. The doctor better know what she was doing. Becoming a cyborg was not in Renna's retirement plan.

"Renna." Her door slid open, and Dallas strode into the room. His eyebrows furrowed as he took in her pale face and shadowed eyes. "Dr. Samil said you weren't feeling well after your test this morning. Any better?"

Renna shrugged. "I'll live. What's the news?"

"The admiral has assigned you a ship and crew. The *Eris* is one of the best small cruisers we have. Weapons functionality is limited, as this is a stealth mission, not an attack mission. But she's a beauty. I'm sure you'll love her."

"That was fast. What's the admiral's game here? Why does she trust me with this?"

"I thought this is what you wanted." He stood in parade rest, arms behind his back, but he watched her warily, as if he was analyzing her every word.

Renna ignored the discomfort of being studied so closely and shrugged. "It was. I just didn't expect to get it. I'm a thief, after all. Don't you military people distrust me on principle?" It felt too easy, somehow, that they would just agree to her proposal.

"The admiral is one of the smartest people I know. Finding Finn and the *Athena* is her top priority, and if you're the one who can do it, she'll go to any lengths to get you what you need."

She was glad they recognized that at least. Too bad they had no idea the problem was in their own organization. "How soon can I leave?"

"This afternoon."

Renna's eyes widened.

"There has been some debate. Dr. Samil would like to keep you under observation for several more days, but the admiral outranks her. We can't afford to waste any more time."

"I always knew I liked you, Major." Renna grinned at him. "I'll pack up my stuff and be ready to go in half an hour."

"Good." He leaned forward, lowering his voice. "I hope you know you can trust me completely, Renna. Right now, my only concern is finding Finn and making sure he's all right. I don't care what other scams you might be running."

She tilted her head and studied his haggard face. "Based on that statement, I'm going to assume *you* don't trust *me*."

"Renna, I know more about your background than anyone else in this organization. I chose you to rescue Myka because I believed in you. And I backed you to find Finn for the same reason. I think you're exactly what MYTH needs, even if they don't know it themselves yet." He paused, his lips twitching at the corners with a grin. "But no, I don't trust you outside my line-of-sight. I know better than that. You should be flattered."

She couldn't help but return his smile. Damn, she was getting soft. A few kind words and she turned to mush.

"That being said," Dallas continued, getting to his feet, "the admiral and her staff don't know you nearly as well as I do. As a condition for this mission, they are requiring ship status reports every twenty-four hours."

The happy glow faded. Dammit. So much for keeping her whereabouts secret from Pallas's moles inside MYTH. "Of course. They're worried I'm going to pull a Finn and steal the ship, huh?"

"You're going to tell me the thought didn't cross your mind?" Dallas asked, tilting his head to study her.

Renna chuckled. "Fair assessment. Fine. I'll report in daily."

"See that you do. You do not want them to send a recall team after you if they decide you've gone rogue. We also equip all of our ships with a self-destruct button, and they're not afraid to use it." He turned to the door. "Finish gathering your things. You leave in an hour."

SIX

R eady to see her?" Dallas asked as he pressed his palm to the hangar bay scanner.

Renna's insides fluttered as she nodded. By the stars, she was as anxious as a teenager on her first date. It was just another ship, just another crew. No need to be nervous.

The door to the hanger slid open, and Renna stifled a gasp at the shiny cruiser sitting on the landing pad. At half the size of the *Athena*, it was still almost as long as a city block.

"The *Eris* runs with a crew of fifteen. It has a fully stocked med-bay and state-of-the-art stealth systems." Dallas puffed his chest out. "One of the best new designs we have."

"Did you have something to do with the design, sir?" she asked, letting her gaze linger over the crisp lines and curves of the beauty.

"I helped, yes, but it was a team effort." He moved into the hangar, but his voice had softened and he smiled at her. "Come, my dear. You don't want to keep your crew waiting."

A dozen men and women stood at attention in front of the ship, while the maintenance crew scurried around prepping the *Eris* for travel. They all wore the gray-and-gold uniforms of MYTH, and most of them were human, but she spotted a few alien faces in the crowd.

Dallas's boots clicked against the cement floor as they approached. "This is Commander Cori Jayla. She's in charge of running the ship and making sure everything goes as planned with the mission."

A tall woman with angular features and a swoop of jet-black hair saluted them. Her dark skin was smooth and unwrinkled, but Renna guessed her to be in her late forties.

"It's an honor to be included in this mission, sir," she said in a crisp voice.

"At ease, Commander. Renna, Jayla has worked for MYTH almost as long as I have and is one of our most trusted agents. She'll help you find Captain Finn or die trying."

"I hope that's not necessary, sir, but I'll do my best." A twinkle of amusement shone in the commander's eyes as she turned to the handsome blond man standing beside her. "This is my executive officer, Lieutenant Alistair Blake."

He saluted smartly, but the grin at the end ruined the military effect. "Welcome aboard, Miss Carrizal."

Renna smiled back. "I look forward to working with both of you."

"Finn must be insane if he left you behind and went on the run with an Ileth pirate," Blake said, with a chuckle. "Either way, his loss is my gain."

Jayla rolled her eyes. "Despite what the lieutenant says, Captain Finn is one of our best. We'll do whatever it takes to make sure he's all right." Jayla's eyebrows furrowed as she glanced at Dallas. "I'm assuming we still haven't heard from him?" Dallas shook his head, and the commander's lips thinned.

Renna shifted on her heels. There was that stupid twinge of jealousy again. She wanted to know more about Finn's life, about what he'd done after leaving Blur's gang. She wanted to know how the commander knew him and if they'd gone on missions together. The urge to know everything about him left her breathless, and a surge of vertigo shot through her, sending the room spinning. She squeezed her eyes closed. Godsdammit. This could stop any time now.

She sucked in a few deep breaths and opened her eyes again when the pain lessened.

And then froze. Her implant had created a glowing text overlay with a full workup on Commander Jayla. Heart rate, blood pressure, height, eye color, birthplace, and rank all scrolled past as she studied the woman. She blinked, and the information shifted a level deeper, into a full dossier on the commander, including statistics, kills, military honors, and missions.

She'd been Finn's commanding officer for two years prior to being reassigned to the *Eris*.

Renna glanced at Lieutenant Blake, and the data shifted instantly. According to the new information, Blake and Finn had been in boot camp together, recruited at the same time by Dallas.

Somehow, when she'd connected with the MYTH database, all of their records had downloaded into her brain. By the blasted stars, maybe this implant thing was going to be useful after all. She blinked again and the heads-up display faded, the personal info disappearing from her vision.

"Everything all right, Renna?" Dallas asked, watching her carefully.

She quickly pushed away her amazement and nodded. "Yes, sir. Sorry, sir." A twinge of panic beat wings against her temples, but she had to look on the bright side. Being able to pull up instant knowledge on anyone could be a real asset in her line of work.

"Commander, is the *Eris* prepped for take-off?"

Jayla saluted. "Ready whenever Miss Carrizal is."

"Very good."

There was a commotion at the hangar door as Dr. Samil darted through it, closely followed by Major Larson.

"So glad I caught you," Samil panted, her pale face flushed pink like she'd been running. "I forgot to give this to you during your checkup." She handed a small silver box to Renna. "We had a breakthrough. It won't stop the integration completely, but I was able to create a compound that should keep the implant stable and the neural connection at bay for now. This is a month's worth of pills."

Renna closed her fingers around the box, the edges cutting into her skin. She glanced up at Dr. Samil, hoping the woman could see how grateful she was. "Thank you, Doc. I mean it."

The corners of Samil's blue eyes wrinkled as she smiled. "Make sure you remember to take them every day. And come back as soon as you start feeling any side effects again. The pills may stop working as your system builds up tolerance."

"I understand. Hopefully, it won't take me more than a few weeks to find Finn. I'll be back for you to experiment on before you know it."

"I'm going to hold you to that, Renna." Samil squeezed her arm. "Be careful out there."

Dallas turned to Major Larson. "Is there something you needed, Major?"

Larson's gaze wandered over the ship like he was looking for something, but after a moment he turned back to them. "I'd like to speak to Renna alone, if you don't mind."

Wariness flitted across Dallas's face, but he nodded. "Very well. Dr. Samil, Commander, follow me." The trio headed toward the loading hatch, leaving Renna and Larson behind.

Larson stood at ease, legs spread apart, hands behind his back. He studied her like he'd studied the *Eris*. Like Renna was just another thing to be used.

She forced her body to stay relaxed. She'd be damned if she let him see how uncomfortable he made her.

Finally, he smiled slightly, baring his teeth. "I'm glad to see I wasn't mistaken about you back on Lenue, Renna. You did what needed to be done with Navang. You rescued the boy and destroyed the threat. I hope you're willing to do the same to Finn and the *Athena*."

"I'm not sure what you mean, sir."

"I know the truth, Renna. I know you blew up the facility. I don't disagree with your actions, but I wish you'd contacted me first." The major shook his head sadly. "It could have saved us all a lot of time and trouble."

Renna stayed silent. The man was going to slip up; she only

had to wait.

"This mission to find Finn and the boy is even more important than your previous one. I can't tell you how critical it is we bring Myka in."

She crossed her arms over her chest. "And why is that?"

"Myka and his technology are the key to our future. To MYTH's future."

She arched an eyebrow at him questioningly, but she held her breath. Could this be it? "How so?" she asked.

"I saw your report. If Navang believed using Myka's DNA could help him build his army, perhaps we can figure out how. We need every advantage we can get. The universe is a dangerous place."

"And you have no problem using an innocent little boy to create a super-soldier? No wonder Finn and Aldani went on the run. They'd want nothing to do with this."

Larson growled and took a threatening step closer, his cold eyes flashing. "You don't understand, girl. There are some things even more important than protecting the innocent. Do you know how many species out there are waiting for the Coalition to slip up? To take over our territories? If that happens, life as we know it will be destroyed. We need to become better than anyone else."

A wave of something sharp hit her in the face. It smelled almost antiseptic, and she wrinkled her nose. What had he been doing in the med-bay?

"If that's what you truly believe, then maybe I don't want to be a part of MYTH after all," Renna said through gritted teeth. Her hands itched to punch the smug look off his face, but she held back. "Or do your superiors know you've been bending their rules to fit your own purpose?"

Larson's lips parted for a fraction before he slammed down his icy expression. "I don't know what you think you know, but I've been a part of MYTH since it was founded. I know the real organization and what they stand for." He lowered his voice. "I'm going to say this one more time, Renna. Your job here is to find the *Athena* and bring that boy back. Or I'll make sure becoming a hybrid is the least of your worries."

Major Larson was nothing more than a bully and a thug, and she knew how to handle those. Renna smirked at him first—for someone like him, there was nothing worse than being laughed at. "Thanks for confirming my suspicions, Major. Now if you'll excuse me, I have a mission to start."

She mockingly saluted him, then spun on her heel and headed toward the *Eris*. She could hear him grinding his teeth as she walked away. The fucker was going to pay—for betraying MYTH, for experimenting on Myka, and for insulting her.

"Everything all right?" Dallas asked as she joined him at the *Eris's* hatch. He watched the major's retreating form. "What did Larson want?"

"He wanted to make sure I understood how serious this mission was. How important Myka is."

"Myka?" Dallas shook his head. "Of course we want to make sure the boy's all right, but bringing Finn in is our goal right now. Where you find one, you'll find the other."

"That's what I thought, too." Renna shrugged. "Perhaps he heard different orders. MYTH is pretty decentralized after all."

He cleared his throat. "Not *that* decentralized. I'll follow up with Larson later and get this confusion settled. The man's always taken too much upon himself. Are you ready to go?"

Renna nodded. "Can't wait."

Dallas's face softened, and he held out a hand. "Good hunting."

She shook it. "Thanks for everything, sir. You won't regret it."

She felt his gaze follow her as she boarded the ship. The urge to tell him the truth was stronger than ever, but she couldn't risk it. She had a traitor to track down before any of them would be safe.

SEVEN

If Renna had thought the inside of the *Athena* was gorgeous, the *Eris* put her to shame. The sleek chrome walls, the smooth leather chairs in front of each console, the navigation map taking up one entire wall of the command center. It was as high-tech as it got. And when Commander Jayla gave the order to take off, Renna barely felt the ship move as they shot through the atmosphere and out into space.

Lieutenant Blake leaned back in his chair on the bridge, grinning at the rapturous expression on Renna's face. "She's a beauty, eh? I won the lottery when I was picked as Jayla's XO."

"I'd say." She lovingly ran a hand along the control panel. "You've been assigned to her long?"

She already knew from her earlier implant scan that he'd worked under Jayla for almost a year, but establishing relationships with the crew was going to be important. And she knew better than anyone that one of the easiest ways to build a relationship with a man was to get him talking about himself. They could never resist.

"Finn and I served under Jayla on the *Athena* for two years. When they gave her this new ship a year ago, Finn got a promotion to captain and his own command. I got picked as XO for the *Eris*."

"That's tough. Did you want your own ship?" She studied him under the guise of paying attention. He was as handsome as Finn, but with spiky blond hair and warm brown eyes instead of Finn's dark hair and blue eyes. But there was something similar about both of them. Maybe it was their military bearing or the upright moral fiber MYTH beat into them. But where Finn had a core of steel, Blake seemed younger somehow. More innocent.

The lieutenant shook his head. "Hell no. What person in his right mind wants that kind of responsibility? I'm perfectly happy serving under a very able commander and not being on the hook if something goes wrong." He pointed to himself. "Having your own command is stressful and I'd hate to damage this handsome face with too many wrinkles. Old age isn't a good look for me."

Renna laughed—for the first time in days, it felt like. "Good point. Wrinkles would definitely take away some of that boyish charm."

"I knew I liked you," he said, beaming. His glance slid toward the commander. "Jayla's going to have my head if I don't get back to work. And she is one woman you do not want to piss off. I think she has bigger balls than I do."

"You going to let me find out?" Renna asked with a seductive smile. She didn't mean a word of it, but flirting was another sure way to hook a man and she'd slipped into her old, practiced personality with ease. She'd perfected Renna-the-flirt years ago after she'd seen how well it had worked in getting her out of tight situations.

Blake flushed a deep red and stammered, "Uh...no...yes... I don't know..."

She bit back another laugh. Well that was unexpected. The guy could dish it out, but he couldn't take it. "Relax, handsome. I promise I won't bite."

Blake cleared his throat. "Er, I really need to get back to work. I'll talk to you later." He almost scurried back to his console.

Commander Jayla crossed the bridge to stand near Renna. "Are you upsetting my XO?"

"I didn't mean to."

Jayla shook her head, her gaze following the man as he took his station. "Alistair's a good kid. One of the best, actually. But he's a lot...nicer...than you'd expect a military man to be. Go easy on him."

"You sound almost maternal." Renna studied the woman's dark skin, her angular jaw. Despite reading Jayla's file, she didn't know anything about her personal life.

Jayla shrugged. "He had an easy life. I don't think he knew what he was signing up for when he joined MYTH. Finn and I have kept an eye on him."

"Is that why Finn got captain and Alistair didn't?"

Jayla nodded. "Blake's not ready for his own command yet. Don't get me wrong, he will be, and he'll be an excellent captain. He just needs a bit more experience under his belt. He's got a different style from most of my crew, and I want to nurture that."

Renna tapped a fingernail against the railing. Interesting. Most military people she'd met were more than happy to beat any sign of emotion out of their recruits. She hoped she was around long enough to see how Jayla and Blake interacted.

"Enough about my crew," Jayla said, shaking her head. "Where are we headed?"

"Costa system. I have a lead on a facility on Crius Beta."

Jayla's brows drew together. "Why would Captain Finn be hiding there? It's a manufacturing system. That doesn't make sense."

"No idea." Renna shrugged. "My research said it was one of the possibilities. Might as well start there."

The commander frowned but nodded. "Lieutenant Tevsi, set course for the Costa system." When she was satisfied they were on their way, she turned back to Renna. "I'll show you to your quarters now and you can get settled in."

Jayla led Renna from the command center through the middle of the ship. Crew quarters were a floor below, and instead of separate officer/crew areas, everyone bunked in the same corridor. It was a pretty ship, well-designed, with barely a noise from the engine room.

"What's it run on?" Renna asked as they passed a pair of engineers working at their consoles.

"It's a fusion core generator with a Peron reactor and an electromagnetic dampening field to help it move smoothly through space. It's a prototype design, but if it works well in the *Eris*, it'll be rolled out to the rest of the fleet." Jayla patted the wall of the ship. "It's quite an honor they assigned her to you for this mission."

"I understand this whole situation is a bit unusual."

"You could say that." Jayla studied Renna, her gaze laser-sharp. "You are also not telling me the entire truth, are you? There's something else going on besides finding a missing ship."

Great. Dallas had passed along his suspicions. Renna would have to tread carefully; she needed this woman on her side. "I promise, as soon as I know something, I'll tell you." She smiled at the commander. "Please know I'd never put you or your crew in jeopardy. I need this mission to succeed as much as you do."

Jayla studied Renna. After a long moment, the commander nodded once. "Fine. But I am the commander of this ship and the safety of my crew is the most important thing, even beyond your mission."

"I understand." Renna turned and started moving again toward the sleeping quarters. "I appreciate you trusting me. I know this is difficult."

"I don't trust you, Carrizal. I trust Major Dallas."

Renna bit back a smile. Now she sounded just like Finn when Renna had first come aboard the *Athena*.

She really needed to stop that. Whatever she had with Finn would have to wait until she'd put an end to Pallas and figured out a way to stop herself from turning into a cyborg. She couldn't afford the distraction, especially if she failed.

And if she failed? Well, none of it would matter then anyway.

Jayla stopped at the end of the corridor and pressed a button on the keypad. "Here's your cabin."

The door slid open to reveal a small room with a single bunk, a table, and a small bathroom. Renna noticed her bag was already on the bed as she stepped inside.

"It's perfect, thank you. Please let me know when we get close to the Costa system, and I'll fill you in on the next steps."

Jayla turned away. "One more thing?" she said, looking back at Renna over her shoulder. "Dallas told me who you are, Star Thief. I'll be watching you." The door slid shut behind her, leaving Renna to stare at the smooth chrome.

Damn the man. Did he have to tell everyone? Being the Star Thief was dangerous enough, but if word got out it was her, she'd be done. Every merc in the galaxy and most of their armies would come after her. It was enough to give a girl gray hair.

She sighed noisily. It would be fairly easy to escape MYTH's clutches and disappear on the next planet, but with this stupid implant taking over her brain, they knew she was trapped. Her only option was to stay here and hope MYTH didn't let the cat out of the bag.

"Dammit," Renna growled and threw herself down on the bed. Her head pounded, and as she rolled over, the hard edges of Dr. Samil's pill box dug into her skin. She pulled it from her pocket and set it on the nightstand where the metal glinted in the overhead lights. Those pills might be the only thing standing between becoming a cyborg and getting a happily ever after.

Renna felt her muscles relax as the pillow cushioned her aching head. She needed to get some sleep before they arrived on Crius Beta. Her thoughts drifted back to Finn. He'd been so angry at her the first time she'd stepped foot on the *Athena*. She snuggled further into the blankets and chuckled. She'd been pretty pissed at him, too, but that still hadn't stopped her from enjoying the view of his ass as he'd marched away from her.

Her body started to relax, and she felt herself drifting in and out of consciousness. The ringing in her ears grew louder, but before she could worry about it, she was asleep.

EIGHT

uzzy. Everything was so fuzzy. A strange dull throb made the back of Renna's head ache, and the taste of metal and star fuel filled her mouth with bitterness. Her weight shifted as the ship around her fell out of light speed. The tension behind her forehead eased as the ship slowed.

The Athena *trembled as Flight Lieutenant Kojima disengaged the FTL thrusters and the flight dampeners re-engaged. On the bridge, Captain Finn frowned at a holomap of whatever system they were headed toward.*

Renna shifted, trying to get a better view of him. His dark hair was spiky, like he'd run his hands through it too many times, and the skin beneath his blue eyes was smudged and shadowed.

"Lieutenant Keva, what's our status?" Finn's voice had a strange metallic tone, but she'd recognize it anywhere.

Her chest tightened and she reached out a hand to touch him, but her arms felt leaden, immovable. When they didn't obey, she focused her gaze on Lieutenant Keva, the Delfine alien who was Finn's XO.

"Krooss, Thasa system. Viktis has a safe house there."

"The third this week." Finn's hands curled around the railing of the CIC. "MYTH is getting better and better at tracking us since we left Forever Station. It feels like we're running in circles, doesn't it?"

The lieutenant nodded. "I hope Renna can figure out what's going on sooner rather than later. I'm not sure how we can stay ahead of the trackers much longer."

"We'll have to try. Maybe our resident pirate has some ideas. He's full of them."

Keva grinned, an unusual sparkle in her violet eyes. "Yes, yes, he is."

Finn shook his head, but a smile tugged at his lips. "Behave, Lieutenant. I'm going to go let Aldani know we've arrived. He needed some more supplies. Make sure he gets everything he asks for."

Keva saluted. "Yes, sir."

The scene faded, but a moment later, Renna watched Finn stride into an equipment-filled med-bay.

Dr. David Aldani hunched over a microscope, but he straightened at Finn's entrance. "Ah, there you are, Captain."

"We'll be landing on Krooss within the hour, Doctor. Have you sent Lieutenant Keva your supply list? I've told her to do whatever it takes to get what you need." Finn sighed and ran a hand through his hair. "I didn't expect to leave Forever Station in such a hurry. We left too many supplies behind."

"I think taking down Kitty Cordoza was more than worth it," Aldani said with a smile. "I saw on the holofeed that they found extensive evidence tying her to a massive slave ring. They said she'll be locked *away for life."*

A slow grin twisted Finn's lips. "Kitty found out firsthand that karma's a bitch. I'm just glad I was there to help put her away." His gaze fell to Aldani's electron microscope, and the amusement slid from his face. "Any news on Renna's condition?"

Aldani shook his head. "Not yet. The tissue sample I took before we left is unlike anything I've seen before. The cells are changing and mutating faster than should be possible."

Finn shoved his hands into his pockets, shoulders hunching. "She's not going to make it, is she?" Renna's stomach twisted at the flicker of pure anguish that crossed Finn's face.

"Of course she's going to make it. She has the best doctors at MYTH working on it. And me. Who knows—maybe MYTH has already found a way to stop the integration completely." He put a hand on Finn's arm. "You can't think like that. Renna's tough. She'll get through this."

Finn nodded, but he didn't look convinced. "Thanks for the information, Doc. I have to get back to the bridge. Let me know if you uncover anything else."

Renna followed Finn as he left the med bay and wandered through the ship. He trailed a finger along one of the smooth polythene walls, and Renna's skin erupted in flames, as if he'd touched her.

But that was impossible. They were millions of miles away.

"Renna, where are you?" he muttered.

She wanted to whisper to him, to tell him she was right there, but the dream had frozen her mouth as well as her body. She used every atom of her willpower to walk toward him, to raise her hand to touch his face, but her body wouldn't obey. She felt impossibly heavy. Immovable.

Around her, the Athena jerked and trembled, and Finn stumbled, catching himself on the wall. Renna shivered again at the searing heat of his hand. Sucked in a breath to say his name...

...and was awakened by Commander Jayla's voice filling her room.

"Good morning, Renna. We should be in the Costa system in under an hour."

Her lungs felt like they'd been squeezed into a teacup, and she took a deep, shuddering breath before responding. "Thanks, Commander. I'll be right up."

She forced herself to sit upright, waiting until the cabin stopped spinning before getting to her feet. Her blood pumped sluggishly through her veins, her mind thick with fog. It felt like she'd been attacked by a rabid moisu. The two-headed creatures rarely left their pray intact.

But she'd seen Finn, even if it had only been a dream. That was almost worth feeling like this.

Renna ran some cool water in the sink, splashing her face several times with the icy water. Damn, that was cold. But it wasn't doing much to wake her up. She was still focused on the longing that ached within her, the touch of Finn's hand on her arm. It had felt so real, so life-like. Like she'd actually been there with him.

Renna studied her pale reflection in the mirror over the sink. Her caramel skin had lost its usual color, and her lips were pale pink. Exhaustion made her look like she was about to pass out.

And then she peered deeper into her eyes. They were even darker than normal, almost black as the pupils swallowed her irises. But as she stared, something flickered deep inside them. A strange glow that wasn't entirely human.

Her fingers curled into the metal sink as everything hit her at once. Acid spiked the back of her throat, and she swallowed back the nausea. It was happening. Beyond the weird mental things, she was *physically* changing. Her implant was turning her into a hybrid.

Renna's knees gave out, and she slid to the floor, her back resting against the bathroom wall. She wrapped her arms around her knees and rocked back and forth. This wasn't happening. Couldn't be happening. She was going to solve this. Everything was going to be all right.

But what if it wasn't?

An angry wail escaped her. It wasn't fucking fair. This wasn't supposed to happen to her, just when she was finally starting her life. She was fucking twenty-three years old. She'd worked her ass off to make it this far, and with one injection, it had all been snatched away from her. Her future, her relationship with Finn, even the money she'd spent the last ten years saving so she could retire and start a new life. What the hell did a robot need with credits?

Bile coated her tongue as another wave of nausea twisted through her. Renna curled into herself further, resting her head on her knees. She'd spent her whole life working so hard to get past her childhood—to become something different, to leave her blasted mother and the tenements behind, to find her own path.

And for what? To die alone and unloved somewhere in a MYTH facility while they experimented on her? Fuck if she was going to let that happen. She'd kill herself first. Maybe she should just do it now and save everyone the trouble.

A sob ripped through her. Giving up would be so easy. She could disappear on Crius Beta. Find a quiet place. End it all. It might hurt Finn for a while, but he'd get over it. He'd understand. And then everyone would be free to move on.

But what about Pallas? She'd promised to stop him, to keep Myka safe. A stupid promise, one she didn't know if she could actually fulfill. One she never should have made in the first place. But it was out there now, haunting her.

Renna raised her head from her knees and scrubbed away the tears wetting her cheeks. Whatever she decided, it would have to be soon. She was running out of time.

NINE

After she'd pulled herself together, Renna made her way to the bridge. Sitting around feeling sorry for herself wasn't really her style anyway. She took up a spot just inside the door, out of the way of the rest of the crew.

Commander Jayla sat in the chair overlooking the command center, while Lieutenant Blake was at his station to her right.

"Entering atmosphere," Flight Lieutenant Tevsi said, adjusting the ship's speed and trajectory. The Delfine pilot glanced back at Renna, raising one of her pale violet eyebrows. "Where to?"

"Hunda," she said. Crius Beta was a modern, well-populated planet. As the ochre-colored ground rushed toward them, Renna could make out the huge manufacturing compounds, shining white and chrome in the late afternoon sunlight. Luckily, she didn't need to worry about finding her way around one of those; they were headed for the main city.

"Dock at Station Twelve, if they have space."

"I'll contact the spaceport now," Tevsi said.

"Thank you, Lieutenant," Jayla said, getting to her feet. "Make sure to keep us under the radar. No need to announce we're with MYTH. Use the fake codes Dallas gave us." Jayla motioned to Renna. "Can I speak with you?" Without waiting for an answer, Jayla marched away from the bridge.

"Are you going to tell me what we're really doing on this planet?" Jayla demanded, stopping in the middle of the corridor. "I did my own research. There's nothing here but a few manufacturing companies and financial businesses. Why would Finn come here? It doesn't make sense." Jayla narrowed her eyes. "Is this some sort of trap?"

Renna sighed noisily. "I'm not sure what else I can do to convince you people. I haven't left yet. Haven't betrayed anyone. In fact, I'm actively trying to help you. Cut me some fucking slack."

A zap of power shot through her brain as her implant kicked on, calculating the odds of her escape from MYTH. She shuddered and threw a hand against the wall to steady herself as the heads-up display appeared in her vision. Eighty-seven percent chance of success if she ran now—they'd never find her on this planet—but there was a ninety-two percent chance she'd never see Finn again if she did.

She squeezed her eyes shut, willing the implant to turn off. That kind of information was not helpful right now.

"Everything all right, Commander?" Lieutenant Blake asked. He walked gingerly toward them, like he knew he was approaching two fighting beasts.

"I don't know. Renna?" Jayla tilted her head, waiting for an answer.

"It's fine." She rubbed the back of her neck. It really wasn't, but the commander didn't care about the implant taking over Renna's brain. "I have a job to do, and I plan on doing it with or without you, so if you're not here to help me, get out of my way."

The commander's lips thinned. "Exactly what do you have planned?"

"Nothing illegal," she said, ignoring the woman's worried frown. "But I'll be impersonating someone else to get inside Titan Industries. If you can't play along, I'll be going by myself."

"Titan Industries?" Blake tilted his head and rubbed a hand along his jaw. "Never heard of them. What do they have to do with Finn and the *Athena*?"

"That's what I'm hoping to find out," she lied.

"Well, count me in." Lieutenant Blake tugged at the lapels of his uniform jacket. "Cloak-and-dagger is my game."

Renna shook her head. "Not if you stomp around like an elephant like the rest of the MYTH soldiers I've met."

Blake shot her a wounded look. "I can safely assure you I've never stomped in my life."

"Really?" Jayla asked, her lips twisting as she tried not to grin. "And that's not you making the whole ship shudder on the way to the mess every morning?"

Blake held up his hands. "I can't be held responsible for anything I do before coffee."

Renna interrupted before the two of them went any further. "Whatever the case is, I need you both to stay out of my way if you come. Understood?"

Jayla's dark eyebrows furrowed like she wanted to protest, but she finally nodded.

"Good." Renna turned toward the hatch. "Let's go find us some intel."

Renna stepped out into the dusty hangar bay at the smaller of Hunda's spaceports and pulled on her knee-length leather coat. Commander Jayla and Lieutenant Blake both followed, dressed in civvies instead of their MYTH uniforms.

The spaceport was at the edge of the city, mostly used by mercenaries and people trying to stay under police radar. Totally her kind of place. She inhaled, letting the smell of the planet wash over her. There was the typical spaceport odor of starfuel and exhaust in the background, along with the scent of food from the nearby bazar and the steel-and-glass tang of the towering buildings at the center of the city. And beyond it all, something she'd never felt before—the faint hum of the communications systems on the planet.

She didn't know whether to be terrified or excited by that addition.

"Where to?" Blake asked, squinting into the distance.

Renna focused on blocking out the noise as she nodded to her right. "The Baji building. It's the blue one over there."

Blake tapped an order into his wrist tablet. "Speeder should be here in a minute or so. You going to tell us what we're up against?"

Renna watched the busy street as speeders whizzed by. A

crowd of laughing businessmen in orange suits hurried back to work at the stock exchange after some corporate lunch. A trio of stylish Delfine women in tight, black dresses walked past on their way to the shopping district. It all looked perfectly ordinary. But that didn't mean it was safe. Blake and Jayla would be better off not knowing the truth, but if she knew anything about MYTH officers, it was that they were as tenacious as a two-headed moisu when it came to information.

She shrugged. "I wish I knew. My research led me to believe there might be a lead on where the *Athena* went and what they're planning. From what I learned, Titan Industries may be a front for a secret MYTH corporation."

"Why would MYTH need a secret corporation?" Jayla asked.

"That's what I hope to find out. I'm going to talk to the man in charge and convince him to give us some answers. Even better, I'm going to walk in through the front door."

Blake let out a noisy sigh. "So no super-spy action on this mission? I have to say I'm disappointed, Renna. I thought I was going to get to play James Bond."

"You realize if you were playing James Bond I'd be one of the villains, right? Spies are not the same as thieves." Though sometimes their jobs overlapped a bit. There was that handsome spy she'd met several years ago. They'd had a fling after he'd fulfilled his mission: catching her.

Renna shook her head. "Besides, why are you still reading that old-Earth stuff? Haven't you heard of Chorwig Deni? He's way better."

"Eh, Bond's smoother. And has a few less tentacles."

Renna rolled her eyes as a speeder pulled up in front of them.

"I'm just going to ignore your bad taste for now. Come on, the sooner we get this over, the sooner we can get back to the *Eris*." And hopefully one step closer to Pallas.

The speeder deposited them in front of the tall, blue building at the center of the city. She stared up at the metal girders curving skyward, twisting as they spiraled the building, and let out a low whistle. The whole thing was made of azure ore from Mali V. Someone had deep pockets.

"So what's the plan?" Blake asked, tucking his hands into the pockets of his dark brown trousers. He wore a cream, open-collar shirt that highlighted his muscled shoulders, and his blond hair was carelessly spiky. He looked like he belonged on a holozine cover somewhere, not in the middle of a military operation. If she wasn't already halfway in love with Finn, she'd have been very tempted.

She cleared her throat and dragged her focus back to the job at hand and not the sparkling caramel eyes waiting for her to answer. She preferred blue eyes anyway. "How about you two wait outside and guard the entrance. I can handle the inside work."

Jayla shook her head. "Not a chance."

"Come on, Commander. You know I'm not going anywhere. I just need a little space to do my thing." She gave the woman her most convincing smile, but Jayla didn't budge.

"We're going with you. Dallas asked us to keep an eye on you, and unlike Finn, I don't disobey orders."

Unexpected hurt stabbed through Renna, and she looked away. Why did it suddenly matter to her either way?

Jayla shook her head. "That's not it. Dallas knew you'd try to do this alone. He wanted to make sure you had backup."

"Excuse me?"

"He's not stupid, Renna, and neither am I. We both know there's something else going on. Why do you think he didn't press you for details?" Jayla smiled. "So despite you trying to push us away, we're going to do this together. Blake and I have your back."

Renna glanced at Blake, who nodded. "What the commander said."

Warmth blossomed in her chest, but she kept her face expressionless. Depending on other people had never been one of her strengths; she'd prided herself on being able to handle everything alone. But in the last few weeks, she'd started to feel...different. Like maybe being part of a team wouldn't be so bad after all. Unfortunately, a weakness like that was a dangerous thing in her line of business. If she was smart, she'd put an end to it before she got hurt.

"Fine." She shrugged. "Follow my lead and keep quiet. You'll know soon enough if we get into trouble."

She tugged her dark hair from its usual ponytail and shook it loose around her shoulders, then unbuttoned the top of her blouse to show some cleavage.

"Let's do this." Renna pulled her tablet from the bag slung over her shoulder, then shoved through the doors into a marble-lined lobby and marched directly toward the pretty Ileth secretary sitting at the front desk. Behind her on the wall hung a large logo in gold metal—a human eye crossed by two spears.

Renna squared her shoulders and spoke as fast as she could. "Excuse me, miss, Monet Green here to see the CEO. I'm with the *Costa Star News.* I need to speak with him immediately on a galactic matter. He'll want to see me at once." Before the girl could protest, Renna pushed past her to the sealed door and tapped her foot impatiently. "Please hurry, young lady. There's no time to waste."

The girl's orange lips parted in shock, and she jumped to her feet to open the security door for the elevators. "I'll...I'll let him know you're on your way up."

Renna smiled at her. "Good girl. What floor is he on?"

"Six." She backed away, and Renna, Blake, and Jayla stepped into the elevator.

"Thank you." Renna nodded at the girl as the doors slid shut.

Blake chuckled softly. "Impressive. Remind me to never try conning you."

"Probably a good idea. I eat nice guys like you for breakfast." Renna grinned at him. "Let's just hope our CEO is as easily fooled. If not, I'm going to need you two to keep everyone out of his office as long as possible."

Renna tugged her shirt lower and flipped her hair again as the elevator stopped, depositing them on the sixth floor.

Another secretary, this one a young blonde human woman with a nice rack, sat behind a large, glass desk. She half-rose to her feet.

"Who are you?" she demanded, her gaze raking over the trio suspiciously. "Mr. Sherle is in a meeting. He's not to be disturbed."

Renna leaned over the desk and stared the woman down, her voice as pointed as the knives hidden in her knee-high boots. "I'm with the *Costa Star News.* I need to speak with him *immediately.*

This is a matter of life or death." She glanced at the office door, and her implant surged on, returning two heat signatures in the next room. One had the slight purple tint of a Trezian alien. Great, just what she needed.

The secretary shook her head. "He's busy. You'll have to make an appointment." She tapped at her console, then said, "Looks like he's free next week."

Renna frowned apologetically. "I'm afraid that's not going to work, miss. Titan Industries is in danger. If I don't see him immediately, you may not have a job next week." Renna tapped on her tablet and pulled up an official looking graph. "See. There's not much time."

The girl blinked and craned her neck to get a better view before Renna yanked the screen away.

"Monet is one of our best reporters," Blake said. "You'd better listen to her."

The girl turned to frown at him, eyes widening as she finally noticed who she was talking to. Her hand drifted up to smooth back her hair, and a soft blush tinged her cheeks. "Are you with her?" she asked.

While Blake distracted the girl, Renna headed toward the office door fighting back a smile. Not bad for a soldier. Blake had a lot of things going for him, not to mention he was exceptionally easy on the eyes.

Without pausing, she thrust open the wooden door and barged into the room.

The tall man behind the desk shot to his feet, his shock of gray hair quivering with outrage. "What is the meaning of this? Lissa! Who are these people?"

The girl appeared in the doorway, breathless and flushed—and not with exertion. She wrung her hands and cast a reproachful look back at Blake. "I'm so sorry, sir, I..."

Renna approached the desk, hand extended. She ignored the angry glint in the man's eyes. "Mr. Sherle, I'm Monet Green from the *Costa Star News*. We're here on a matter of urgent business." She glanced at the Trezian, then back to Sherle. "We need to speak privately. Now."

His face turned purple, and he opened and closed his mouth before finally exploding. "Get out! I will not have reporters in my office!" He pointed toward the door, finger quivering. "You have thirty seconds before I call security."

She stepped closer to him, lowering her voice. "Trust me, you're going to want to hear this. I'm with MYTH. We have reason to believe you're in danger."

The man's jaw snapped shut. "Godsdammit. Lissa, show Mr. K'Zergi to my private waiting room and get him whatever he wants." He turned to the alien with a bow. "My sincerest apologies, Relge, this will only take a few minutes."

The Trezian folded two of his arms across his broad chest. "You are trying my patience, Sherle. I will return tomorrow, and you had better be ready for our discussion." He lumbered to his feet, towering over the humans in the room before stomping out.

Lissa muttered her apologies and shut the door quietly behind him, but not before first shooting Renna a death glare.

Mr. Sherle slammed a fist on his desk. "What the hell are you doing here? MYTH only contacts me over holovid. They've left me to run this business as I see fit."

Renna lowered herself into the chair the Trezian had vacated and crossed her legs. She smiled slowly, all urgency gone. "Please have a seat, Mr. Sherle. There's no need to shout."

He froze, his face going a deeper shade of purple. After a long moment, he dropped back into the chair behind his desk.

Jayla and Blake took up positions on either side of the door. The commander's hand hovered close to her blaster, while Blake crossed his arms over his chest. Renna ignored the way his white shirt stretched over his muscles and his full lips curved into an amused smile. At least someone was having fun.

"I demand you tell me what this is about," Sherle said.

"Then I need you to tell me who your contact is at MYTH." Renna leaned forward and rested her elbows on her knees. The position also allowed a clear view of her cleavage.

Sherle's gaze didn't even waver from her face. "Why?"

Well, it had been worth a shot at least. Renna straightened again and tried a different tactic. "Mr. Sherle—or may I call you Epher?—your company is about to be investigated by the Coalition Association for Scientific and Technical Research for illegal research practices. MYTH wants to leave you swinging in the wind, deny all involvement, but I'm here to help you."

"And who are you exactly?"

"I'm a MYTH special agent. I'm trying to track down whoever sold you out, and I think they're inside the organization. You scratch my back, I'll scratch yours." She let her gaze linger on him, slightly suggestive. The man flushed and dropped his gaze.

Ah, good. She was finally getting through.

Sherle pulled up a set of charts on his monitor. "MYTH funding accounts for sixty percent of our budget. We were formed from a startup company five years ago by the medical arm of the government, but our mandate changed three years ago to focus on manufacturing and design of networked computer systems that can be used for long-range communication."

She nodded, pretending to already know that information. "Correct. And tell me, how often do you have contact with the MYTH shareholders? Who directs your production and costs?"

"Twice yearly we send a shareholders' report on our progress to MYTH. As long as we keep making strides toward finalizing the comm plan, Major Larson leaves us alone." He paused. "I don't understand why we're in trouble with the CASTR. We operate above board, within the rules of the Arlon Treaty. Why would they be investigating us?"

Renna twitched with excitement. He'd named Larson as one of the contacts. She was on the right track. "I'm afraid there is some internal turmoil within MYTH that is affecting certain special projects. I suggest you search for new shareholders and reduce your dependence on MYTH funding. If you're caught in the crossfire, it will destroy this company."

His eyes widened. "But..."

"I am telling you the truth, Mr. Sherle. Don't trust any communications from MYTH or their subsidiaries. In the meantime, I'll do what I can to delay the investigation."

"Why do you care?" He placed his hands on his desk and leaned forward to study her. "Why are you helping me?"

She smiled slyly. "This is where we get to the back-scratching part." Renna stood up and moved toward the desk. "I need access to your files and network."

His jaw gaped. "What? No."

"Just for a five minutes. I need to run a scan. I promise I won't leak any of your info. I'm looking for something specific."

"What?"

"I can't tell you that. It's classified. But I promise I'm not here to audit you. Your secrets are safe, Mr. Sherle."

The purple had faded from his face, turning it ashen. "Absolutely not. Those files are confidential."

Renna sighed and got to her feet. Why could people just never do as they were told? It would make everything so much easier.

He glared at her. "Now if you'll excuse me, I have some shareholders to contact."

"I'm afraid not, Mr. Sherle." Renna crossed behind the desk and pulled out a small white packet. She opened it, and a small pile of light blue powder sat in the middle.

"What is that?" Sherle demanded.

Renna smiled and blew the powder into his face.

He spluttered in panic and waved his hands around, trying to brush the powder away. "What did you do, girl?"

"Took care of a complication. Goodnight, Mr. Sherle. It was a pleasure to meet you."

A moment later, he slumped over his desk, sound asleep.

"Lieutenant, can you get him out of the way please?" Renna asked, glancing over at Blake who stood stock-still beside the door.

His eyes had gone wide, but he nodded. "Yes, ma'am."

TEN

D id you really have to drug him?" Jayla asked, frowning at Sherle's motionless body. Blake had stretched him out on the low couch in the corner before returning to his post at the door. "That's not our usual method of handling these situations."

Renna had already booted up the computer, and her fingers drummed against the smooth wood as she studied the hologram of his family on some off-world vacation. A pretty wife and two cute girls. They looked nice and normal. Hopefully she hadn't made him one of Pallas's targets. The traitor would not appreciate Sherle giving up this data.

"I didn't have time to talk the guy down," she said with a shrug. "Just easier to keep him out of the way."

Jayla's lips thinned, but she merely said, "Interesting that Major Larson is involved. I wonder what he has to do with Titan Industries."

"Or what *that* has to do with finding Finn," Blake added, arching an eyebrow at Renna.

Finn. Her heart clenched, catching her off-guard. Right. They thought her primary concern was looking for the *Athena*. Could she risk telling them the truth now? She was usually a pretty good judge of character, but if either of them were involved with Pallas, she'd be putting Finn in terrible danger.

But they were running out of time, and it was clear she couldn't do this alone. She didn't have much choice. Renna cleared her throat uncomfortably and typed a command string into the computer. Silence stretched until the room throbbed with it. Finally, she said, "Titan Industries is tied to MYTH, that's true. But I'm not here to investigate Finn. I'm after something bigger."

Jayla nodded. "We already guessed that, Renna."

Renna felt her body tense like she was about to dive off of a high ledge. She met the woman's gaze. It was now or never. She nodded, ignoring the twist of unease in her gut. She'd do what she had to, even if that meant trusting these people with the most important things in her life.

"What you don't know is that there's a traitor inside MYTH. Someone with the codename Pallas was behind Navang's facility, and if we don't find him, he'll use that hybrid army to destroy the whole organization. Maybe even the coalition government."

Blake's jaw dropped. "That's impossible."

"This man is devious, Lieutenant." Renna glanced down at the computer. "He's spent years working on this plan. The problem is I have no idea where or when he'll strike. Or even what he really wants."

"And you think Larson is involved?" Jayla asked, gritting her teeth. "I always hated that man. He pinched my ass once. The only reason I didn't punch him in the balls was because he was a superior officer. But I can't believe he'd go as far as treason."

"Commander, I'd bet my life that this man is one of Pallas's moles within the organization. Draven Navang named him as a contact, and here he is showing up again, involved with Titan Industries. But I need to find real proof before I can accuse an officer of treason."

Worry flashed across Jayla's face, but she nodded. "Then do what you need to. We'll make sure you're not disturbed."

Quickly, Renna searched through Sherle's email, but nothing stood out. Next up were his network files. She pulled up several dozen earnings reports, a list of investors from the past ten years, and a shareholders' report from last year. Digging a little deeper, she found the list of personnel who'd worked at TI and downloaded them to her disk. She'd have to run it through her scan later and see if any MYTH hits came up.

"Finding anything?" Jayla asked, opening the door to peer out at the lobby. "I think Miss Secretary is getting a bit antsy."

"Almost done." Renna moved on to the last year's R&D reports and read over them quickly. Her fingers paused on the keyboard as she caught a paragraph that tugged at her memory.

The latest prototype for Titan Industries is a long-range communicator that runs on the electromagnetic energy between stars. Designed to allow almost instant communication between star systems with no lag, it holds great promise in uniting the great expanse of space. And would make TI one of the foremost experts on this type of communication.

Her skin erupted in goose bumps. With the neural network

that Dr. Navang had developed for his hybrid army, a device like this could give someone complete and instant power over all the soldiers anywhere in the galaxy. They could send troops to any planet, commanding them in real time, while safely out of the line of fire.

Even more worrisome was the thought of the sleeper agents Navang had created. With instant communication, they could react immediately to threats or other orders. They'd be undetectable and unstoppable.

Renna swallowed and copied over the design plans. It was all here, she just needed to figure out what it meant. She wasn't stupid, but Pallas had woven his web carefully, the parts moving like chess pieces across a board she couldn't see.

Across the room, Commander Jayla suddenly went stiff. She pressed the comm below her ear. "What's going on, Tevsi?" Several seconds passed before she nodded. "We'll be right there."

Like a switch had been flipped, Jayla's spine straightened, and her voice took on a clipped, military tone again. "There's been an attack on MYTH HQ. We have to report in. Now." She met Renna's gaze. "It looks like you were right."

Lieutenant Blake jumped to his feet. "But that's impossible. MYTH defenses are state-of-the-art. We have three Peron cannons guarding each facility, along with comm towers, electromagnetic barriers, and guards everywhere."

Renna followed as they headed down the hallway to the elevator. MYTH's defenses might be state-of-the-art, but if there was someone on the inside, it wouldn't matter if they had the newest tech in the galaxy.

They'd all die anyway.

ELEVEN

Back on the *Eris*, Jayla paused in the CIC to address her crew. "Prep for immediate takeoff. Once I've debriefed with Major Dallas, I want to be ready to head directly for wherever he assigns us." Jayla was completely in control and in command, but beneath her confident exterior, Renna saw the flash of fear in the woman's eyes. Someone had attacked her family. She was getting ready for battle.

The crew scrambled to complete her orders, and Jayla turned to her pilot. "I'm headed to the comm room. Patch Major Dallas through, Tevsi."

The pilot nodded, but the commander had already spun on her heel and marched toward the back of the ship. Renna exchanged a worried glance with Blake, and they followed close behind.

Jayla took her place in front of a console in the comm room

in parade rest, but every line of her body sung with tension.

Dread gnawed through Renna's gut, nervous energy making her muscles twitch. If she'd been alone, she would have paced back and forth in the small space, but Jayla looked like she was about to crack. Setting the woman off would not help the situation. Instead, Renna played with the ends of her hair and stared at the smooth, chrome walls. Pallas had to be behind the attack. But why had he finally struck?

Renna's fingers froze, wrapped around her dark strands. Sherle's files. Dammit. She hadn't even thought to check for a tracer. Fucking rookie mistake. What the hell was wrong with her?

The image of Major Dallas filled the screen as the hologram shimmered to life. Renna tried to focus instead of cursing at herself.

"Commander, where the hell have you been?" he demanded. Behind him, the air was hazy, as if filled with smoke.

Jayla saluted. "Sir, we were following a lead on the *Athena*. We returned to the ship as soon as we got word. What happened?" She stood stiffly, her spine locked into perfect military posture, but one boot tapped against the metal floor.

Dallas's lips thinned. "Our facility has been attacked. The place is in chaos. Major Larson is missing, along with several high-ranking officials." He paused, and his gaze finally steadied on Renna. "As well as the entire medical team."

Renna's lungs clenched as all of the oxygen was sucked out of the room. "Dr. Samil?"

"Gone. Along with all of the experimental drugs she was working on. Including yours."

Renna sat down heavily on the chair beside her as her knees gave out. Pallas knew. This was retaliation for Renna's investigation. Could she risk telling Dallas the truth now, too? Could he help them stop the traitor?

But the thought still haunted her—what if he was the traitor himself? What if this was all an act to get her to slip up and show her hand? She'd already told Jayla and Blake. That had to be enough.

Jayla flashed Renna a look of worry but turned back to Dallas. "What's going on there? What do you need?"

"I need you to get to the bottom of this. I'm starting to wonder if it's connected to Finn and the *Athena*. What did you find out on Crius Beta?"

The commander glanced between Renna and the holocomm. Waiting for Renna to tell him the truth.

Fear stroked its icy fingers against her neck, and Renna shivered. She couldn't do it. She couldn't have those lives on her head if Dallas was the traitor. She'd have to stall him somehow.

"Sir," she started. "We discovered Titan Industries, a manufacturing company, is a MYTH front for scientific research. They're developing a communication device that will allow instant communications across the galaxy."

Dallas eyebrows furrowed. "What does that have to do with Captain Finn?"

Renna stood up, forcing herself to remain calm. "Nothing as far as we know, but it may have something to do with the hybrid army Dr. Navang was building."

"I thought that was finished," Dallas protested. "Navang is dead, and his facility is destroyed. There are no more hybrids." He paused. "Other than you and the boy."

"But what if he was working with someone else? Someone who's not ready to let the plan go?" Renna suggested. It was as close to the truth as she could get without spilling everything to him.

Jayla frowned at her but stayed silent, thank the gods.

Major Dallas sighed noisily. "Whatever the hell is going on, we need to figure it out now. Before another facility is attacked."

"Do you have any leads on who could have done this?" Renna asked.

"It had to be an inside job, I'm afraid. No one else could have gotten past our defenses." His forehead wrinkled with a frown. "But it doesn't make sense. Why? Who?"

Lieutenant Blake met her gaze across the room and nodded at her imperceptibly. Relief flooded through Renna. They were going to play along for now.

"Perhaps they're all connected," the lieutenant suggested. "If someone inside MYTH was working for Navang, it would explain why they were able to get a hold of Myka Aldani in the first place and how they knew about his...alterations."

Dallas was silent, and Renna glanced at Blake in surprise. The guy was hot *and* smart.

"You may be right, Lieutenant," Dallas finally continued. "But while we try to uncover what's really going on here, I have a different mission for you. Find and rescue the medical team. It's the only thing we have a lead on right now and the only thing that will keep Renna alive long enough to help us figure out the rest of this."

"A lead, sir?" Jayla asked.

"Yes, this came in a few minutes ago." The holoscreen flickered as Dallas typed something into the controls. The image solidified into a woman with blonde hair sitting in front of a screen. Her features were blurred enough that Renna couldn't quite make her out, but as soon as she opened her mouth, Renna sucked in a sharp breath.

"This is Dr. Thana Samil. I am issuing distress code VANI. Please rendezvous at the following coordinates as soon as you can." In a trembling voice, she rattled off a series of coordinates, then shifted closer to the camera. A dark bruise marred the left side of her face, and her eyes looked bloodshot and exhausted as they flicked to someone off camera. "It's a matter of life and death," she whispered before the screen went black.

"How did she get this out to you?" Renna asked. "If she was kidnapped, why would they have let her near a comm device?"

Jayla chewed her bottom lip. "I don't know, but I don't like it. It feels like someone is setting a trap."

"Damn straight it does." Dallas's image reappeared on screen. "But that's a chance we have to take. Samil is too important to MYTH. And she's the only one with the formula for Renna's drugs. Retrieving her is our number one priority right now."

Renna's whole body twitched with unease, but he was right. And maybe with a little luck she could turn the trap around on Pallas.

Even better, maybe Major Larson would be there. Kicking his ass would totally make her day.

"What's your plan?" Renna asked.

"Samil used code VANI in her message. That code is only used when there's no other option. It means search and destroy.

Scorched earth. Whatever it takes."

She sucked in a breath. The doc's bright eyes and warm smile flashed through her memory. Pallas had gone too far. This woman had done nothing but help Renna, and now she was going to die?

"Dr. Samil just signed her own death warrant? No. There has to be some way to get her out of there."

"That's what I'm counting on you for, Renna," Dallas said, leaning closer to the screen. "And if Blake is right and there's a traitor inside MYTH, the three of you are going to have to do it alone. Top secret. I'll try to hold off the destroy order as long as I can, but you're running out of time." His voice quavered, and he glanced away from the camera. "The most I can give you is twelve hours. Please do whatever you can."

Fear formed a lump in her throat, but Renna swallowed past it. "I'm the only girl for the job. I won't let you down, Major." She paused. "I'm going to need all the intel you have on that planet and any facilities near those coordinates."

"I'll get you anything you need, Renna. Just ask."

She smiled at him. "I'm going to hold you to that."

TWELVE

R enna sat at the small round table in her room, reading through the data Dallas had sent to her tablet. She took another sip of scorching coffee and held the liquid in her mouth for a fraction of a second—until her tongue started to burn—before swallowing. Sometime in the past few days, she'd started doing stuff like that, letting herself experience feelings she'd normally ignore. Like each time might be her last.

She shoved the coffee cup away, brown liquid sloshing onto the table.

Stop that.

But the haunting possibility was always there in the background. She might not make it through this. She'd thought that plenty of times before, when a job had gone tits up or she'd found herself faced with an angry merc, but she'd never really believed it.

Seeing that strange metallic reflection in her eyes had changed everything.

Even if she did find a way to stop the implant from completely taking over her body, it would still change everything. She'd be different in some very fundamental ways. How the hell did you deal with something like that?

Renna buried her head in her hands, rubbing her temples. She'd dealt with becoming a different person before. When she'd left the Izan tenements, she'd created a new persona, changed herself to survive. She could do it again.

But first she had to save Dr. Samil, and sitting here feeling sorry for herself wasn't going to help. She straightened her shoulders. So. First order of business: rescue Dr. Samil and her team. Second: destroy Pallas. Third: find Finn and live happily ever after.

Totally doable.

And if she was lucky, she might be able to take care of step one and two at the same time. Obviously letting Samil get a message out to MYTH was a trap, but Renna had a few of her own tricks to play. If Pallas and Major Larson had kidnapped the med team, maybe she could take them both down.

She studied the dossier. New Angeles was the smallest planet in the Vorti system. Its only claim to fame was the small scientific community that had sprung up around a series of ancient ruins. The mystery of who'd built them and why sent thousands of archaeologists and university students there every year. Small towns had popped up near each site to provide support services, goods, and food. But the rest of the planet was wild and empty. The perfect place for a hideout.

According to the holomap, the surface terrain looked rocky, with low jagged hills and gray dirt. The biggest outpost was the Tholi spaceport, crouched in a valley between two large hills. It served as the central base for most of the excavation operations in the area and had a bustling warehouse district for storing food, supplies, and ships.

Renna typed in the coordinates Dr. Samil had given, and a glowing holomap of the city sprang to life over the table. She pinched her fingers together, zooming in on what appeared to be some sort of squat bunker with a rounded roof. She changed the angle, but her heart sank. She'd seen these before. One door. No windows. No other way in.

If this was where they were keeping the med team, she was completely screwed.

Renna threw her tablet down on the table and got to her feet. The frantic drumbeat in her head picked up strength as she paced her cabin. She'd only get one shot at this. But how could she break into an impenetrable building without getting the hostages killed instantly? Frontal attack was a no-go. They didn't have a big enough team. And the clock was already ticking. The MYTH bombers could show up at any time.

Did she say screwed? More like completely and utterly fucked.

Renna rubbed the back of her neck. *Godsdammit.* She hated working without a safety net or an escape plan. Especially with whatever was going on in her head. Things could go wrong in a freaking hurry if she wasn't perfect. And if her implant chose the wrong moment to go haywire? She could get all of them killed.

Jayla's voice came over the intercom, jerking her out of her thoughts. "Renna, ETA on Tholi is twenty-three minutes."

Shit. She'd officially run out of time *and* ideas. Renna rubbed her sweating palms on her thighs.

Time for plan B: making it up as she went.

She slipped into a pair of tight leather pants and a black sweater and pulled on her knee-high boots. She strapped a holster around her shoulder and another around her waist before grabbing her leather military jacket from the chair where she'd dropped it earlier.

She paused, staring at her fingers curled around the smooth black leather.

She'd gotten it from MYTH when she'd first joined Finn's team. The special coat, given only to MYTH agents, was made of reinforced leather that was bulletproof but moved like a dream.

And only a few people in the entire galaxy had access to one.

She smiled as the beginnings of plan formed in her mind.

"You want me to do what?" Commander Jayla asked as she and Renna strode toward the cargo hold.

Renna kept her gaze forward and her voice steady. "I want you to be my prisoner."

Jayla stopped dead in the corridor. "No way. If you're wrong and this goes... what is that phrase you use? Tits up? I do not want to be out of commission."

Renna paused, turning to face the commander. "You won't be. But bringing you in as a trophy might be our best and only chance to get inside that bunker."

"What makes you think they'll let you inside in the first place, with or without me?"

Renna gestured at Jayla to keep moving. "Because someone has a grudge against MYTH that's big enough to destroy an entire headquarters. Getting their hands on one of their top officers will be a chance they can't resist."

The women cleared the cargo hold hatch, and Renna headed for her arms locker. She grabbed some extra clips for her blaster and slipped them into her pockets. "Not to mention, if this is a trap, don't you want to take down whoever did this yourself?"

Jayla smoothed the front of her uniform jacket and glared at Renna. "You know I do. This is personal now."

"Then we don't have time for subtle. You heard Dallas. MYTH will be sending strike teams any minute."

Jayla cleared the chamber of her pistol to check it before slipping it into its holster. "I wish I knew what's going on. Who this Pallas is and why he's doing this."

"Don't we all?" Renna strapped a knife to her thigh and slipped another one into the special slot on her left boot. She was all about stylish *and* functional.

The commander narrowed her eyes. "If our resident thief thinks this is the only way, then I'll have to trust you." She frowned at Renna. "But don't try to pull anything."

Renna threw up her hands. "I promise. I'm a reformed woman. A MYTH girl, you could even say. I've got too much riding on all of this to play games." She patted her pockets one last time. "Ready to go? My implant says the bunker is a ten-minute walk through town."

Lieutenant Blake joined them at the hatch. His full lips were twisted in a pout, and he crossed his arms as he leaned against the opening. "I don't like this. I should be coming with you. Damn, the whole team should be coming with you. There's no way you're going to get out of this alive."

"Then I guess you'll be captain," Jayla said, clapping him on the shoulder. "Don't worry about us, Lieutenant. I need you keep the ship ready for immediate take off. If we're not back in two hours, get the hell out of here before the strike team arrives."

"But, Commander, this is insane." His gaze flitted between them, a frown puckering the skin between his eyebrows. "I can't agree with this plan."

Renna chuckled. "You don't even know what the plan is. But if you did, you'd like it even less."

Blake's frown grew deeper. "Commander..."

"You have your orders, Lieutenant." Jayla smiled at him, then marched from the ship.

Renna waved to Blake and followed. He sighed nosily as the hatch slid shut behind her.

In the *Eris's* hangar bay, Renna slapped a pair of exovises around Jayla's wrists, fastening them loosely in front of her, but the commander still didn't look much like a prisoner. Renna wrinkled her nose at the gray dust coating the ground and any flat surface.

"I wish this was at least clean dirt," she said, picking up a handful of the gritty sand. It immediately turned her fingers gray. "Sorry about this." Renna rubbed a handful across the back of Jayla's dark uniform, then turned her around and smeared another handful across her front.

"What the hell are you doing?" she demanded.

Renna arched an eyebrow. "I couldn't capture you without a struggle, right? We might need to mess up your hair a bit. And maybe add some strategic dirt to your face."

Jayla took a step back and raised her shackled hands. "Oh, hell no. You are not putting that in my hair."

"Fine. At least let me pull some strands out of your bun. I want you to look disheveled."

Jayla's shoulders slumped, but she didn't protest as Renna pulled some of the commander's dark hair from her bun to curl wildly around her face.

"Hey, you have nice hair. Why do you always wear it back?"

"This is not the time to go all girly on me, thief. We need to focus."

"Talking about hair is always appropriate." Renna dusted off her hands, careful not to get any of the dirt on her own clothes. "You can get to the key, right?"

"It's right here in my pocket." Jayla patted her hip. "We've been through all this all ready. Are you stalling, Carrizal?"

Renna smirked. "Is it that obvious?"

"A little. Now come on. We have MYTH soldiers to save."

Jayla marched out of the hangar in front of Renna before she could stop her. Renna scurried to catch up, pulling her pistol and shoving it into Jayla's ribs as they started down the street. The Tholi spaceport was a shithole if she'd ever seen one. Dirty streets, even dirtier humans. The air smelled of dust and garbage and human stench. Renna wrinkled her nose.

Leading the stately commander through the slums earned them quite a few wide-eyed stares and a couple of cat calls from the men who lounged against the peeling buildings. They spat long strings of black liquid between stained teeth, and Renna shuddered as one landed feet away from them. The Eridu aliens had a special herb that calmed the nerves and supposedly made people happy. The poor of the community chewed it like gum, but it also gave them a vacant expression and black teeth. Not exactly her idea of attractive.

"Hey, baby, why don't you tie *me* up, like that?" one man called, leering at them through watery eyes. "Even better, I'll tie you both up and have some fun."

"Pretty sure your penis isn't big enough for one of us, let alone two."

He spit again. "Got a big mouth on you, huh? How about you come over here and show me what you can do with it?"

"I'd rather suck off a Russka." Renna smiled sweetly. "But you'd know all about that, wouldn't you, handsome?"

He growled and pushed himself off the building.

"Renna, behave," Jayla muttered. "I don't want to have to take down this guy with my hands tied. We don't have time for a brawl."

Renna shrugged, glancing back at the man. "Fine. I was just hoping to blow off some steam. A good fight always settles my nerves." A good screw was even better, but Finn was safely tucked away in one of Viktis's safehouses. Hopefully.

"I'm pretty sure we'll have a fight on our hands before we know it. Now behave."

The man followed them for half a block, but when Renna didn't respond to his taunts and name-calling, he fell back and left them alone. They cleared the slums, sped through the market, and headed for the alley across from the bunker.

"Over here." Renna crouched behind a stack of supply boxes and studied the building. The door was made of thick, worn wood with a heavy electrolock. It was an older model but still serviceable. It would take Renna at least sixty seconds to hack it, time they couldn't spare if they were trying to escape. She'd have to figure out a way to disable it on the way in if she could.

Pain sliced across her vision, and she gasped, squeezing her eyes shut against the throbbing. Images flashed through her mind, like the implant was searching for a workaround to the lock problem.

Finally, it focused on the lock's base, showing a glowing four-digit lockcode. Renna studied the image. There! A switch to keep the lock from engaging if you entered the right code. Now she had the right code. And a fucking headache. But at least it seemed like the implant was trying to be helpful. Now if she could only get the hang of using it.

"You all right?" Jayla asked, studying Renna's pale face with a frown.

"I've been better. Let's get this over with." Renna shoved the commander forward, and they crossed the street. At the door, she quickly input the code before pressing the comm button on the door.

Her heart felt like it was trying to claw its way through her chest, and she took a deep breath to get it under control. Her acting skills would have to be impeccable for this one.

"Who is it?" a gruff male voice called. "What do you want?"

"I have a delivery."

"We don't need no deliveries. Go away."

She pitched her voice to sound slightly annoyed. "Look, I don't have time to stand here all day. Pallas told me I'd get fifty-thousand credits for any MYTH officer."

"Pallas did?" He sounded confused, but a moment later, there was a buzz as the door slid open. Two men stood on the other side, guns pointed at Renna and Jayla. Galivant model rifles if she wasn't mistaken. The high-tech guns were unusual for merc gangs who operated in this part of the galaxy. Someone was paying them very well.

A heavy man with sandy hair and a jagged scar across his cheek glowered at them from inside. "Who are you?" he demanded.

"Dene Hally. I'm a merc from Anat. Caught me a MYTH commander when I was escaping the planet last week." Renna jerked her head at Jayla. "Found out she's some sort of leader there. Pretty sure Pallas will pay extra for this one."

The man frowned, his thick mustache covering his upper lip like a fuzzy caterpillar. "Pallas didn't say nothin' about more deliveries."

"You think I'm lying? Look at the woman's uniform. Can't you put her with the others and pay me? I'll be on my way, and you'll get the credit."

He exchanged a glance with one of the other men, who lowered his weapon. "Can't hurt, I suppose. Take her away."

Renna stepped in front of her bounty. "I don't think so. Money first. You know how this works, handsome." She gave him a sweet smile and let her gaze sweep the bunker's entryway. There was a small room off the entrance she guessed was the security room, and another a bit farther in that probably led into the main body of the bunker. That had to be where they were holding Dr. Samil and the MYTH med team.

Now if she only knew where Pallas was.

She waited for the buzz of her implant to scan the building for heat signatures or alternate entrances, but nothing happened. Of *course* it wasn't working now. She was going to have to do this the hard way.

"Quite the setup you guys have here." She studied the room more overtly before letting her gaze travel up and down the man's beefy body. Renna leaned forward suggestively. "Pallas must really trust you to put you in charge."

Despite his obvious suspicion, the man puffed out his chest. "And I won't do anything to jeopardize that trust."

"Good man." She stepped through the doorway and pulled Jayla with her. Another step and she was close enough to touch the man's arm. "I didn't catch your name, handsome."

His face flushed, and he jerked away. "It's Rico. But keep your distance. I need authorization from the boss before I pay you anything."

"Pallas keeps tight tabs on the purse strings, eh?" Renna leaned against the cool steel wall and crossed her arms, ignoring the two men with their guns still trained on her.

"Nah, Pallas is too busy to worry about mercs begging for credits. One of the other men is in charge here." Rico jerked his head toward the back. "Chrandy, go get him."

The man closest to the door disappeared through it, but not before Renna caught a glimpse of the wide open space of the bunker behind him. Completely empty.

What the hell? Usually these things were used as warehouses, stuffed full of supplies and people. She snapped her attention back to Rico. "So tell me, how'd you get involved in all this? Pallas doesn't exactly recruit on the open merc channels."

"I ran with Arker's gang in the Apollo system. A few years back, Pallas contacted us to see if we wanted some extra work. I ended up staying after the job was done."

"Smart man." This time when she inched closer, the man didn't even flinch. "And what happened to Arker? I'm assuming he didn't like you defecting."

The man grinned wolfishly. "Pallas let me take over his territory after we killed him. It was time for new management in that sector anyway."

"Brutal. I like it." She was close enough now to run a hand down his arm. "I wish I would have met you before I joined up with Viktis Korrik. What an ass."

Rico growled. "That Ileth stole my fucking ship. I'd do anything to get back at him."

"How come I'm not surprised?" Renna laughed lightly. "Viktis isn't exactly good at making friends."

She sucked on her lower lip, a move that usually didn't disappoint. Rico's gaze drifted lower, and she smiled slowly. "I have an idea." Then she shook her head as if it was too stupid. "Never mind."

"No, tell me," Rico said.

"I'm looking for a change of scenery. You handsome men hiring? I'm pretty good at what I do. Even better, I can help you get back at that damned Ileth. Teach him to fuck around on me."

"Now that's an interesting suggestion." Rico leered at her, studying her tight pants and even tighter sweater. Renna arched her back slightly to show off her...assets

"A *very* interesting suggestion." Rico chewed his lip, making his mustache move on his upper lip like it was alive. "I bet the boss would be happy to have someone with your...skills on our team."

"Oh, handsome, you don't even know how skilled I am," she purred, moving close enough that the rancid sweat staining his clothes made her nostrils burn.

He wrapped a meaty arm around her waist and pulled her toward the door. "Let's go find out."

The other man interrupted, holding up a hand to stop him. "Quit thinking with your dick, Rico. What do I do with this one?" He jerked the gun at Jayla.

"Bring her with us and throw her in the cell. The boss can sort it all out later."

"I'm not sorting out anything. Kill them both."

Renna froze.

Major Larson stood in the doorway, a smirk twisting his angular features.

THIRTEEN

Fear clawed its way up Renna's spine as she stared into Larson's icy eyes. Now that she was standing here, facing him, the reality slammed into her like a Trezian's fist.

Larson really was a traitor to MYTH.

"Nice to see you again, thief," he said. "I'd hoped you'd be joining us. I didn't count on the added bonus of Commander Jayla, however."

Jayla glared at the man. "You'll pay for this, Larson."

Renna stepped forward, hands held in front of her. "Let Jayla go. She has nothing to do with this. I'm the one you want." Her skin crawled as the two guards' guns tracked her, ready to fire at any sudden movement.

"You don't know what I want," Larson said. "But luckily, you're exactly right. Pallas will be pleased."

"Why are you doing this? Why betray MYTH?" Renna asked.

Across the room, Jayla's whole body went rigid as she waited for his answer. Right. His betrayal was especially personal to the commander who'd spent years at MYTH.

Larson shrugged, drawing Renna's attention back to his tall frame. "MYTH abandoned me when I needed them most, but Pallas offered me an opportunity to become powerful. To make a difference. MYTH has lost its way, but we're helping it get back to what's right. And this cybernetic army will make us unstoppable. We'll be able to protect our people."

"You sound like a crazy fanatic," Renna scoffed. "No matter how idealistic you try to spin it, the truth is you want to take over the galaxy with your hybrid army. You want to destroy rather than protect." She shook her head. "You're nothing but a thug, and I've met plenty of those in my line of work. They all die badly."

"It doesn't matter what you think. I believe in Pallas's vision, and I'll do what I need to to make sure it comes true. And if I get to have a little fun torturing our enemies in the process…" Larson smirked. "Then so be it."

"Then take me to him," Renna demanded. "I want to face him myself."

"Oh, you will. Trust me. But I plan on having some fun with you first." Larson nodded at one of his guards. "Take her guns."

This was not how she'd planned for it to go, but it looked like there was only one way to get to Dr. Samil and the kidnapped scientists now. Through Larson and his men.

She was going to enjoy this.

Renna met Jayla's gaze across the room and nodded slightly.

One of the guards approached, and Renna held out her

blaster. With her other hand, she slowly pulled a knife from beneath her jacket. As he took the gun, she slammed it into his midsection. His eyes widened as the blade slid between his ribs without resistance.

Renna used the momentum to grab his arm, spinning him to use as a full body shield.

He screamed in pain, and the other men reacted instantly, opening fire. The impact of the bullets hitting the man's body made him shake against her.

Major Larson screamed at his men. "Don't kill her! Pallas needs her alive."

The guards jerked the guns out of aim. The bullets went wide, spraying against the metal bunker walls in a staccato screech.

Across the room, Jayla slipped out of her cuffs. With a sweep of her leg, she took down the man closest to her, stomping on his neck when he hit the floor. It crunched loudly and he went still.

But she couldn't worry about the commander; Renna had her own men to worry about. She snatched her gun back from the dead merc and fired off half a dozen shots. One of the other guards dropped to the ground amidst the ricocheting bullets.

Two down, two to go.

A sudden pounding in her head made her vision go blurry. Gods, not now! She blinked away the fog and yanked her knife from the dead man's chest.

Larson raised his blaster, set to stun, and she sent the knife flying across the room.

It missed, thudding into the wooden door beside his head. His finger tightened against the trigger, and Renna jumped out of the way as he fired. Her shoulder cracked as she tumbled toward the door to the warehouse, and her breath whooshed out in a rush of pain.

Fuck.

Renna's right arm throbbed and burned as she scrambled to her feet. Across the room, Jayla struggled with the final guard, but the commander would have to fend for herself. Larson's murderous expression sent shivers down Renna's spine as he stalked toward her. She was going to need all her skills to take him down.

Renna darted deeper into the warehouse toward the only furniture in the space—a heavy, metal desk. She slid behind it just as Larson marched through the door and quickly scanned the space. Light filtered in from windows high on the wall, driving away some of the gloom. Boxes were stacked in the far corner, but otherwise, the space was empty. Where the hell was the med team?

"You can't hide from me," Major Larson called. "There's no-where to run."

"I don't need to. You couldn't hit the side of a transport ship with that thing." Her bravado sounded false even to her, and she grimaced. Her arm throbbed in time with her head and she want-ed to curl into a ball, but right now, that wasn't going to happen.

Shifting her weight, Renna clutched the gun even tighter. She straightened from her crouch, pointing it at Larson. "Drop the weapon."

He chuckled and shook his head. "I admire your fight, thief, but you're trapped. There's nothing you can do."

"Where are the MYTH soldiers?" she demanded. "Where's

Dr. Samil?"

"Right where Pallas left them." A smug smile split his face. "I can't believe you fell for it. I didn't think you were that stupid."

"Did you even consider we might have walked willingly into the trap?" she asked.

The door beside him opened, and Larson glanced back, then saluted crisply. "So glad you could join us."

Renna's gaze snapped to the figure standing beside him, and her arm lowered on its own account.

FOURTEEN

The very doctor Renna had trusted with her life stepped further into the warehouse, a soft smile on her face. "I'm glad to see I wasn't wrong about you, Renna. Being here in person will make it so much easier to verify your death."

"Dr. Samil?" Renna's words were barely a whisper.

"Looks like the drugs haven't worked quite yet, but that's all right. I'm excited to study you as the change happens." Samil's expression was calm and friendly, like this was just another med visit.

Renna's right arm burned where she'd landed on it, her head felt like it was stuffed with shrapnel, and confusion twisted her insides so tight she thought she'd burst. "I don't understand, Doctor. What are you doing here? Why are you working with these people?"

"I'm not working with these people, dear. They work for me."

Major Larson saluted. "And it's a pleasure, ma'am."

Samil smiled at him. "You've done well, Major. Now please wait at the ship. Renna and I have a few things to discuss."

Larson glared at Renna, but eventually nodded. "Yes, ma'am. Call me if anything changes." He marched away through a side door, back ram-rod straight.

But Renna barely noticed as the blood rushed to her head and she put out a hand to steady herself against the desk. "What are you saying?"

Samil shook her head regretfully. "I suppose I should forgive you for not understanding. Those drugs I gave you actually sped up the process instead of slowing it down. I'm sure your brain feels like mush right now."

"You lying bitch," Renna hissed.

"I did what I had to do, dove. You should understand that."

Fear was an iron band around Renna's lungs as she tried to suck in a breath. She'd never even seen this coming. It wasn't possible.

Dr. Samil was Pallas?

"Why don't you make this easy on both of us, Renna?"

"You should know by now, the last thing I am is easy." Renna tried to rotate her injured shoulder and winced as a flash of pain shot down her arm. "How about another way out of here?" she muttered to her implant. But of course there was no surge of knowledge, no indication the damn thing was even on.

"Poor choice of words. Look, Renna, I don't want to hurt you. I need your special physiology to finish my experiments. Let's talk this through. We have a few more minutes before the MYTH bombers arrive on planet."

"And then we'll *all* be dead," Renna snapped. "I can live with that." She pulled the chair out from the desk and sank into it. This was a fucking nightmare. The woman she'd thought was trying to save her had been behind Myka's kidnapping, the hybrid army, even the experiments Navang had conducted on Renna. But why?

"What do you want, Doctor? Or should I call you Pallas? Why are you doing this?"

Samil brushed back her hair and glanced down at her watch. "I'm not sure we have time to do this now, and I don't know that it really matters."

"It matters to me. If you're going to turn me into a monster, don't I at least deserve to know why?"

The doctor sighed. "Very well. I joined MYTH ten years ago. I was young, just twenty-three, and terribly naive. When I got my first assignment, I was proud to be part of this organization, proud to help protect the galaxy. But after a few years, MYTH became too powerful, too corrupted, and they started using their own troops as experiments."

Samil's face darkened. "When they destroyed the thing most important to me, I knew it was time to stop them. And you are the key to revolutionizing this organization once and for all."

Renna's arm had begun to shake as she tried to hold her gun level with Samil's chest. "If you think I'm going to help you, you're sorely mistaken. MYTH knows about you, and we know how to stop you."

Samil chuckled and shook her head, her blonde hair grazing her shoulders. She looked so kind, so innocent. How could she be the one behind all of this?

"Have you forgotten that ticking time bomb in your head?" Samil asked. "Besides, I've been working on this plan for almost five years. It's flawless. When I'm done, MYTH will be destroyed, and the galaxy will be changed forever." Her words rang with conviction.

Great. Another fanatic.

"Look, doc, I respect you," Renna said, holding her hand out. "I even thought we were friends. Instead of going all vigilante on MYTH, why not just tell a reporter and have them do a smear story? You know how well that works on the politicians. Imagine the blow up with a government operation. They'd be shut down in seconds."

Samil shook her head, her pink sweater at odds with the ice in her voice. "I don't want them shut down. I want to use them. But they must be cleansed first. And you're part of that, dove."

"Hate to disappoint, but I have other plans."

"Not for much longer." Samil pulled a small gun from her vest pocket and fired it at Renna before she could even blink.

Renna gaped at the feathered needle sticking from her arm. "What the hell did you do?" Her fingers trembled as she ripped it away. For the first time since they'd arrived on this planet, the possibility she might fail hit her. Pallas would win, and they'd all die. Or worse.

The gun was suddenly too heavy to hold, and she let it sink to the top of the desk. She'd wasted way too much time talking to this woman. She should have just shot first, but she'd wanted to understand Pallas's motives. She'd needed to know why the woman was doing this. Renna gripped the edge of the desk as the room started to spin. Look where that had gotten her.

"I need you alive, Renna. Your body is mutating Navang's experiments in ways even Myka's didn't. You will be the lynchpin of my army."

"Army? We destroyed it with Navang's facility." The room was going gray around the edges, like fog rolling in, and Renna blinked furiously to clear her vision.

"You didn't think that was the only facility I used to produce my army, did you?" Samil laughed, loud and girlishly high.

Renna clutched the edge of the desk even harder as her whole body started to tremble. "I should have guessed."

"Yes, you really should have." Samil took another step closer. "Give in, dove. There's no need for heroics. I don't plan on killing you."

"Stay where you are." Renna tried to raise her gun again, but her arm wouldn't obey.

"Another minute now and you'll be out. You and I will disappear, and when MYTH finds the charred remains of my team, unidentifiable because of the bombs, poor Major Dallas will assume you're among them." Samil gestured to the back of the warehouse.

Renna's gaze followed the woman's finger to the heap of bodies piled in the shadowy corner. All wearing gray MYTH uniforms. "You killed them," she whispered, pressing a hand to her lips.

As she watched, a trail of crimson blood snaked from the shadows toward Renna. It trickled across the pavement at first, gaining speed as it flowed through the warehouse. Her eyes widened as the thick blood flowed faster, picking up pace as it turned into a river of death. Headed directly for her.

Renna jumped to her feet and lurched away from the oncoming storm. Samil dashed forward to grab Renna's arm, but she wrenched away from the doctor. Renna stumbled, her foot slipping in the viscous liquid, and she landed on her ass with a jarring thud.

"I'm gonna...killllll..." Renna's words slurred as her mouth filled with cotton wool, and she tried to swallow.

Godsdammit.

Terror surged through her in one last burst of mind-clearing adrenaline, and she scrambled to her feet. She threw herself at Samil, her left fist connecting with the woman's jaw. With Renna's momentum, the two women landed in a heap on the floor.

Samil screamed as blood streamed from her nose, and the door behind them slammed open, two more guards surging into the room. As they crossed the threshold, Commander Jayla jumped from somewhere behind them, cracking the butt of her pistol against one of the men's skulls.

He went down like a ton of rocks, and Jayla pointed her gun at the other. "Don't move, asshole."

The doctor scrambled to her feet and raised her own gun at Jayla. "I'm sorry you got involved, Commander. You've never been part of this plan. You were one of the good ones."

Renna blinked up from her position on the floor as the whole room spun drunkenly.

Samil's grip tightened on her gun and Renna opened her mouth to scream a warning at the commander, but her lips didn't move.

Samil fired off a tranq shot, hitting Jayla in the neck.

Jayla furrowed her eyebrows. "Dr. Samil? What are you doing?"

Before the doctor could respond, a low vibration filled the air, growing louder. "Looks like I'm out of time. Come along, Renna. We have an appointment with a medical facility far from here."

Jayla dropped to her knees with a thud. Her gaze met Renna's across the room. Terror had stretched her features into a stiff mask.

"I'm sorry," the commander whispered before she toppled to her side, unconscious.

The throbbing grew louder as the ship approached the bunker, and Samil hooked her hands under Renna's armpits and pulled her toward the door.

"Damn, you're heavier than you look," she muttered.

Renna glared or, at least, tried to. Her muscles just wouldn't respond. Maybe there was some way to slow the doctor down so she was caught in the bomb blast as well. She'd sacrifice herself if it meant stopping Pallas for good.

Renna's eyes had turned to sand, her eyelids growing heavier by the second, but she forced them to stay open, to stay focused. She was not going out like this. There had to be some way to fight it. Coldness seeped through her limbs. She would have liked to have said goodbye to Finn. To see him one last time. But this way he'd be safe. He'd get over her.

The doctor hit a rough patch on the floor, jarring Renna, and she gasped as fire shot through her bad shoulder. The pain cleared her mind for a split second.

Her holo interface blipped into focus. Maybe her implant had reset. Maybe she could use it against Samil. Another bump and the heads-up display flickered off. Shit.

Renna fought for consciousness and for control of the implant. At the next bump, the display slid into focus. Something low and insistent blinked behind her left eye, and she forced herself to read the letters. It felt like trying to decipher an alien language, but eventually she got it.

The approaching ship wasn't the MYTH bomber.

It was Lieutenant Blake and the *Eris*.

FIFTEEN

L et the drugs take you, Renna. You won't feel a thing."
Samil smiled down at her, then pressed a finger to her
ear communicator. "Larson, I need someone in here
now! We need to evacuate." Samil paused, a frown marring her
pretty features. "Where the hell is everyone?"

The door slammed open, and Blake stood there, his blaster
aimed at Samil's heart. His blond hair was disheveled, and with
his brown eyes flashing, he looked like some kind of avenging
angel.

"Dr. Samil? What are you doing?" Confusion furrowed his
eyebrows as he glanced at Renna and the commander both motionless on the ground.

"Oh thank god, Lieutenant," Samil said, her voice going soft
and trembling. "Larson tried to kill them. We have to get help."

"I can radio MYTH. They'll stop the bombers if they know we're here." Blake lowered his gun and pressed a finger to his comm unit.

"Good idea. I'm going to go get my med kit. I'll be right back."

Renna tried to thrash and scream, to warn Blake, but her whole body felt like it was coated in cement. Things were getting dimmer by the second.

"This isn't over, Renna," Samil whispered, before darting away through the open door.

Renna gasped for breath, the words echoing over and over in her mind.

Pallas. *Dr. Samil* had escaped.

Blake crouched beside her and placed two cool fingers against her neck to check her pulse. "Hang in there, Renna. Help's on the way."

She felt her eyelids grow heavy, and he shook her shoulder. "Stay awake. You don't need any beauty sleep. You're gorgeous enough already."

Blake spotted the feathered needle beside Renna and picked it up to study. His long fingers dwarfed the tiny barb. "Shit, that's a Marko tranq. Takes at least twelve hours to wear off." He stood to search the warehouse. "Where the hell did this come from, and where the hell is Dr. Samil?"

Renna tried to answer, tried to break free of the drug trapping her mind. She gasped for air, ordering her arm to move.

And then everything went dark as the tranq took over.

Cold. She was so cold.

The air felt strange—heavy somehow. As if a piece of metal mesh was draped over her like a blanket. Slowly, her vision cleared and she blinked at the lights glowing brightly in a ship's corridor.

A happy sigh escaped Renna's lips. She was back on the Athena. *The familiar walls and controls of the CIC surrounded her and the tension slipped from her muscles.*

Lieutenant Keva sat at her station, busily scanning the sector displayed on her holomonitor. Viktis stood behind her, peering over her shoulder at the screen.

"Looks all clear," he said. "I think we should have a safe run through the system. Once we get to the nav point, switch over to the hyperdrive and follow those coordinates."

Keva nodded, the bun of silver hair on the top of her head swaying slightly. "Kojima said the stealth system was working again. Gheewala was able to reprogram it on the new frequency."

"Good, we're going to need it to get in and out of that system without MYTH detecting us."

Keva's already thin lips all but disappeared as she frowned. "I hate this."

"I know," Viktis said, squeezing her shoulder. His hand lingered a bit longer than was acceptable. "But Renna's working on it. You'll be back in the fold in no time. I'm sure of it."

Keva jumped as Finn's heavy boots sounded on the stairs to the CIC, and Viktis dropped his hand.

"Status report," Finn ordered, his impatient gaze raking over the

crew.

The lieutenant scrambled to pull up the information on her console. "We're approaching the Leporis system. Viktis thinks we can get through without anyone the wiser if we use our stealth drive."

"Do it." Finn turned to Viktis. "Any word from Renna?"

The alien shook his head, the sharp planes of his face deepening. "Not yet. It's only been two weeks, Finn. Give our girl some time."

A muscle jumped in the captain's jaw as if he wanted to snap at the Ileth, but he turned away. "I want to know the instant you hear anything."

Viktis clapped a hand on Finn's back. "Look, Cap. We're all worried about her, but you know Renna can take care of herself. She's fine."

"I'm not so sure. I've had Gheewala scanning the frequencies for MYTH transmissions. The base on Titus Beta was hit."

Viktis's amber skin paled. "Pallas."

Finn nodded. "That's what I'm afraid of. But I don't know if that's where they took Renna or if she was even still there. What if her cover's blown already? What if she's dead?" He stared off over the CIC, clearly caught in some nightmare in his own mind.

"Renna's smart. She knew the risks." Viktis glanced at Finn from the corner of his eye. "And she's too stubborn to be dead. I've seen her get out of worse spots than this."

Deep lines were etched into the space between Finn's eyebrows as he scowled. "We all knew the risks. Doesn't mean I like them." He turned and started back down the stairs. "I'll be in my quarters. I want to know the second anything changes."

Keva and Viktis exchanged worried glances.

"He hasn't been the same since we left Forever Station," the lieutenant said. "I don't know what to do to help him."

"There's nothing we can do. It's all up to Renna now," he answered. *"But I know what I can do to help you."* Viktis winked, and Keva flushed violet.

"Meet you in my quarters later?" she asked softly.

"You better count on it."

Surprise shot through Renna at their exchange. She'd never in a million years have guessed Viktis and the uptight lieutenant would be attracted to each other, but it made sense. The pirate needed a good influence, and Keva needed to loosen up.

Renna grinned. She would give Viktis such hell the next time she saw him.

Around her, the Athena shuddered as the FTL spun up. Pressure built inside her head until her ears felt like they were going to explode. Another blink, and she was on the flight deck with the Athena's pilot, Lieutenant Kojima.

"Dammit. What the hell is wrong with these sensors? They're off the charts." He tapped a command into his communicator. *"Sergeant Ghee-wala, check them again. It's still not working."*

Kojima's fingers flew across the controls as he rearranged the flight path. Renna recognized their destination. Viktis had contacts in the small merc colony on New Rhea. The Athena would be able to hide for several weeks safely there. She wouldn't have to worry about them.

But that damn longing surged through her again.

The only thing she wanted was to be back on the Athena. To be with Finn and Myka and Viktis. It felt strange to say, but for the first time in her life, she'd felt like she was finally home when she was on that ship. She sighed softly, and suddenly the sensors on the flight deck went crazy.

"What the hell is going on?" Kojima pounded on the console, but the

numbers blinked and spun like they were possessed. "Captain Finn! Flight deck now!" *he shouted into his comm.*

Kojima struggled to get the ship under control as it rocked and shuddered. The navigation console lit up bright red as warning sensors went off across the Athena.

Finn thundered into the deck. "What is it? What's going on? Did we hit something?"

Kojima shook his head, too busy trying to regain control to salute his superior officer. "She's gone crazy. I've completely lost control of her. It's like someone reprogrammed all her nav systems. She's set a course for the Coro system."

Finn grabbed the back of Kojima's chair as the ship shuddered again.

A sharp ache started behind Renna's eyes, and she squeezed them shut. What was going on? Were they in danger?

"What the hell is in the Coro system?" Finn demanded as he studied the system specs.

"Nothing. There's a small backwater colony on Tartarus, but that's it." Kojima typed a few more commands into his console before finally throwing up his hands. "It's completely locked. I can't even get into the command prompt. We're tied to this course until whoever has control releases us."

Finn's face went pale. "Too dangerous to send out a distress signal?"

Kojima nodded. "We're in MYTH space. They get word and it's all over."

"Fuck." Finn's hand trembled as he raked it through his hair. "Keep trying to regain control. I'll prep the team for evasive maneuvers and get Aldani and the kid loaded onto one of the escape shuttles."

Kojima turned back to his console, while Finn stared out the window at the blackness surrounding them.

"Dammit." Kojima flipped on the comm. "Crew, prepare for jump to light speed." He turned back to Finn. "I've never seen this before. It's like the Athena's come to life. She's got a mind of her own." More beeps from the nav system as it recalculated. "And she's not backing down."

"Keep it together as best you can, Kojima. And let's hope whoever is in control of our ship knows what they're doing."

Renna reached out to touch Finn as he passed, but her arm wouldn't obey. All she wanted was for him to know she was okay and for them to be safe. She wanted him to know how much he meant to her, even if she couldn't say the words out loud. But so much distance separated them. Even in her dreams she wasn't able to reach him.

A searing pain shot through her as the ship jumped to light speed and Renna gasped.

Everything went black again. Except the streaming of the stars around her.

SIXTEEN

Is she going to be all right?" Lieutenant Blake asked softly. Renna tried to force open her eyes, but her body was trapped in a foggy softness.

"I hope so. I think she got a bigger dose of the tranq than I did, but she still should have been awake by now."

Commander Jayla sounded worried, and Renna struggled even harder to pull herself out of the blackness holding her down.

Vibrations from Jayla's pacing trembled through Renna's body. So she wasn't dead. Always good news.

Blake spoke, a smile in his voice. "The poor girl's probably exhausted. She's had a lot going on." He chuckled. "Besides, Finn won't let her sleep much longer anyway. I thought he was going to throttle me when I said he had to wait to see her."

Jayla chuckled. "The man's got it bad. I've never seen him like this."

"Hope she doesn't break his heart. Renna doesn't seem like the settling-down type." Blake sighed. "Not that you meet a lot of those kinds of girls in this job anyway."

"Lieutenant, are you getting romantic in your old age?"

"Gods no. Who has time? I have a galaxy to save." Blake's footfalls approached the door. "And if that was a hint, I'm on my way back to the CIC. Sir."

Renna tried to claw her way out of the fog before they left, but her eyes remained closed, her body still. She wanted to scream, to tell them she was listening, but her voice wouldn't obey. She was trapped here in the dark, in her own mind, as it slowly disappeared into...nothingness.

"I'm sure she'll wake up when she's ready," Jayla said, sounding troubled. "In the meantime, Finn and I have a lot to discuss."

Finn? He was here? Renna's mind thrashed, but she still didn't wake. She felt the throb of the ship around her, the machinery running through the floor and walls, but she couldn't feel her own fucking body.

The soft swish of the door sliding shut behind them left Renna alone in the room with her screaming thoughts. She tried to force her consciousness to wake, to listen to the commands she was giving it, but instead, she grew more and more tired, her limbs heavy like lead. Until she drifted off to sleep again.

Renna jolted awake as a warm hand brushed against her face. She'd been dreaming again. Of ships and stars and men she'd thought long dead. And right now, she had no idea what was real and what she'd made up in her head.

Renna licked her cracked lips and opened her eyes. It took a moment for them to focus on the face hovering above her. A face from her dreams.

"Finn," she croaked.

"Shhh." He smiled down at her, expression full of concern. "Don't talk, just take it easy. You're going to be fine." His fingers brushed a strand of hair away from her cheek, and her skin erupted in goose bumps.

If she wasn't so weak, she'd have thrown herself at him. Instead, she ordered her own hand to touch his. It resisted at first, but eventually it moved and Finn curled his fingers around hers.

The touch lent her enough strength to ask, "Are you really here? *How* are you here?"

He gave her one of those heart-twisting half-smiles of his. Maybe she'd died and this was heaven. Maybe this was just another dream. But damn, if that was the case, she never wanted to wake up.

Her tongue felt like a wad of cotton in her mouth. Gods, when was the last time she'd brushed her teeth? She gestured to the glass of water on the table beside her bed. Finn helped her hold it to her lips, and she drank thirstily.

When her hand started to shake, Finn gently took the glass from her and set it on the table. "I was hoping you could tell me that," he said, brushing back another strand of her hair. His gaze softened, making him look young and vulnerable.

An electrical jolt shot through her with an emotion she didn't want to name. Putting her feelings into words would make them too real.

"The *Athena* brought us here on her own," he said. "But Gheewala said she could sense your electronic signature on the ship. We didn't have much choice but to believe her. And then we arrived in the space port and saw the *Eris*." He studied her for a long moment, his expression curious but wary. "How did you do it?"

Renna frowned at him. "I don't understand. Do what?"

"Control the *Athena*. You brought us here."

What did he mean? The dull ache was back again, and she let her eyelids drift closed. It was so much work to keep them open right now, so much work trying to figure out what was going on. Sleeping was so much easier.

"Hey, Renna. Stay with me, love." Finn's warm hand cupped her face, and she struggled back to consciousness.

"I'm here."

"That's my girl. Was it the implant? Did it allow you to contact our ship?"

Renna forced herself to focus on his worried face. "I don't know. Maybe? Once, before you went on the run, I thought I could feel the ship inside my head. Maybe we connected somehow because of the implant or the drug. But I couldn't have controlled her. It's not possible."

Except that wasn't true. She'd longed for Finn in her dreams, but maybe they hadn't been dreams. Maybe she'd actually been there, a part of the *Athena*.

Finn stroked a finger gently down her cheek. "Well, whatever happened, we'll figure it out later. Right now you need some rest. I'll be waiting for you when you wake up."

"Promise?" she asked.

Finn took her hand, settling back against the wall beside her on the bed. "Promise."

SEVENTEEN

The murmur of low voices woke Renna a few hours later. This time she was able to stretch in bed, to curl her fingers into her palms and yawn as she drifted awake. She turned her head on the pillow toward the voices. Dr. Aldani and Finn stood at the open door of the cabin, the light from the passage giving them both halos.

"Why is it taking so long for the drug to get out of her system?" Finn's words were clipped and short.

Aldani shook his head. "I don't know. Her blood levels are fine. The pressure in her brain has eased. There's no reason for her to still be comatose."

"Is it the transition? Is her implant killing her?" Finn's voice cracked.

Aldani put his hand on Finn's arm. "We don't know that. She's strong, Finn. We're going to find a way to get her through this."

"But you said…"

"I know what I said. The drugs Samil gave Renna have caused some neural damage. They may have caused the implant to start integrating even faster. But it will take time for me to try to work out a new formula from what little data is left of Navang's experiments. I only have a partial code."

Renna's fingers twisted in the sheets as she clenched them into fists. Dr. Samil. *Pallas.* The woman's betrayal rushed through her, aching and painful like a physical wound. Her pulse thundered so loudly it drowned out Aldani's voice. She'd let herself trust the woman, and Samil had done worse than betray her. She'd tried to kill her. Not that Renna was any stranger to death, but at least in the merc business, you usually knew who your enemies were.

And after walking right into Samil's trap, the woman had still escaped. How was she going to find Samil again? How was she going to stop her before the implant took over? Before she turned into a monster.

A stupid Shakespeare quote popped into her head: *Nothing in his life became him like the leaving it.* Macbeth.

With a groan, she pushed the thought away. She was proud of her life—she'd done some amazing things. She certainly wasn't giving up now. And why the hell were useless quotes the only thing she remembered from her few years of school? That was some quality education right there.

Except wait. Renna paused. Shakespeare.

Something tugged at her memory and she sat bolt upright. "I know someone who might help," she croaked.

Both men jumped at the sound of her voice, spinning to face her. She would have laughed at their expressions if she hadn't been so tired.

"Renna." Finn was at her side in an instant, perching on the edge of the bed to take her hand. "How are you feeling? Can I get you something?"

She smiled weakly. "I'm all right. Calm down, Finn." She looked past him to David Aldani, whose dark eyebrows were knit together with worry, too. "There's a merc on Lenue who took a sample of Navang's original drug. He might give us the formula if we give him the right incentive."

"Viktis's contact. I remember." Finn squeezed her hand. "I'll have the *Athena* head out immediately."

"No, wait. We need to think this through first. Samil knows I'm on to her. She knows the *Eris* will be tracking her. What she doesn't know is how or if you're involved. The *Athena* needs to stay off her radar for as long as possible, and Myka needs to stay safe. She's determined to continue building her army and she could still use him." Renna swallowed against the cotton balls that felt like they were clogging her throat. "Water?" she asked.

Finn poured her a glass from the pitcher beside the bed. She downed the glass in three large swallows, then dropped back against the pillows. Her heart raced like she'd fought a band of thieves, not taken a simple drink. "Doc, what's going on? Why am I still so tired?"

Aldani shook his head. "I can only guess your body is trying to repair itself, to fight against the implant taking control. There's a war going on inside you, and both sides are evenly matched."

"Which is why we have to get that drug right the hell now." Finn shot to his feet. "Samil or not."

Renna shook her head. "Listen to me, Finn. The *Athena* and the Aldanis need to disappear. You can't get caught in the middle of this. We'll take the *Eris* to Lenue. Hopefully that'll keep Samil off your trail a bit longer."

"I don't like this. There has to be another way." Finn paced the room, arms behind his back. "I need to talk to Viktis. He'll have some ideas."

Renna's eyes widened and she turned to Aldani. "Did he just say he was going to voluntarily ask the pirate for advice, or is my implant fucking up my hearing, too?"

The doctor chuckled. "I think they've become friends. It was quite touching to see both of them so worried about you."

She shook her head and turned back to Finn. "I think Viktis will agree with me," she said.

The captain shrugged. "There has to be another way. I'll be back as soon as I can." He pressed a kiss to Renna's forehead and strode from the room.

Gods he was beautiful. She could've stared at him all day. And the fact that he was here, with her? She was selfishly ecstatic. He should be far, far away, safe from Pallas or Samil or whoever the hell the woman was, but just his presence had already made her feel better.

When the door slid shut behind Finn, she turned back to Aldani. "So how about the truth now, Doc. What am I looking at? Hours? Days?"

The man sank into her desk chair, the lines around his mouth deepening with his frown. "I wish I knew. Your body seems healthy. There are no signs of physical rejection yet. The bigger problem is your nervous system. As far as I can tell, the implant has started to fuse and take over some of your basic bodily functions and systems. The drugs Samil gave you have accelerated that process, but your body is fighting it as hard as it can. Unless we find some way to make them both work together, you..."

"Won't make it."

Aldani shook his head. "You'll make it. You'll just be something... different."

"What do you mean something *different*? Different how?" A boulder sat on Renna's chest and she struggled to prop herself up against the pillows so she could breathe.

Aldani wouldn't meet her gaze as he continued. Instead he chose to stare at the white tiled floor. "Myka is a hybrid. Part-human, part-machine, and while both of his systems have integrated and work together, they're still separate, like with most cybernetic additions people have installed.

"But what's happening to you is different. The machine is starting to take over, to *become* you. When this process is finished, your implant will be another organ you need to keep you alive. It will simply be an extension of yourself, and the connection you feel with the *Athena*, with other mechanics, will deepen.

"Navang thought Myka was the apex of his work, but you have far surpassed him. You'll be something new. The implant will become inseparable, indistinguishable from your own systems. Constantly evolving and changing. Growing on its own, even." Aldani rubbed his clean-shaven jaw. His dark skin had gone ashy as he finally met her gaze. "You'll be a new species. The genesis of something new in this galaxy."

Renna's mouth went dry. She opened and closed it, but there were no words. How did you respond to something like that?

Aldani got to his feet. "But we're going to stop that from happening. We're going to make sure you stay in control of this and not the other way around, okay?"

Easier said than done. If she'd commanded the *Athena* while unconscious, the implant was already taking control of her brain, her body. Was she even herself anymore?

"Stop looking like that," Aldani chided. "Finn will have my hide if he comes back to find you pale and terrified."

Dear gods. Finn. Her heart twisted in her chest, and Renna sat up. "Don't tell him," she pleaded. "Whatever happens, I don't want him to know. I'll disappear first, find some way to put an end to being a monster, but he can't know."

"Renna... I... "

"Please, doc. I want him to remember me as I am, not some... robot. I am going to do my damnedest to beat this, but if the worst thing he thinks is that I died because of the implant, so be it. I don't want him to see me changed. What if I don't recognize him? What if I hurt him?"

"Let's not worry about that now, okay? We've got time, and if you think this man can help you, we still have hope." Aldani squeezed her shoulder. "I wish I could go with you, but I know you're right. I've met Dr. Samil; I am familiar with her work. She's cunning and if she gets her hands on Myka again, she'll be unstoppable. You're our only hope now."

Renna nodded. "I know. Myka's still okay, right?"

"He's perfect and dying to see you. Hopefully you'll be up for it later."

He let himself out of her room, leaving Renna to stare at the ceiling. Cold dread made her limbs heavy. Was he right? Could all of the weird things she'd experienced lately mean she was changing into something else? What had Samil done to her back in that warehouse?

There was only one way to find out. She took a shaky breath and closed her eyes, forcing away the fear and focusing on the *Athena*, the feelings she had for Finn, the crew, the ship itself. She pictured the smooth walls and metal floors, the spacious bridge. The dull ache started again as she slid deeper into her imagination.

And then she felt the tremble of the ship around her, the slight shudder that told her she was there. Part of the ship. Watching. Waiting.

This time, if she focused hard enough, she could feel it. The brush of air against the hull, the feel of the engineers working on her core. Even the whispers of the two crew members as they sneaked a kiss in a secluded corner.

Renna stretched out the tendrils of her connection and focused on the nav computer in the CIC. Viktis leaned against the railing, talking to Lieutenant Blake about a poker game he'd won on Forever Station. Lieutenant Keva sat at her station, listening, a knowing smile on her face.

Finn had taken up his usual military stance off to the side. He pretended not to listen, but he couldn't resist interrupting Viktis to fill in parts of the story.

Viktis described the station, and Renna recognized some spots from the old days. The last time she'd seen it, she was with him. They'd finished their last job together there. Little did she know then, the next job Viktis took would be killing her.

A strange sadness pinged through her. What if things had been different? What if she'd let herself fall in love with Viktis instead of dropping him for the next handsome merc who'd come along because she'd been scared of her feelings? Would he have turned down the job? Would they have had something special?

A small part of her would always wonder with regret what might have happened between them. But while she loved Viktis as a brother now, she was pretty sure she was *in* love with Finn. And that scared the hell out of her. Renna sighed and felt the ship shudder around her.

Wonder surged through her. She'd made it do that. But how? Controlling ships was not part of what was supposed to happen here, but if she could use her implant for that, what else could she do if she learned to control it?

Slowly she pulled back out of the *Athena*, risking one more look at the three men on the bridge. Finn laughed at something Viktis said, his worry lightening for a moment, while Blake chuckled and clapped his friend on the shoulder.

And then she was gone, back in her bed on the *Eris*. Alone.

Renna blinked at the ceiling as she settled back into her own body. It felt strangely tight, claustrophobic even. Maybe if worse came to worse, she could lose herself in the *Athena*. At least she'd be able to watch over Finn and his crew.

Stop that, she scolded. *You're being creepy.*

Right. She was going to beat this and have her happily ever after. MYTH owed her a retirement on a garden planet and a fat stack of credits.

Steeling herself, Renna swung her legs over the side of the bed. Time to get moving. She had a mercenary to convince to help her. And knowing the type, any sign of weakness would have him circling like a shark.

EIGHTEEN

"Well, look who's up." Viktis grinned at Renna as she sank into a seat at the table in the comm room. He leaned back and crossed his arms. "Nothing like scaring the old man half to death," he said, jerking his head toward Finn. "I thought he was going to..."

"Enough, pirate," Finn interrupted as he entered the room. Pink tinged his cheeks, and he didn't meet Renna's gaze as he slipped into the seat beside her. "I'm glad to see you're feeling better."

"Me too." She smiled. It didn't hurt that being around him again made everything feel better. Gods, when had she turned into such a sap?

Commander Jayla tapped a fingernail against the table. A bruise darkened the skin beneath her left eye, and a cut sliced across her cheekbone, courtesy of Samil's men.

"Let's get started," she said, pulling up a holo of the bunker where they'd faced Samil. "MYTH bombed the place not long after the *Eris* escaped. I wasn't able to radio HQ in time. Any evidence Dr. Samil might have left behind has been destroyed. We're running blind here."

Lieutenant Blake nodded from the other side of the table. "We tried to track her ship's signature, but Samil and Major Larson were able to block it. They disappeared without a trace."

"Major Larson, a traitor. I still can't believe it," Finn said. "He had everyone fooled. And the doctor…" His voice trailed off as she shook his head

Jayla grimaced. "He even fooled the admiral. Larson was part of her advisory group. The things he knows about MYTH could destroy us. I don't even want to talk about Dr. Samil. How could we have missed something so huge?"

Finn gazed around the table as if to dare anyone to disagree with what he was about to say. "Well, whatever we think about Larson and Samil, the first thing we need to do is get Renna healthy."

Jayla opened her mouth to protest, but Renna held up a hand. "Before this turns into a discussion no one can win, I have my own suggestion."

Viktis groaned. "The last time you had a plan, I had to go on the run with our esteemed captain here. If this means I'm stuck alone with him for another two weeks, I quit. The guy can't handle his liquor or his women." He rolled his eyes but shot Finn an impish grin.

"Keep it up, pirate," Finn warned good-naturedly.

"Boys, behave." Renna fought the urge to stick out her tongue at them, but that would only lead to more childish behavior. "Viktis, you'll be relieved to know this plan has nothing to do with leaving you in Finn's clutches. I need your help with Wall. He's the only one left who has a sample of the medication Navang developed."

The unsaid words were there, heavy in the air around them. The only thing that might be able to keep her from turning into a cyborg.

The pirate nodded. "Makes sense. I should have thought of that right away. I'll put out some feelers. Last I heard, Wall and his crew had left Lenue after the attack."

Aldani steepled his fingers. "In the meantime, I'll continue my own research. There may be other alternatives we can use to keep Renna's implant stable."

"I appreciate the help." A warm glow curled through her. How had she gotten so lucky to have these people on her side? "I don't know what tricks Samil has up her sleeve, but I'm worried. I'd like to get moving on this as quickly as possible. Viktis, can you get a hold of Wall as fast as you can? Doc, if there are any genetic stabilizers you can think of, I'd be willing to give them a try until we get a real cure."

She glanced around the table at the people she'd come to care about. Blake lounged in his chair, looking unconcerned, but his fingers drummed a nervous tattoo against the table. Jayla had her commander expression back on—calm and composed, though Renna was sure she was anything but. Even Viktis, usually the most laidback man she'd ever met, sat on the edge of his chair.

Gods. Sometime in the last few weeks these people had become her family. How had that happened? She'd spent so long keeping to herself so she didn't get hurt, yet here she was, terrified for all of them.

Renna took a deep breath, trying to focus on the task at hand instead of her feelings. "Listen. Despite what's happening to me, Samil is still out there. And she's still gunning for MYTH. We need to figure out what her plans are before she can strike again. Whether or not we find a way to stop my implant from taking over."

Finn opened his mouth to protest, but she cut him off. "Hear me out. I think our number one priority is getting the doctor and Myka to a safe house and away from anything MYTH-related. Samil can't use him if she can't find him."

"Consider it done," Viktis said.

"We'll use the *Athena* to take them to the safe house. We know the ship is still off MYTH radar and is safe for now. Once they're settled, the two ships can rendezvous on Lenue and figure out our next steps."

Finn scowled at her. "You're not sending me away on some errand, Renna."

"I wasn't planning on it. I want Keva to lead that mission. I need you and Viktis as back up when we visit Wall."

Finn opened his mouth to argue, then realized what she'd said. "Oh. Right. Works for me."

"What about me?" Blake asked. "You can't leave me behind. I saved your life."

Renna grinned at him. "You're my hero." Beside her, Finn frowned at them. "But I need you and Commander Jayla to stay behind on the *Eris* and watch our backs."

Blake grimaced. "Left on the sidelines again. Seems to be my lot in life."

"Buck up, soldier, at least you won't ruin that pretty face of yours in a firefight." Renna smirked. "I mean, it's not like you have much else going for you."

"Hey..." Blake protested, but his eyes sparkled. "I thought we were friends."

"Are you two quite finished?" Finn asked coldly.

Renna glanced at him in surprise. Was he actually jealous? "I think so. Are we all clear on the plan?" Everyone around the table nodded. "Good, then I'm going to head to the mess before I pass out. I'm starving."

Finn got to his feet with her. "I'll come with you."

Together, they left the comm room. Finn matched his long stride to hers, and Renna was glad. Her head still felt swimmy, like the whole ship could tilt at any moment. Keeping herself together in that room had taken more out of her than she'd expected. His odd behavior hadn't helped either.

She let her fingers trail along the cool metal of the walls as they walked, sneaking glances at Finn from the corner of her eye. It had only been two weeks since she'd seen him last, but it felt like everything had changed. She didn't even know where they stood anymore. Or what her own feelings for him were.

Lies.

She knew exactly what her feelings were. She cared about him. She wanted the time to get to know him again, to see if anything more could happen between them. She wanted him. But not like this. Not with this alien tech in her brain turning her into a machine. Not with Samil chasing them.

Renna sighed.

"What's wrong?" Finn placed a hand on her lower back, and she shivered at the warmth of his touch.

"Everything is so strange now." She was too much of a coward to meet his gaze and studied the white tiles on the floor instead. "I hate feeling so awkward around you."

Finn stopped in the middle of the passageway and tugged at her hand, turning her to face him. "There's nothing to feel awkward about." He smiled down at her, unusually earnest. "I worried about you every minute we were gone."

Renna forced herself to look up at him, her insides heating at his concerned expression. "Why? I was perfectly safe." Until she'd walked into Samil's trap. She'd been too damn cocky.

"Anything could have happened. MYTH could have locked you away. There was no guarantee they'd believe you."

Renna's eyes widened as she remembered. "Finn!" Her hand clutched his. "Dallas is alive. He made it off Hesperia before it was destroyed."

Finn's grin split his face. "That's the best news I've heard all day. I hate that he thinks I'm a traitor, but at least he's alive."

Renna shook her head. "He doesn't. He knows you better than that. I wanted to tell him everything, but I didn't know if I could trust him or if he was working with Pallas."

"Never. And he might be the only one who can help us now."

Renna chewed her lip. "Maybe we can find a secure channel once we're at Wall's. I don't want to use the MYTH frequencies in case one of Samil's spies is listening in."

Finn's gaze swept the narrow corridor. "But what if there's already a traitor on board? What if someone on the *Eris* is working for her?"

"Then I guess we're already too late." Dread curled through her, heavy and thick. "I don't know what to do anymore, Finn. I don't know which way is up or who to trust. I don't even know what to do next. I always have a plan." She hated that her voice cracked on the last word.

Finn pulled her into his arms and stroked her hair. She rested her head on his chest and took a deep breath, inhaling his scent.

"It's going to be all right, love," he said. "You're not alone, Renna. We have a team of people behind us. And we're going to make Samil pay for everything she's destroyed."

"But I don't know where to go next. She could be anywhere." The thump of Finn's heart was strong and steady in her ear. His arms tightened around her, and she felt safe for the first time in days.

"I don't think that's going to be a problem," he said, his voice vibrating low and sexy. "Samil will find us, long before we're ready. But that's okay. Maybe we can use that to our advantage."

"We set our own trap?"

She felt him nod. "But before anything else, we have to get your implant stable." He tilted her chin up so he could look at her. "I need you at your best, Star Thief."

She chuckled. "I don't feel much like stealing anything right now."

"Except my heart," he deadpanned.

Renna moaned and pushed away from him. "I can't believe you actually said that."

"But at least I got you to smile." He brushed away a strand of hair from her face. "Let's go get you some food, and then you're going to rest some more. Aldani will have something for you soon, I'm sure of it."

Hopefully he was right. She had too much to do to give up now.

NINETEEN

The mess was empty except for the matronly woman stirring something in a pot on the stove, and the little boy who sat at one of the nearby tables chatting with her.

As she entered, the boy looked up, pausing from kicking his feet against the chair legs. A grin split his face and he launched himself at her. "Renna!"

She braced herself for impact as he threw his arms around her, rocking her back on her heels. "Hey there, kid. How've you been?" She smiled down at Myka's dark, curly hair and hugged him back. An unexpected warmth spread through her.

He pulled away, grinning up at her. "Better now that you're here."

"Well, of course. I make everything better." She winked at him and sat down at the table, smiling over at Miss Mary, the cook, before she turned back to Myka. "So tell me all about your adventures since I've been gone. Did you keep that pirate Viktis in line?"

He sat down across from her. "He's not that bad, I guess. And he showed me how to play Costa Five Poker. I won twenty credits from Uncle David." He preened, and Renna tried not to laugh.

"I'm going to have to keep an eye on you, aren't I? You may give me a run for my money some day."

"Nah, I'll go easy on you. I owe you." He stuffed a handful of crackers into his mouth, talking around them. "Uncle David said you were sick. They wouldn't let me see you. What happened?"

Renna glanced at Finn over the boy's head. How much had they told him? Finn nodded, and she let out a breath. "Well, back at Navang's, he injected me with that drug to see if my implant would integrate with my nervous system. Looks like it's trying, but the rest of my body is fighting it. I've been pretty tired."

Myka nodded. "Yeah, I remember feeling like that, too. But it gets better. And then we'll be the same." His eyes lit up hopefully. "It'll be cool to have someone else like me around."

A pang of sadness shot through Renna. It must be tough for the kid, knowing he was different. But if he could deal with it, so could she. And even better, Myka hadn't changed too much. Maybe there was hope for her yet, despite the drug cocktail Samil had given her to change the way her implant worked.

She ruffled the kid's hair. "Right? I mean the rest of these people don't get how cool it is to be part-machine. I can't wait until some of those super powers you were talking about kick in. Running extra-fast or being extra-strong could sure come in handy in my line of work." Hell, she'd just take being able to turn the damn implant on and off when she wanted.

Myka frowned. "Well, yeah, it's cool. But I thought the captain said you weren't going to do that stuff anymore. He and Viktis got in a fight about it last week."

Renna glanced up at Finn and raised an eyebrow, but he looked away. "Guess I'll have to see what else there is out there for a washed-up thief, then," she said with a smile. "Don't worry about me, kid. We'll figure it out. Now, I'm starving. What do you recommend?"

"Miss Mary made up a big pot of stew. It's the best."

"Then I'll have that. Why don't you go ask her for a bowl?" She needed to have a little chat with Captain Finn about her future.

Myka darted away to the kitchen.

Renna leaned back in her chair and tilted her head to study Finn. He glanced away and tugged at his collar as he leaned against the table.

"Care to tell me what that was all about?" she asked.

"It was just a discussion Viktis and I had. I didn't know Myka overheard us."

"And what did you two *gentlemen*—" she emphasized the word slightly, "—decide about my future?"

Finn cleared his throat. "Nothing, really. I assured Viktis you were done with mercenary work and wouldn't be interested in any other contracts. That you had given up that sort of thing. That MYTH could trust you."

"You assured him, huh?" She raised an eyebrow. "And how did you know that?"

Finn tugged at his collar again. "I thought... since you were working for MYTH…"

"That I'd give up the only job I've ever been good at?"

"I…"

"Save it, Finn." She shook her head. "Neither you or Viktis know anything about my future plans. And to be honest, right now my only plan is surviving this mess. After I know I'm not going to die, I'll think about what comes next."

She'd spent most of her life planning what would come next—an early retirement on a vacation world. But she knew no matter what happened, that could never work for her now. If she was really honest with herself, she was hardly the type to settle down. Either in life or relationships. Which made her current situation all the more confusing. Part of her wanted to see what happened with Finn. Part of her wanted to run the moment this was over. She wasn't sure which part would win at the moment.

Finn's voice deepened, and he leaned forward to rest his hands on the table across from her, his gaze at her eye level. "I've been thinking about what comes next since we went on the run." He looked like he wanted to devour her for lunch.

Renna swallowed.

"I hate that you left as we were getting to know each other again. I missed you, Renna." He smiled wolfishly. "Obviously you missed me, too, if you took control of the *Athena* to get us back here."

Heat blossomed in her face. "That had nothing to do with you," she protested, getting to her feet. "I was unconscious. I didn't even know what I was doing."

Finn circled the table, and Renna backed away from him until she hit the wall. The expression on his face made heat pool between her legs and her mouth go dry. He stopped, just far enough away that he wasn't touching her but close enough she could feel the heat from his body.

His blue eyes bore into hers. "Look at that. The Star Thief's afraid," he said softly.

She shook her head, her tongue darting out to lick her suddenly dry lips. Finn's gaze dropped to watch. Once upon a time, she would have used that to her advantage, to seduce him and turn the tables. To take control of the situation. What the hell had happened to her?

She inhaled Finn's scent—citrus and sandalwood. Damn him, he was right. She had missed him. But with everything going on now, she couldn't afford to let him distract her. She couldn't think about the future. There was only the present.

Damn, she wanted him, though. Now. On the freaking mess hall table.

Finn's gaze trapped hers as he caressed her jaw with one of his long fingers, letting it drift lower down her neck to brush butterfly-light against her collarbone.

Renna's skin tingled with fear and desire and lust until she could barely see straight.

And then he lowered his lips to hers. Just a soft brush of skin at first, but heat zapped through her and she sucked in a breath.

Finn took that as an invitation, smiling before he kissed her again softly. The feel of his mouth against hers sent a blaze of fire through her. Renna curled her hands into his arms, and he jerked her to him, deepening the kiss. He forced her mouth open, stroking her tongue, teasing her until she moaned.

"Finn," she whispered, pressing herself against him, her fears forgotten for the moment. His hands tangled in her hair, and he kissed her until she was dizzy, until her knees trembled—along with other, more intimate parts of her.

He pulled away slightly to press kisses to her jaw, sliding his tongue against the sensitive skin beneath her ear. They were tangled in each other, his hard strength holding her against the wall. And she felt an even harder part of him pressed against her.

Another surge of heat shot through her. Gods, she'd missed him. She didn't care what it meant at that moment. "I want you."

"I know." He nibbled on her earlobe before capturing her mouth again.

"Hey, what are you guys doing?" Myka's voice made them shoot apart so fast that Renna grabbed the wall, using its strength to hold her up so she wouldn't slide bonelessly to the floor.

"Why do you always have to kiss like that? It's gross. It's like you're eating her face or something." He grimaced at them and then dropped a bowl of stew on the table. "Miss Mary said she'd bring out some biscuits in a minute, and you'd better eat before it gets cold." He put his hands on his hips like a mother hen, his gaze shifting between the pair.

Finn ran a hand through his hair, making it stand on end. "Better do what he says, Ren. You don't want Myka and Miss Mary to gang up on you. You need to eat to keep your strength up." A feral smile curled his lips. "For later."

TWENTY

Renna ate her stew and tried to ignore the desire burning in places she didn't even want to think about. Somehow she was able to hold a halfway coherent conversation with Myka, but that might have been because he was full of stories about being on the run. She just had to nod her head and look interested.

She wanted to kiss Miss Mary when the cook called the boy back to the kitchen to help with dinner.

Myka threw his arms around Renna and squeezed. "I'm glad you're back." Before she could respond, he disappeared through the kitchen door.

What the hell was she going to do now? She couldn't lock Finn in his cabin and have her way with him while he and Jayla were busy planning their next steps. She was too keyed up to sleep. And staring at the walls in her cabin would send her right over the edge.

The only thing left was blowing off some steam in the ship's weight room. She quickly changed into workout clothes and pulled her arms behind her back, enjoying the pop of her joints as she stretched. She swung them back and forth. Interesting. Not a twinge from injuring her shoulder back at Samil's warehouse. Aldani must be a magician.

She'd have to ask him about it later. Right now, the only thing she wanted was to imagine Thana Samil's face on the punching bag in the corner.

She switched on the machine and took a few jabs at the floating, stuffed orb. Her fist connected with the synthetic white ball over and over, her muscles burning with the exertion. The punching bag dodged as she struck, but her hits struck dead center. It was as though her fists had a homing device inside the orb as she pummeled it with powerful strikes.

Renna stopped to stare at the hovering machine, a frown furrowing her eyebrows. "What the hell is going on?"

She plucked it from the air and turned it over to check the controls. The float mechanism was supposed to be randomized so you had to work for the sweet spot, but she was hitting the damn thing like it was standing still.

A quick check confirmed it was set up properly, and she set it back in the air, letting it rise to face height. "Okay, little guy. Let's try this again."

She threw a right hook, but her fist still connected with the bag dead center. Left hook, right hook, uppercut. Each one landed with precision.

Renna blew her escaping hair from her eyes. Did the bag have a faulty mechanism? "Screw this. I'm done," she said. Before she could grab the thing to switch it off, it gave a low beep and fell to the floor as the grav thrusters cut off. She blinked at the now-deactivated device before stooping to pick it up. She switched it back on and it hovered in front of her, waiting for her next command.

She raised her arm and faked a punch. The thing seemed to throw itself in the way of her punch, instead of away from her. Like it knew exactly where her fist was going to land.

Off, she thought.

The beep sounded again, and it fell to the floor with a thump.

She rubbed a shaking hand over her face and glowered at the ball on the floor. Since when could she connect to gym equipment with her implant?

A heads-up display instantly appeared across her vision with calculations, charts, and dates. Renna froze, staring at the details as her hands went clammy.

A green date flashed in the center of the display. According to her implant, this new talent had started three days ago. Around the time Samil had started giving her the new drugs. Somehow they'd increased her neural connections. That had to be how she'd controlled the *Athena,* too.

A tingling started in her chest, and she pressed a palm to her ribcage as if she could stop her heart from beating its way out. Yet another piece of evidence that she was changing. That her implant was transforming her into something else. She needed to find a way to stop it before she lost everything that was important to her. Before she lost herself.

A man's voice jerked her out of her downward spiral. "Usually

ATHENA'S ASHES | 155

people come here to use the equipment, not stare at it."

Renna spun around to find Lieutenant Blake leaning against the hatch, a smirk playing across his lips. He wore MYTH-issued workout clothes—a gray top and close-fitting pants made of some shiny material that grazed his tight muscles. His blond hair was still carefully messy, and sandy stubble shadowed his chiseled jaw.

"Maybe it was staring at me." She forced her racing heart under control and smiled at him. No need for him to see how freaked out she was.

"I could see why." His gaze took in her figure-hugging shirt and leggings.

Renna took the bait, slipping into flirting as an easy distraction. She preened a bit, pushing out her chest and turning her hips. "I specialize in gorgeous."

He pushed himself off the doorway and stalked toward her. "And how about combat? Are you as good at fighting as you are at bragging?"

"Better," she said with a slow smile. "Wanna try me out?"

Despite his good looks, Alistair Blake was no Finn, but fighting was an even better distraction than flirting. And being physical always made her feel better, even if it wasn't the type of physical action she craved.

"Oh, most definitely." Blake circled her, seemingly relaxed and at ease, but his gaze followed her every move. "I can go easy on you. I'd hate to hit an injured woman."

"Don't worry, love. I like it hard and fast." The innuendo slipped from her lips, part of the trash-talking of the sparring ring. She shivered. The only one she wanted hard and fast was Finn. She craved him like a drug and that scared the hell out of her.

Blake chuckled as they slowly spun around each other. "Don't forget you asked for it then." He lunged, his fist missing her jaw by centimeters.

Renna jumped out of the way. "Handsome and deadly. Why aren't there girls lined up at the door for you?"

"I'm too much for most girls to handle." Blake smiled, a dimple flashing in his cheek.

Renna struck back, darting around his defenses. Her fist landed squarely in his abdomen and the lieutenant grunted. But he followed up before she could recover, landing a quick jab on her jaw.

Her head snapped back and stars danced in her vision. "Not playing around, are we, Lieutenant?"

"Call me Alistair. You're not MYTH yet." He took a step back, swinging his shoulders a bit to keep them loose. "And you should know I never play at fighting or beautiful women."

A grin snuck to her lips. "Good to know." The guy was a charmer, that's for sure. Quite a difference from the steamy, intense lust Finn's very presence caused. Another surge of hunger shot through her.

Focus, Renna.

She danced around Blake for a few more heartbeats, gaze locked with his. They were close enough that his hot breath whispered against her neck, and she shivered.

He took that moment to throw an uppercut, bringing him even closer to her. Renna blocked it and grabbed his arm, twisting it behind him until his hard back muscles were pressed against her chest.

Blake struggled, the veins in his biceps standing out, and with one smooth move, he reversed their positions, flipping her around until he had her in a chokehold.

"How the hell did you do that?" she wheezed, bucking against his chest. His scent enveloped her—spearmint and spice and something sweet she couldn't place. It was a clean scent, one that reminded her of bright summer days. Far different from Finn's sexy sandalwood.

Something that felt like desire stirred inside her like a waiting beast. Gods. It had been so long since she'd been with Finn. Damn Jayla for keeping him away so long.

"I'm very talented," he said, a smile in his voice, jerking her attention back to the fight and away from the heat growing inside her. Blake's arm loosened ever-so-slightly, and she took her opening.

Renna twisted away from him, breaking his grasp before spinning to face him again. "Want to show me exactly how talented you are, handsome?" she asked teasingly. Her gaze dropped lower, to his muscled thighs, then traveled back up to his face. She wanted Finn more than she'd ever wanted another man, but damn she wasn't dead yet. She could still admire the view.

He blinked at her, cheeks turning pink. "No. I didn't mean…just forget I said…"

She grinned. "You're a tease then?"

He stumbled a bit as they circled, catching himself before he went down on the mat in a tangle of arms and legs. "I don't know what you're talking about." He threw a clumsy punch to cover his embarrassment that Renna sidestepped easily.

Well, well. Flustering the adorable Alistair Blake might be

her new favorite thing.

She attacked again while he was still distracted, bluffing with a jab and striking with an uppercut. He blocked her first punch and missed the second. Renna's hand connected with his jaw with a satisfying *thunk*.

"Ow," he said, rubbing his chin and glaring at her with puppy dog eyes. "That hurt."

She winked at him. "Sometimes love hurts, handsome."

"Is that so?" He cracked his knuckles. "Then let's get serious. I'm not going to let a wispy thing like you take me down."

"Keep talking like that, and I'll do more than take you—" She let her gaze drop to his waist again with a suggestive grin. "—down."

Blake sucked in a breath, then started coughing. His face turned a mottled red, and she bit back a grin. He was so easy to set off. She was having way too much fun with this.

"Put your hands up, woman," he said once he'd gotten his breathing under control. "Let's do this."

He settled into his fighting stance, and she couldn't help but admire the way his arm muscles flexed. He was almost as muscular as Finn, but there was something about him that seemed to lack Finn's edge of danger. Blake just needed a few dangerous missions to toughen him up. He needed to get out of his comfort zone.

"Come get me, baby." She curled her fingers at him, beckoning him toward her.

They attacked at the same moment, throwing punches at each other in a frantic bid to win. Renna felt her fist connect with Blake's washboard abs, then grunted in pain as his hook caught her across the jaw. They flailed for a good minute, neither giving ground, until Blake feinted and she fell for it, throwing her whole weight behind a punch that totally missed him.

He grabbed her arm, spinning her back into a hold against his body. Her face was inches from his as they panted, and the strong beat of his heart raced against her chest. The sheen of sweat highlighted his chiseled cheekbones and shimmered across his nose.

He lowered his head a fraction, dropping his gaze to her mouth.

Was he going to kiss her?

For a nanosecond, a tiny part of her wanted it, wanted to see what his full lips would feel like on hers, how he'd taste. But she couldn't do this. Not to Finn. Renna struggled in Alistair's firm grip for three ragged breaths before she maneuvered enough to push him away.

Goose bumps rippled across her skin, and her head swiveled slowly toward the door as Finn stepped across the threshold.

"What the hell are you doing?" Finn asked.

She blinked at him as the ice in his voice sent a shiver down her spine.

Blake raised an eyebrow. "What does it look like? We were sparring."

The captain strode into the room, fury in every tense muscle of his body. His glare alternated between Renna and Blake, but finally came to a stop on her.

He fisted his hands together in front of him, as if he didn't think he could control himself. "I trusted you, Renna. I believed you when you said you'd changed. I should have known better."

He turned to Blake and poked a finger into the man's chest. "And you! I thought you were my friend. A brother. That wasn't sparring. That was..." He broke off and shook his head. "What else have the two of you been doing since I've been gone?" His furious gaze froze them both where they stood.

Renna opened her mouth to protest, to redouble Blake's proclamation, but he cut her off with the wave of a hand. "I'm done here. I don't want to hear your excuses. There's nothing left to say." His whole body quivered with barely suppressed rage.

Renna's heart shattered at the hurt in his eyes. "Finn. Stop it. It's not like that," she protested. But he was already out the door. Her mouth went as dry as a desert. Finn still didn't trust her. That hurt more than even the prospect of turning into a robot.

Blake put a hand on her arm to stop her from following. "He's too angry right now. He won't listen to a word you say. Give him a little time."

She exhaled, her whole body deflating. "As much as I like you, you know nothing is ever going to happen between us, right?"

He smiled. "I know. I'm way out of your league."

Despite herself, she chuckled. She swallowed past the lump in her throat. "I'm going to go get cleaned up. Thanks for the fight."

"Any time." Alistair paused and, just before Renna left the room, said, "Renna?"

"Yes?"

"Finn's a very lucky man. Don't let him forget it."

TWENTY-ONE

Renna marched down the *Eris's* corridors to her cabin. Emotions swirled and battled inside her, swinging between fury that Finn thought she'd cheat on him and disbelief that he could be upset when they'd never agreed to stop seeing other people. Even worse, he'd involved someone else in this mess. Poor Alistair had simply been in the wrong place at the wrong time.

She opened her cabin door and slipped inside, staring sightlessly at the bed. A few minutes ago, she'd wanted Finn more than she'd ever wanted another man. But if he couldn't trust her, if he didn't accept her personality for what it was, could she really be with him?

Renna peeled off her workout clothes and stepped into the shower, turning up the temperature as hot as it would go. Her skin was glowing pink and her fingers puckered before she finally switched it off. Her muscles felt a little more relaxed, but her brain was still spinning.

Fuck this. She wasn't going to wait around for Finn to feel like talking to her. He'd just have to deal with her now, whether he liked it or not.

She quickly dried off, then threw on a sweater and a clean pair of leggings. She was going to tell him the truth about what happened. It would be up to him after that.

Renna crossed to the hatch. A knock stopped her, hand half-way to the control panel.

"Renna? We need to talk."

She blinked at the door. Finn hadn't been able to let more than an hour go by either. "Are we going to talk or are you going to throw accusations at me?" she finally asked.

"Please open the door. I don't want to do this standing in the hallway."

Renna pressed the control pad, then crossed her arms and stepped aside as the door slid open. "Fine. Come in."

Finn took up a spot beside the table, his gaze resting on her for a moment before sliding away.

Silence stretched between them, and she clenched her fists. She was damned if she was going to talk first. He'd come to her room. Let him make the first move.

Finally, he sighed heavily and raked a hand through his dark hair. "Look, I'm sorry I jumped to conclusions about you and Blake. I saw the two of you pressed together like that and thought the worst." He met her gaze. "I was jealous."

Renna raised an eyebrow. "That's no excuse for acting like an asshole. Nothing happened between Blake and me. Ever."

Finn nodded. "I know. Blake told me the same thing."

Her chest tightened. "What?"

"I asked Blake about it. He said you were sparring."

She dropped her voice until it was dangerously low. "You went to Blake first before coming to talk to me?"

Finn blinked as he realized his misstep. "No. I, uh. See…"

Renna threw up a hand. "Don't even try. How can you scream at me about trust when you didn't even have the common decency to come talk to me about the situation?"

"Renna, that's not it."

She cocked her head. "No? Then would you care to explain? 'Cause that's how it looks from my end."

Finn growled. "Look, I've spent the last two weeks worried about you. I had no idea if you were safe, if I'd ever see you again, or if you'd even done what you said you were going to do."

"If I *what*?" Renna gaped at him. Had he really just said that? "You've never trusted me, have you?"

The walls of her room closed in, making it feel no bigger than a closet. Her legs itched to pace, her hands curled into fists, ready to strike out at something, but she was trapped here against the door, staring at someone she thought had loved her.

Finn yanked a chair away from the table and sat down heavily. "You know my past. You know that I've always had a hard time trusting people. I was burned too many times—by Blur, by the gang, even by people I thought had my back. It's easier for me to expect the worst. That way I'm not hurt if it happens."

"Join the fucking club."

He nodded. "I know. You haven't had it easy either. I don't know what to say but that I'm sorry and I want to fix this."

"Fix this? I didn't think anything was broken until you freaked out on me for no reason." She glared at him. "I'm not going to do this."

His gaze snapped to hers. "Do what?"

"Dance around your feelings and try to figure out what it is you want from me. Let me tell you a few truths. I'm a thief. I always have been, and even if I give it up and walk the straight and narrow, I always will be. Obviously you still have a problem with that. With trusting me."

"I don't..."

"You do," she insisted. "You've already planned out my life when this is over. Some boring desk job where you can make sure I behave while you go out and have your adventures. It's not going to happen, Finn. I could never be that person. And I don't want to be with someone who wants that for me either."

Finn stared down at his hands clenched together on the table. She didn't think he was going to answer, but he finally spoke softly. "I don't want that for you, Renna. At least not consciously. I just don't want you in danger. I want you to be safe. I care about you, and it scares me. And when I get scared, I try to control things."

"No kidding." The words slipped out before she could stop them, and she winced. Being sarcastic right now would not help the situation.

But Finn didn't respond to her taunt. "It was easy to jump to conclusions about you and Blake because it was something else to focus on, something I could control. It was right there in front of me, and I could get angry about it. Do something about it. I can't do the same thing with Samil or MYTH." He finally looked up at her. "But I do trust you. I know you'd never betray me or MYTH."

"Damn straight. I gave you my word. Everything I've done since you found me a month ago has been to help you and your damned organization. And look where it's gotten me. I'm turning into a fucking monster. You'll have to excuse me if I've been a little preoccupied. I don't have a lot of extra energy to spend on figuring out how to make you happy."

She blinked back the sudden tears that burned her eyes. Was Finn so focused on his own feelings that he couldn't see how terrified she was herself? "I don't know what you want from me, Finn. But I don't have anything else to say to you right now. To be honest, the only thing I want to do right now is tell you to fuck off and kick you out of my cabin."

It was so much easier to be on her own, to not have to answer to anyone else. Now that she cared about what Finn thought, it felt like she'd given him too much power over her. Having to deal with someone else's expectations pissed her off.

It would be so much easier to walk away now.

"Kicking me out won't solve anything, will it?" he asked. "So what do we do?"

She shrugged. "Fuck?"

A smile tugged at the corner of his lips but he shook his head. "There's nothing I'd like more. But that's only a temporary solution. I care about you too much to let this go, Ren." He met her gaze, blue eyes full of pain. "But you're a hard woman to love. It's like trying to hold sand in your hand. The tighter you squeeze, the faster it escapes. You fascinate and terrify me at the same time. The only thing I do know is that I'd like to be with you when this is all over so we can figure *us* out."

Renna stared at the dark stubble that shadowed his jaw, the slump to his shoulders. What was she doing here with him? With these people? She was becoming someone she didn't even recognize.

The only thing she'd ever been good at was running away. But if she stayed with Finn, she'd have to choose to move forward. She'd have to learn how to face her problems instead of pushing them away. She'd locked away her feelings for so long, pretended they didn't affect her. Could she even change at this point?

Renna stared down at her hands. Was fighting for Finn worth it? Or was fighting Samil the only thing she should focus on right now?

Her pulse thudded sluggishly in her ears. Maybe they were the same thing. Maybe by choosing to move forward with Finn, she was fighting for herself and her future. Choosing to take back her power from Samil.

There were no guarantees in life; she knew that all too well. She and Finn might never make it, but if she didn't try, if she didn't give their relationship a chance, she'd regret it for the rest of her life. She couldn't let fear win.

If Renna ran from this like she always had, that's exactly what would happen.

She met Finn's gaze, fingers twisting in the hem of her sweater. The words felt like marbles in her mouth, like she could barely speak around them, but somehow she got them out. "I want to be with you, too. I want to figure out what's between us."

Finn's face softened with his smile.

Renna continued before he could interrupt. "But you have to trust me, Finn. I would never cheat on you or betray you. I never have, and I've had plenty of opportunities. We're in this together—at least until we decide we're not."

There. She'd said it. And the world hadn't come crashing down around her. She smoothed the front of her shirt where she'd twisted it into tiny hills.

"Do you forgive me?" he asked hopefully.

Renna nodded. "We're both new to this relationship business. We're going to make mistakes, but we have to talk about them, okay?

"Promise."

"Promise." Renna met Finn's gaze across the room, and the atmosphere in the cabin went from tense to something else in a matter of seconds. She'd never been in a relationship long enough to have make-up sex, but she'd heard fantastic things about it.

Finn's eyes darkened, and they threw themselves at each other at the same moment, bodies crashing together as their lips made contact like heat-seeking missiles, an explosive fusion of skin and scent and passion. Finn pushed her back against the door, pressing his body to hers, covering her completely. Their tongues warred and caressed each other, and she tasted him—citrus and sandalwood.

She had the instant thought that this was what home must feel like, but it was gone a moment later, pushed away by the feel of his muscles beneath her fingers. Finn jerked her tightly against him, the pressure of his mouth, his tongue, sending shivers down her spine as he deepened their kiss.

Renna's hands drifted up to tangle in the hair at the base of his neck. She never wanted to let go, but Finn broke away, gasping for breath. Their gazes met, and he smiled slightly.

She shoved a strand of hair behind her ear and tried to normalize her breathing. "So, Captain. What are you doing for the next few hours?"

"Hopefully you?"

"Smart man. I plan on taking up most of your schedule. Good thing I've had a birth control implant since I was thirteen."

"A very good thing." With a wolfish grin, he scooped her up and carried her to the bed. Renna settled between his arms as he lowered both of them to the mattress. Finn's eyes searched hers and something twisted inside her, taking up residence in her heart, filling it with what felt suspiciously like love. She wanted to look away, to break the connection between them. It was too much, too raw. But she didn't. Especially after the conversation they'd just had. If she *was* falling in love with this man, she wanted to be with him for real, for however long she had.

With a low growl, Finn captured her lips with his again, his tongue dipping into her mouth, teasing her with what was to come. His arms caged her, supporting his weight above her, and Renna slid her hands beneath his shirt, feeling the smoothness of his skin, the ridges of muscles, the faint scars left from his past life.

Her hands drifted higher, grazing his nipples, and he sucked in a breath. Renna grinned against his lips and did it again, before yanking his shirt up and over his head.

Finn grabbed the hem of her shirt, and she struggled to free herself as his tongue traced patterns across her abdomen. He stared down at her breasts, still bare after her shower, then lowered his mouth to one of her nipples.

A burst of heat flared through her as he worshiped her with his mouth. Renna arched her back, whimpering as pleasure wound tighter and tighter in her midsection. He flicked her nipple with his tongue, and she gasped as heat shot through her in a blaze that left her breathless.

"I love that sound," he said, raising his head to meet her half-lidded gaze. "Should we see if I can make you repeat it?"

She could only nod as he moved to her other breast. A moan escaped her again as the wave of pleasure started to build, and she buried her hands in his hair to hold him close to her.

His hardness pressed against her, and Renna let her hands drift down his hard abs until she found the waistband of his trousers. Slowly she unzipped them, sliding her hands beneath the fabric to touch him. He was hard as steel and soft as velvet, and all she wanted was to feel him inside her.

"I want you," she whispered.

Finn responded instantly, going even harder than she'd thought possible. In seconds he'd stripped off his pants and pulled hers off as well. They tangled back together like magnets, skin to skin.

Renna kissed him deeply. As if she could make him feel how much she cared for him without saying the words. Her hands slid down his body until she found his cock, hard and ready for her.

"I need you," she whispered. "Now."

With a growl, Finn rose above her, positioning himself between her thighs before thrusting into her. She gasped as he stretched and filled her, deep enough that she could feel him at her very core. Slowly he slid himself in and out, teasing her, testing her. Each movement made her body convulse, heat and pleasure surging through her until her eyes rolled back and she let herself escape into the feelings.

His fingers traced her jaw, and he lowered himself to kiss her again, still keeping up the slow, intense thrusts that were driving her insane.

Renna's whole body trembled at his touch, screaming for release. She moaned against his lips, then grabbed his ass, hoping to force him to go faster, to ride her until she exploded.

"Please, Finn," she begged, arching her back and trying to climb inside him.

He stroked her cheek with a single finger. "Only if you call me Nick."

Her eyes flew open. "Nick?"

"My name. No one uses it. I'd like you to be the only one."

Something warm and soft flowed through her chest. Was she worthy of this kind of intimacy? Especially with him? She pulled his mouth back to hers. "I want you, Nick," she whispered as she kissed him.

He groaned, thrusting hard and deep, and all other thoughts flew from her mind. Renna gasped as he gathered her into his arms and flipped onto his back. "Ride me, Renna. I want to watch you as you come apart."

She smiled seductively. "My pleasure." Renna slid down the length of him, her fingers tracing his nipples as he filled her. She could feel him, rock hard inside her as she rocked against him.

He grabbed her hips, holding her to him, then thrust into her, harder and harder until they were both panting. Finn captured her hands in his and pulled her down until their foreheads touched and their breaths mingled. As their gazes met, something wordless passed between them. Something she hadn't felt in years. Love. A promise of more.

Renna's heart clenched as emotions flooded through her, emotions she thought she'd buried long ago. But being with Finn had awakened them, had opened her to them again. And this time she wasn't going to deny them.

Beneath her, Finn began to move again, his eyes never leaving hers. The pressure built inside her like a glowing star, and with one last thrust, it went supernova, shattering her from the inside out. She let out a low cry and shuddered as wave after wave of pleasure flowed through her. Finn's gaze wavered as his own release neared, and a moment later he went stiff, groaning as he came.

Renna collapsed, draping herself over Finn's body. She rested her head on his chest, listening to his heartbeat. Her eyelids drifted shut, despite wanting to caress every plane of his body and then begin again.

Finn brushed her hair back from her face and kissed her forehead. "I missed you, Renna."

"I missed you, too, Nick."

She felt him smile against her skin. "I like hearing you say my name. Knowing that you're the only one who uses it. It's like a secret."

"I like it, too." She slid off him, nestling herself against his body, snuggled securely under the covers with her head still on his shoulder. "Don't go anywhere. Just need a few minutes to rest my eyes."

"Sounds like a plan," he agreed, pulling her even closer.

Renna smiled as she drifted off. She felt content for the first time since this whole thing had begun.

TWENTY-TWO

Renna jerked awake the next morning as Jayla's voice filled the room.

"Crew, we'll be landing on Hera III in an hour. Please prep for landing."

The intercom snapped off, and Renna snuggled her cheek against Finn's bare chest. His arm tightened around her.

"Just think," she said. "We get the drug from Wall, Dr. Aldani does his thing, and I'll be back to normal. And then we can get on with hunting down Samil."

"I'm going to enjoy making her pay for all of this," Finn said. "I trusted the doctor. I thought we were friends. For her do to this…"

"I don't understand it," Renna said, tracing a finger through the dark hair that dusted Finn's chest. "She has everything. What could MYTH possibly have taken from her?"

Finn shook his head. "I wish I knew. Samil kept to herself when she served on the *Athena*. She was always friendly, but never gave any indication she wanted to get personal, so I left her alone. Now I wish I'd made the effort to get to know her."

"We'll figure it out. Maybe it doesn't even matter. She's evil and has to be stopped. Simple as that."

"Fair enough," he said, voice rumbling beneath her ear. "I'll be happy to put this all behind us."

"I think we all will." She raised her head to look at him. "In the meantime, I think we have a better way to spend the next hour than talking about her, don't you?"

Finn grinned. "I certainly do."

When the *Eris* landed at the spaceport in New Queensland, the crew immediately started the prep for a quick take-off. Commander Jayla and Lieutenant Blake stayed on board, while Renna, Viktis, and Finn trekked to the edge of the city to find a speeder.

Wall had agreed to meet them in his new compound and had sent the coordinates to Viktis through a secure comm channel. When the spaceport on Lenue was destroyed in Navang's attack, Wall had relocated his drug production facility to Hera III, a tiny planet on the edge of Coalition space.

The government had tried terraforming it, to bring in settlers from Earth, but the planet was as stubborn as its indigenous species—a willowy group of aliens who called themselves the

ATHENA'S ASHES | 175

F'Obon. They towered over the humans at seven feet, with long thin necks and perfectly round heads. Their leathery skin protected them from the harsh winds that blew across the dusty terrain.

The humans who stayed behind when the Coalition left formed a settlement in a protected valley, where they harvested the spindly cactus-like plants to use in medical dispensaries. New Queensland had roughly fifty-thousand residents, squished into apartments and adobe houses, who spent their days either searching for or processing the plants for shipment off-world.

It was the perfect place for Wall to retreat to.

"What the hell is taking so long?" Finn growled, crossing his arms.

Viktis lounged against the crumbling rock wall that marked the edge of the dusty plain and the beginning of civilization. He shrugged. "The settlers on this world run on their own time. No sense in getting impatient."

Renna scanned the dirt-streaked dockworkers who were taking a break nearby. "Speak for yourself." Her skin pricked with unease, and she shifted her weight from foot to foot, hand on the handle of her blaster. "I sent the order half an hour ago. I don't like this." At least Keva and the *Athena* had already left to take Aldani and Myka to the safe house. They'd be safe, no matter what happened here.

"Just a busy day." Viktis yawned. "It'll show up soon."

Before she could complain again, the hum of an approaching speeder filled the air and Viktis raised his eyebrow in an I-told-you-so smirk.

Finn's hand twitched near his holster, and Viktis pushed himself off the wall. He stayed relaxed, but the set of his shoulders told her he was still on guard.

The speeder pulled to a stop in front of them, and the driver's door opened with a hiss. The driver grinned at them, his left front tooth missing. "Speeder as ordered. Bring it back by the end of the day or you'll be charged double."

"And you'll be taking off an hour from our bill, since you're late, right?" Renna asked.

"Not my fault. Traffic jam on the other side of town." He slid from the car and headed toward the seedy bar at the end of the street. "Have a nice day."

"Traffic jam, my ass," she muttered, heading for the driver's seat.

"Where do you think you're going?" Viktis asked. "I'm the pilot here."

Renna smirked. "You haven't piloted a ship in five years. Besides, I already have the map of the city in my head. You know, crazy implant and all."

Viktis's eyes narrowed. "I don't need an implant to help me find my way around. You know, my impeccable sense of direction and all."

Both Finn and Renna burst out laughing. "You keep telling yourself that," she said, climbing into the speeder.

Viktis huffed. "Fine. But I'm not sitting in back."

They sped through the shit-hole of a town, passing slums and tenements on the way to the more wealthy part of the city. A thin layer of yellow sediment coated the buildings and streets, giving it an odd, dusty glow. Even the skin of the humans living there was tinged yellow.

Renna parked the speeder. When they got out, they approached Wall's compound, a rambling set of buildings hidden behind a high steel wall. She eyed the barbed wire with a frown. The security measures seemed a bit excessive.

"You sure he's waiting for us?" she asked, pressing the buzzer on the gate. There was no answer.

Viktis stared through the bars of the gate into the silent compound. "When I spoke with him on the holo earlier, he said he'd have a man on point to let us in. Try again."

Renna leaned on the buzzer for a good thirty seconds before letting go. The shrill scream of the bell echoed through the courtyard, but there was no sign of movement. The skin between her shoulder blades prickled, and she unsnapped her holster. On either side of her, Finn and Viktis pulled out their blasters.

"I'm going to hack into the system," she said, crouching in front of the lock. "Watch my back."

The two men nodded, and Renna went to work on the gate. With a quick glance she could tell it was Rege Rail model—but this one was different.

"Schematics," she ordered her implant. Her pulse jumped with excitement as the holo image of the lock appeared in her vision, the plans pulling apart to show her the various components.

When this implant thing worked like it was supposed to, it was amazing.

As her gaze switched between the real lock and the virtual one, her frown deepened. Wall had altered his lock in some way. This was going to take longer than she planned.

Renna pulled her tools out of the small case she carried on her belt and inserted a probe into one of the chip slots. There was a soft beep as her program ran through the system.

While she waited, she peered through the gate into the dirty courtyard. A long, low building sat directly in front, guarded by a thick wooden door. Two larger buildings flanked the main building, long and low. Warehouses, she'd guess.

A gust of wind blew down the street, bringing with it the arid scent of dust and smoke. Her hacking tool beeped again, and Renna glanced down. A few tweaks in the code and the gate clicked as it unlocked.

"We're in," she said, pocketing her tools and grabbing her blaster.

Finn readied his gun as he pushed open the gate. He took several tentative steps into the courtyard, sweeping the space for anything unusual. Viktis and Renna followed close behind.

"What the hell is going on?" Viktis muttered. "Where is everyone?"

"Wish I knew." The prickling of her skin was getting worse by the second, and she forced herself to take a calming breath as she pointed to a thick metal door in the interior wall of the courtyard. "I think Wall's lab is through here."

It opened immediately, the heavy lock already disengaged. She glanced at Viktis, whose eyebrows had furrowed until they were almost touching.

He shook his head and shifted his blaster in his hand. "That door should have been locked. On your guard."

Renna nodded and stared down the long, narrow corridor made from rugged stone. Her skin erupted into full-fledged goose bumps as the trio crept down the corridor. There were still no signs of life or movement from anywhere.

"Show heat signatures," she ordered. Why did she keep speaking out loud? Her implant responded to thoughts as well as words now. Old habits die hard evidently.

"Anything?" Finn asked.

She shook her head as they moved farther down the corridor. At the far end she spotted another heavy door, this one slightly ajar. Finn pushed it open and Renna slipped past him into what looked like a kitchen.

Or, at least, it had been before someone had ransacked it. The cupboard doors had been ripped from their hinges and broken terracotta plates were smashed on the floor in piles of orange dust. Dry goods and food were scattered everywhere, leaving a trail of white powder and shattered eggs. She took a step farther into the room and grimaced as her feet squelched in some sort of slick cooking oil.

Renna clutched her gun tightly. Beside her, Viktis's amber skin had turned pale, and the bone plates in his head quivered with anger.

What had happened here?

"Through there?" She pointed at the door across the room. Her hand shook as she pushed it open onto another long room.

"Gods," Viktis whispered.

Electronics and machinery were smashed and scattered across the floor like someone had taken a sledge hammer to the entire contents of the room. Holovids and communicators were barely recognizable pieces dusting the floor. Electrical chips and shards of glass crunched under Renna's boots as she approached the center of the space.

Her unease was at full force now, like an icy hand pressed against her spine. Where was everyone?

"His lab's got to be through there," Viktis said, gesturing at the final door.

"There could be anything waiting for us behind there," Finn said softly. "Whoever did this could still be here."

"I hope they are," Viktis growled.

Renna ordered her implant to scan for heat signatures. "There's nothing alive behind that door," she said with the shake of her head.

Finn's hand tightened on his blaster. "Still doesn't mean there can't be danger. Are you both ready?"

Renna and Viktis nodded.

"Let's do this," Viktis said. He kicked the door open, and Renna and Finn burst into the room, guns sweeping the space. She froze at the utter destruction that had turned Wall's neat lab into an apocalyptic scene. The space was cavernous, built of steel and cement. Fluorescent lights glowed overhead, casting stark shadows over the rows of smoking machinery Wall had used to produce the black market drug, clay. The drug that had destroyed Renna's childhood

Its burnt-sugar scent mingled with the copper stench of blood. It clogged Renna's throat and made her stomach convulse. And then she saw them.

Six of Wall's men hung from the steel rafters by their ankles.

Blood dripped from where their heads used to be, and the floor beneath their bodies was a crimson lake that had already started to coagulate.

Acid burned her throat, and Renna swallowed it back as she turned away from the grisly scene. Viktis and Finn had already moved farther into the room, their guns at the ready.

Renna pulled her shirt over her nose and followed them toward the other end of the room where a wall of flickering holo monitors loomed.

As they cleared the last stack of destroyed crates, Finn flung out his arm. "Stay back." His voice went hoarse, and dread curled tightly in Renna's chest.

Viktis pushed past her, only to stop dead.

Oh, gods.

There was nothing Renna could do but step forward as well. And then she wished she hadn't.

It was Wall. Or had been before whoever'd killed him had split him open from neck to navel. He lay prostrate, arms and legs extended in a grotesque mockery of how they'd found Myka back in Navang's lab.

His face had been sliced off, leaving only a bloody skull behind. His insides spilled onto the floor beside him in a pile of pink, slimy mush. A single holoscreen had been inserted into the cavity to take the place of his heart and lungs.

The iron-rich scent of his blood mingled with the odor of decay already rising from his body. Renna pressed a hand to her lips, revulsion making her unable to look away. As she stared, the holoscreen in Wall's chest cavity flickered on. Light glowed behind the streaks of Wall's blood that dripped down the corner of the monitor, but it wasn't enough to hide the horror of what played there.

It was Renna.

Lips parted, she watched herself hack into the MYTH computers and copy files to her optical drive. Oh, gods. Someone had recorded this the day Dallas had gotten her access to the MYTH files.

"I had permission to be there," she protested. "Major Dallas knew about this."

The scene continued with a list of files scrolling across the screen. Finn's eyebrows drew together. "He knew you were accessing those?"

"I was searching for Pallas's information. Of course he didn't know. He thought I was searching for clues to find the *Athena*."

On the screen, she furtively copied over more information, then bent down beneath the bank of computers before finally leaving the room.

The scene fast-forwarded several hours according to the time stamp across the bottom of the screen. And then the images slowed again. A spark of something burst from below the computer bank, creating a small puff of black smoke.

As they watched, the whole room exploded.

Renna gasped and stepped back. "I was picking up the holodisk that I dropped," she protested. "I didn't plant that bomb!" Her mind spun with everything that had happened in the last few days. Wall's horrible death, Samil's trap on Tartarus, the explosion in the MYTH facility that took down the defenses.

Dr. Samil had played them all.

Her gaze focused on the body holding the holomonitor, and a cry tore from Renna's lips. She turned away from the man's desecrated corpse, from the image of herself doing the unthinkable, from the questions in Finn's eyes, from Viktis's sick expression.

Finn grabbed her, pulling her face against his chest. "Shhh. It's okay, Renna. It's going to be okay."

She sobbed against his shoulder. "It's never going to be okay."

Viktis gingerly removed the disk from the holodevice, then turned back to them. "Pull it together, Ren," he said. "You need to get into Wall's safe and see if your drugs are still here."

Finn stroked her back. "You can do this. And then we can get the hell out of here and kick Samil's ass."

She took a shaky breath, still breathing through her mouth to avoid the scent of death, and tried to push away the horrors around her. She had a job to do. She'd seen things as bad as this before. They just hadn't hit quite so close.

Renna nodded into Finn's shoulder. "All right. I can do it. I'll be okay." Without looking around, she headed directly for Wall's safe.

Her heart sank when she saw it was a state-of-the-art model, like all of Wall's tech, but she squared her shoulders and crouched in front of it, concentrating as hard as she could on the keypad and electronics. Not the eerily silent warehouse of the dead around her.

Two minutes later, the safe cracked open. With a stifled scream of both anger and disgust, she kicked the door shut so hard it sprang back open.

Wall's severed hand lay palm up on the bottom of the safe, an empty vial clutched between his cold, stiff fingers. Renna's drug was gone.

"I'm going to kill that bitch if it's the last thing I do." Her voice shook, but this time it was fury, not horror.

Finn wrapped an arm around Renna and pulled her back toward the door. Viktis surveyed the warehouse one last time, letting his gaze drop to his former friend's body. "When you do, I want to be there to watch."

TWENTY-THREE

Renna crawled into the speeder, not protesting when Finn took the driver's seat. As they drove off, she stared out the window, unseeing. Her skin crawled, and all she wanted was a hot shower and a stiff drink.

And some way to erase the images of the warehouse from her mind.

Samil had done some horrific things, but this attack had changed everything. She'd made Renna look like a traitor and tortured an innocent man.

Each scene in the warehouse had been specifically created to taunt Renna. The men hanging from the rafters mimicked a job gone wrong back on Baeno, where her team had been beheaded and hung when they'd been caught. Wall's positioning had been the exact same as Myka's. And the hand in the safe… She bit back a shudder. The Seralline Star Sapphire job on Treze.

Samil wanted Renna to suffer. To let her know that she knew more about Renna's past than anyone. Every nerve ending in her body twitched. What else did she know about Renna's life? Who else was in danger?

Finn pulled the speeder to a stop in front of the *Eris's* hangar. He cut the power, but didn't move to get out of the car. Instead, he shifted so he could look at her.

Renna's stomach lurched. She'd never seen that expression on his face before.

"Renna, I need to ask this. What happened back at MYTH? What were you doing in that room?"

"You still don't trust me?" She couldn't hide the disbelief in her voice. Hadn't they just had this conversation? Hurt made her lungs ache, but she forced herself to look him in the eye.

"I *do* trust you. That's why I need to hear it from you." He smiled. "MYTH is going to throw everything it has at you if Samil leaks this. I want to be able to protect you."

Her tension eased a bit. "I don't need your protection. I can take care of myself."

"We all know that, Ren, but we're a team." Finn squeezed her hand. "Let us help."

From the back seat, Viktis nodded in agreement. "Never thought I'd say it, but pretty boy is right."

Renna took a deep breath. "Fine. Dallas got me into the archive. I told him I needed to look for information that would help me track the *Athena* down. I accessed all the personnel files for everyone on board, but before that, I did a sweep of the system for information on Pallas. Exactly what we discussed before I left you guys."

"I remember," Finn said. "But how did she get footage of you planting a bomb?"

"I told you. I dropped my OSD, but somehow Samil edited the footage to make it look like I was planting something. The bitch has more resources than the devil."

"What game is she playing?" Viktis asked with a frown. "She doesn't seem like the kind of woman who does anything without a reason."

Finn tapped his fingers on the steering controls. "I have no idea, but whatever it is I don't like it." He pushed open the speeder door. "Let's get back to the ship and meet up with the *Athena* at the rendezvous point. We have a lot to discuss."

The trio boarded the *Eris*, and Commander Jayla met them at the CIC. She took one look at their faces and turned toward the comm room. "Inside. Now."

Lieutenant Blake followed, closing the door behind them. "What the hell happened? You look like someone murdered your best friend."

Renna let out a gasp, and Viktis's hands curled into fists.

Blake's eyes widened as he took a step back. "What the hell did you find?"

Finn raked a hand through his hair and sat down heavily. "Samil got there first. Wall's dead. The drug is gone. She's playing a game with us, but I can't figure out what she's after." He glanced at Jayla. "We need to regroup with Aldani and see what else we can do. Renna needs that drug."

Renna put out a hand to stop him. "Renna is fine. What we need to do is stop Samil before she goes any further. She's enjoying herself too much with this. She thinks she's smarter than all of us, and until we prove otherwise, her taunts will only get worse." And she couldn't live with herself if someone she cared about was the next target.

Finn slammed a hand down on the table. "I don't care what she wants. She's dead."

"Captain, take a deep breath," Jayla said, frowning at him.

"Sorry, ma'am." Finn dropped his hands back into his lap, looking chastised, and Renna bit back a smile despite herself. Always nice to see someone else could get Finn to toe the line.

"I agree that the first step is meeting up with the *Athena*," Jayla said. "We need to get Dr. Aldani working on a cure for Renna. Then we need to tell MYTH HQ what's going on. If Dr. Samil wants to destroy us, I'd say she's already got a good start. They need to start working on a plan to stop her. We can't do this ourselves."

Blake nodded. "Let someone higher up figure this one out. This isn't on you, Finn. Or Renna."

"What if Samil is still gunning for Myka?" she asked. "What if Dallas orders you to return to HQ? The kid'll be in danger."

Viktis paced between the table and the wall. "There's no reason for them to know we have Myka or Aldani. Leave them at the safe house. They'll be hidden there, and Aldani can continue to work. I'll have supplies sent to him."

"I think that's the best bet." Finn nodded. "I don't want to disobey a direct order from the major if I don't have to."

Blake grinned at him. "Little too late for that, isn't it, buddy?"

Finn narrowed his eyes. "Still think you're a comedian, don't you, Alistair?"

Blake smirked at him, and Renna cleared her throat. "I'm still not sure about this. We know Samil has spies inside MYTH. What if Dallas is one of them?"

"I can safely say that he's one of the good guys," Commander Jayla said. "But I understand your caution. Lieutenant, take Viktis to the comm room and set up a secure channel for him to use to connect with Dr. Aldani. We'll set course for the rendezvous point immediately."

Blake saluted and followed Viktis from the room, leaving Renna, Finn, and Jayla behind.

"You're excused, Renna. I'm going to want to debrief the captain on his mission," Jayla said. "I'm still his superior officer after all."

Renna scowled at both of them. Why did the commander want her gone? Until this point they'd all worked together. "I'd prefer to stay if you don't mind."

Jayla shook her head. "I'm sorry. We'll be discussing classified information. But I'll have him back to you in no time." She smiled, giving Renna no choice but to get to her feet.

"I'll come find you when we're done here," Finn said reassuringly.

Renna didn't bother to answer as she left the room. If nothing else, at least she could spend some quality time in her bunk. That hot shower was calling her name, and she had her own plans to make. As she cleared the area, she spotted a small, dark-haired woman bent over one of the consoles. Renna paused.

"Sergeant Gheewala?"

The woman looked and smiled. "Renna. Nice to see you."

"Hey, you used my first name." Renna grinned at the woman.

It had been a joke between them on the *Athena* that Renna would only be considered part of the team when they remembered to call her by her first name.

"I've been practicing." The woman's shy smile made Renna's heart glow.

"So why are you on the *Eris*? Did Finn reassign you?"

Gheewala's gaze still darted anxiously around the space before she spoke, but when she finally focused on Renna, she seemed a little less stressed out. "Commander Jayla and Captain Finn agreed that my services would be most useful on the *Eris* where I could track your EMP signature if anything happened at Wall's facility."

"Oh."

Gheewala nodded. "If we were walking into a trap, Jayla wanted to know the instant something went wrong, and reading your new signature is as good as a comm device. Did you know you transmit on the same frequency as the *Athena*? As most of the MYTH ships, actually."

"Um. No. I did not." Renna wasn't even sure what that meant.

"I can pick you out of any electrical reading instantly. It's quite fascinating to see. Your implant has a distinct subfrequency that seems to be in harmony with the *Athena's*. I was able to recognize it when your implant took control of the ship yesterday. Luckily Captain Finn believed me."

"Of course." Renna chewed her lip before asking the next question. "So if my implant now has a ship's frequency, can I communicate with other ships?"

Gheewala frowned. "I'm not sure. Obviously you can with the *Athena*. You will have to try with the other ships. It seems likely, especially if your implant has morphed into a communication-based relay system."

Renna chuckled. "Care to explain? You forget I don't talk empath."

Gheewala giggled. "Right. I forget you don't see things the same way. Since I'm a tech empath—specifically engines, drive cores, and communication devices—I can read those things. Some ships use dark matter to communicate with each other and with other planets; others use a relay system based on connections set up between ships. So only ships within the same fleet can talk to each other. It makes for a secure comm line. Unless I'm around."

"So you're a technical spy," Renna said, eyebrows rising.

"I suppose so, yes." Gheewala continued. "Your case is interesting in that you seem to be able to do both—send and receive communications between networked ships, as well as non-networked. It's strange. You're like a conduit."

"I'll take your word for it," Renna smiled. "But what does it mean?"

"I'm not sure. Nothing for now. Just an interesting skill to be able to copilot a ship from across a star system."

"Interesting and freaky as hell. I still have no idea how I did it."

"Well, if you can learn to control it, I'm sure MYTH would never let you go."

A shiver of dread curled around Renna's heart. Was that Samil's plan, too?

"Can we keep that between the two of us for now?" she asked. "I'd like some time to do some of my own research before bringing it to anyone's attention."

Gheewala looked troubled, but eventually she nodded. "I won't say anything unless someone questions me directly."

Renna squeezed the woman's arm. "Thank you, I really appreciate it. I'll let you get back to your monitoring."

"Renna, it was good to see you. I know this is all difficult for you, but if you need to talk, I'm around. I know how it is to be... different."

Renna smiled gratefully, surprised at the woman's kindness. "I know you do. I'm glad you're aboard, Sergeant. I feel better knowing you're here."

TWENTY-FOUR

R enna set down her tablet as Finn stepped into her
room. "Everything all right with the commander?" she
asked.

His face was strangely pale, but he nodded. "Fine. Just had to
go over some MYTH business. Necessary evil."

"If you say so." She pointed to a chair. "Sit down before you
fall down. You look exhausted."

Finn sank into the seat. "I've felt better. But we'll be docking
at Forever Station in thirty minutes. I'll be fine once we're settled.
Didn't think I'd be back here so soon."

"Oh?"

"Viktis and I were here less than two weeks ago. Took out
Kitty Cordoza."

"That was you?" She shook her head. "How the hell did I not
know that?"

Finn smiled tiredly. "We've been a little busy with other things. I promise I'll tell you the whole story soon. You'll get a kick out of it. Viktis won another ship."

She chuckled. "Can't wait to hear that story. Have you talked to Viktis by the way? Did he contact Dr. Aldani?"

"Yes. They're safe and secure. Viktis assures me no one will ever find them if something happens to all of us."

Renna got to her feet, relief flooding through her. "Good. I have a bad feeling about this, Finn. Really bad."

"About what?"

"Everything. It's all gone wrong from the moment I stepped foot on the *Athena* to save Myka. Samil has been pulling strings we didn't know even existed. What else does she have planned?"

"Whatever it is, we'll get through it together." Finn took her hand and pulled her toward him. "It's going to be okay."

Renna straddled his legs and rested her forehead against his. "Is it? I'm not so sure any more. If we're going to fight this woman, we may have to start using her tactics. She's ruthless, Finn."

Finn brushed her hair back from her face, tracing her cheekbone. "So are we. And I've got too much to lose if we don't stop her, so I'm not even entertaining other options. Besides, I owe you a long vacation somewhere."

"Damn straight you do." Renna grinned down at him. She shifted on his lap, and his eyes widened as she ground her hips against him. "But in the meantime, I think we could find a little relaxation here to tide us over." Renna cupped his cheeks in her hands as she lowered her lips to his.

Finn melted into the kiss, pulling her closer. She kissed him again, nibbling at his lips, teasing him with her tongue, and when he moaned, the sound sent liquid fire through her.

Finn yanked her head back down, kissing her greedily. His hands slipped beneath her shirt, traveling up her ribs, and she shivered as his rough skin brushed hers. With a quick twist, he had her bra off and dropped it to the floor. He gently cupped her breasts, thumbs gently caressing her ribcage between them. Just far enough away that her nipples ached for his touch.

She shifted again, feeling him grow hard against her. Her hands traveled down to unbuckle his belt, and she skimmed them over his flat stomach.

Finn sucked in a breath at her touch, then stroked his thumbs over her nipples.

"Oh, gods," she whispered, arching her back as the wave of sensation rushed through her. She could only sit frozen as he gently caressed and fondled her breasts. And when he tugged her shirt up, she quickly pulled it over her head.

"You are so beautiful," he said, gazing at her before lowering his lips to her breast. He stroked her gently with his tongue, and pure heat shot through her midsection. She gasped, pulling him closer.

His tongue teased her, flicking against her nipple and making her moan with pleasure. She buried her hands in his soft, dark hair and let him explore her with his mouth until she thought she'd explode.

Finn's hands drifted lower until he slid one into her pants, brushing her soft curls. Gently he stroked a finger there, just over her slit until she couldn't stand it.

"Nick, I want you," she whispered. She wanted all of him. Now.

His finger slowed, and in one movement he rose to his feet, bringing her with him. A moment later they were both naked, trousers in a pile on the floor. Renna wrapped her legs around his waist and devoured him with her mouth, her whole body throbbing with the feel of his skin against hers.

Finn slipped a finger inside her and groaned. "Gods, you're so wet." She felt him harden against her as he sank back down on his chair and positioned her over him.

Renna smiled down at him as she slid onto his member. Her eyes fluttered shut at the rush of pleasure she felt with him inside her, but Finn cupped her cheeks and she opened her eyes.

He kissed her again, and Renna began to rock against him until they were both gasping.

The pressure built inside her until it felt like pure starlight thrummed through her veins. She pulled her lips away from his and stared into his eyes. Her breath came in gasps, but she didn't break his gaze until the final thrust pushed her over the edge.

"Oh, gods. Nick!" She shuddered and trembled as she came, her whole body a flood of feelings.

Finn groaned and thrust into her one last time. Their eyes met, and she realized with a shock she felt closer to him than she'd ever felt with anyone.

With a deep chuckle, Finn picked her up and carried her to the bed, curling himself around her. "Damn," he said, his breath hot in her ear. "I think I'm still having aftershocks." His whole body shuddered again as if to punctuate his words. "Renna, you do things to me I never thought I'd feel."

Renna smiled into her pillow. "The feeling is mutual."

TWENTY-FIVE

N ice to see Forever Station never changes," Renna said as she and Finn left the *Eris* and headed toward the main dock. The spacer landing area was as dirty and seedy as she remembered, with worn cargo crates stacked in corners and flickering hololights casting their strange fake glow over the space.

"Well, we did park in Cheapside. The government docks are quite a bit nicer," Finn said, stepping gingerly around a wet pile of...something.

Renna grinned. "I wouldn't know. The only way I'd have seen one of those docks was on a prison ship, and I did everything I could to avoid that fate." They made their way toward the door. "So what are we doing here then?"

"The *Athena* is waiting for us in the next bay. Jayla wants to contact Dallas from there. Says it's a gesture of good faith from me." He grimaced as they cleared the hangar and headed down the corridor to the other bay. "I keep forgetting he thinks *I'm* the traitor."

"You still think it's safe to talk to him?" she asked. "What if he doesn't believe us?"

Finn draped an arm around her shoulder and pulled her to him. "You worry too much. I'm sure everything will be fine. And if it's not, we'll come up with a plan. We're not going to let Samil get away with this."

Renna smiled up at his cheerful expression. She wished she could believe him, but her senses twitched in a way she was more than familiar with. It was the same feeling she got when a job was about to go bad. Only this time the feeling screamed a warning at her as loud as an angry Trezian battlemaster.

Jayla, Blake, and Viktis had already boarded the *Athena* and were waiting with Lieutenant Keva in the comm room. Finn saluted Jayla as they entered and then slipped into a seat at the head of the table. Renna took the one beside him.

"Everything safe, Viktis?" she asked, noticing he was sitting a bit closer to Lieutenant Keva than was proper.

He nodded. "Safe as stars."

She bit back a smile at the old code they'd used so many years ago. "So what's the plan?" she asked Jayla. "Have we heard from Major Dallas?"

The commander glanced away from Renna, looking troubled. "He's been trying to contact the *Eris* for about an hour now, but I wanted us all together when we spoke with him."

Blake leaned back in his chair and crossed his arms behind neck. "The old man must have a wasp in his britches from the admirals. It's four hours past Renna's check in time. If we don't touchbase soon, they'll be so freaked out they might initiate the *Eris's* self-destruct sequence."

Renna frowned. "Damn. I'd forgotten all about that. But with everything going on at HQ, would they really care?"

Jayla switched on the holocom. "I guess we're about to find out."

A fuzzy image of Dallas solidified into his virtual presence. He paced in front of the comm monitor, a frown creasing his face. "Commander Jayla. Report."

"Yes, sir. We've found the *Athena*, sir. Captain Finn and his crew are safe and sound with us."

Dallas's shoulders visibly relaxed, and he turned to the screen to stare at them. "Welcome back, Finn. I trust you'll have a tale to tell. But first I want to review some disturbing information we recently received."

"Sir, I'd like to report..." Finn started.

Dallas held up his hand, his voice going cold. "Let me finish, Captain." He turned his steely gaze to Renna. "We know the truth. We know you've been working with the traitor all along."

"What?" Renna demanded. "That's impossible. Dr. Samil is the traitor! She's been working inside MYTH to bring it down for years. She drugged me and tried to kill me. Why the hell would I work with her?"

"I'm sure that's what you want us to believe. But I have proof that you've been working with Dr. Samil for months."

Renna's gaze darted around the room. Jayla's eyebrows touched her hairline, and Blake's brown eyes were wide and shocked. Even Finn's jaw had dropped.

"That's not true, sir. I only met Samil a few days ago."

Dallas frowned into the holo. "You've lied to us from the beginning, Renna. You knew about the traitor inside MYTH. You knew she'd been plotting against us for years."

Renna jumped to her feet. This couldn't be happening. "No! I swear, sir. We only learned about the existence of the traitor Pallas at Navang's facility."

"That's enough of your lies, girl," Dallas roared. "I have the proof." He hit a button and his image was replaced with the same grainy video Renna had seen at Wall's.

"But, sir, Renna said she had permission to search those files," Finn said, interrupting the playback. "She was looking for a way to stop Pallas." He squeezed her hand under the table.

Dread curled like a snake in Renna's stomach as she waited to see what Samil had done this time.

"She did not have permission to do this," Dallas said. The screen cut out again, this time to an image of the black market on Lenue. Renna recognized it from when she'd first met Wall.

Oh, gods. *No.* She'd intended to sell the communicator chips she'd stolen from Dr. Aldani's facility but had stumbled across Viktis first. She'd decided to hold on to them, to help MYTH. She'd chosen the right path. But now, here on the screen, she watched as her holo-self stopped at one of the booths and passed something over to a vendor.

"That doesn't prove anything," Viktis said. "She could have been buying a sandwich."

"Wait," Dallas growled.

Across the room, Jayla had leaned forward to watch the video. Blake's hands were clenched together on the table, his knuckles turning white. She didn't want to even glance at Finn for fear of what she'd see in his gaze.

Renna watched as the scene continued with her walking away, then cut to the man she'd supposedly sold something to. He went inside his shop and plugged a chip into his computer. The image on his computer filled the screen.

She curled her shoulders forward, hunching against the weight of the evidence against her. That was the data she'd gathered on the MYTH leaders and headquarters she'd gotten only a few days ago, plus detailed schematics on defense systems, technology, and troop movements that she'd never seen before. All there for viewing by the highest bidder. She knew how it worked. He was pulling together a sell list. She even recognized a few of the names as buyers she'd sold to in the past.

Somehow Samil had spliced together different footage to frame Renna perfectly.

"We were able to intercept the man's comm and retrieve the data, but this breach of security is grounds for treason," Dallas growled.

"Major, I can assure you that wasn't me. I copied data from your database to use to hunt down Pallas. That's as far as it went," Renna protested. "You have to believe me. I want to stop her, not take down MYTH."

"I believed you when you said you were working for us. I believed you when you said you were looking for Captain Finn. I believe now that you've lied to us from the very beginning."

"Sir, if I may—" Jayla started.

"You may not." Dallas's voice was like a whip, cutting through her words. "I am not discussing this any further over a holocom.

Commander Jayla, you will bring in Captain Finn and the *Athena* immediately to MYTH HQ. And you will bring the traitor, Renna Carrizal, in wearing cuffs."

"What about Dr. Samil?" Renna demanded. "She's still out there. She's still trying to destroy you. And Major Larson is with her. He's been feeding her information for years. He was on the admiral's board, for fuck sake! Why aren't you going after *him*?"

"We have upgraded our systems and removed all of Dr. Samil's access. Major Larson has been dishonorably discharged and all of his access removed as well. Admiral Usamov is confident the threat is contained. Right now, you're our biggest problem. A problem I can't wait to deal with," he said ominously.

She could feel the fury coming off of him in waves, even through the holo. Too bad there was no way in hell she was going back there to face him in person.

Finn stood up to face the holo. "Sir, please..."

"I've had enough out of you, Captain. Get your ass back to base before I try you for treason, too." Dallas glared at them all and then snapped off his communicator.

Renna stared straight ahead. She couldn't stand seeing the distrust and hatred on everyone's face. Samil had succeeded in turning everyone against her.

"Renna, how could you?" Jayla asked accusingly. "We trusted you."

Her gaze flew to the other woman's. "You don't believe that do you? You know how devious Samil is. She'd do anything to protect herself, and I'm a convenient scapegoat."

Jayla shook her head. "It was on the screen, Renna. You saw it yourself. Why do you keep denying it?"

"Maybe there's another answer," Blake suggested. His brown eyes were troubled. "You wouldn't betray us, right, Renna?"

"Of course not," she snapped. "This is all Dr. Samil's doing. You should know me better than that."

"But you copied that information yourself. How else did it get there, along with the chips you stole from Aldani?" Finn asked, not meeting her gaze. A muscle jumped in his jaw.

Renna jumped to her feet and crossed her arms over her chest. "You're kidding, right? You're all walking right into Samil's trap. This is what she wants—me locked up, Finn and the *Athena* grounded. And when there's no one else to fight her, she'll strike. She'll destroy everything. You can't let her win."

She stared at each of them in turn, willing them to believe her, to trust her, but every gaze dropped as she met it. Her body went cold. She should have known better. No one ever trusted a thief, no matter what they said.

"Finn. You promised me..." Her voice broke when he wouldn't meet her eyes, instead staring at a spot on the wall. Spots danced in her vision.

"Fuck this," she spun on her heel. "I thought better of you all." She stared straight at Finn as she said it, hurt making her heart beat sluggishly. Everything he'd said about trust had been a lie. He'd never believed in her. Had it all been an act?

"Renna. Wait. We need you to stay on the ship. Dallas's orders," Jayla said apologetically. "I can't let you leave."

"Then I guess I'll be in my bunk, waiting for all of you to come to your senses." She slammed her palm against the button that opened the door and marched out, spine straight, face expressionless. This was bullshit and they all knew it.

She wasn't going to wait around for Dallas to decide she was a traitor. She had a real traitor to stop. And that meant getting the hell off the *Eris* without getting caught. Luckily they were on Forever Station, and she knew the bowels of that place like the back of her hand.

When she was safely back in her room, she grabbed her duffel bag and shoved a few changes of clothes into it, along with her tools and tablet. She pulled on her leather coat and hid half a dozen knives in her boots and the slots in her sleeves. Where she was going, it never hurt to be heavily armed.

Now she just had to get off the ship without Finn, or anyone else, stopping her.

The pain of his betrayal hit her again like a punch in the gut, and she wrapped her arms around her waist. Her knees gave out, and she fell onto her mattress, biting back a sob. How could she have been so wrong about him? After everything they'd been through. Everything they'd said. Hell, she'd almost told him she loved him less than an hour ago.

She curled her hand into a fist and punched her pillow.

Damn him. Damn them all. She didn't need them. She'd done perfectly fine without them until now; she'd be fine working alone again. She'd take down Samil if she did nothing else before she turned into a cyborg.

Someone rapped softly at her door, and Renna froze. Shit, they'd come to lock her in the brig already. She didn't want to resort to violence, but there was no way they were taking her in. Quickly, she dropped her duffle beside the bed and kicked it beneath the mattress.

"Who's there?" she demanded.

"Renna, open up. It is Viktis."

She glowered at the door. He was the one unknown in this whole situation. Did he believe her? Or was he siding with his new friend, Finn?

"What do you want?" she demanded through the door.

"To help you," he answered softly. "I can get you off the ship without anyone knowing."

"And why would you do that?" she asked.

"Renna. Stop wasting time! It's me. You know I have your back."

She opened the door. "Just checking. I didn't know how your bromance with Finn had affected your senses."

"The captain's a fucking idiot if he believes that video. Now get your stuff. We don't have much time before Jayla puts the ship on lockdown."

Renna grabbed her bag from beneath her bunk and noticed Viktis already had his own duffel slung over his shoulder. "A little conspicuous," she said, nodding to it.

"Not if we're on shore leave." He grinned, his amber eyes sparkling. "Let's go. We have a station to get lost in."

Renna followed him through the sleeping quarters and to the cargo bay hatch. The bay was empty, all of the technicians still finishing up their own duties docking the ship and prepping it for a quick getaway, per Jayla's orders.

Viktis opened the hatch, and the pair slipped out into the metal docking tube that led to the main station. None of the port crew paid them any attention as they picked their way over cables and around carts of tools. Renna followed closely behind Viktis, but they kept their pace casual, two engineers off for some shore leave on the most infamous station in the sector. They cleared the docking bay and headed for the elevators at the end of the warehouse.

"Where to?" Renna asked. "I'm assuming you have a plan in mind?"

Viktis smiled slowly. "You know me so well. I have an apartment down in the Merrin district where we can lay low until I get a hold of my ship. I'm assuming you've got your own ideas?"

She grinned back at him. "The ship you won in a poker game? Finn said there was quite the story behind it. I can't wait to hear it."

"All in good time," he said with a chuckle. "Let's get you safely out of here first."

Renna nodded. "My plan is to go after Samil, but I need some information first. Every advantage I can get." A dull throb started behind her eyes, wiping the smile from her face. "Shit."

"What's wrong?" Viktis asked, eyebrows shooting up. "Are you all right?"

She shook her head. "My implant has a built-in comm, and Gheewala will be able to track me using my EMP signature as soon as they realize I'm gone."

"Can you shut it off?"

"I don't know, but I'm going to try." Renna focused on the signature of her implant. Gheewala had said it was unique, but if she could turn it off or blend it with some of the other communications in the station, maybe she could hide her presence.

She took a deep breath and felt herself slip into the comm network. Her mind moved sluggishly as she pushed through the electromagnetic field. Definitely not the easy connection she'd made with the *Athena*. Energy sparked through her mind, but after a minute she found the comm line. With a few tweaks to the energy signature, she closed off the ship's communication access to her implant. That should keep them from contacting her for the time being. Now hopefully she could find a way to keep them from tracking her, too.

Renna slipped deeper into the station's network, searching for something she could use as a shield. If she hid her signature behind a stronger one, maybe that would be enough. The sensation of travelling through the wires and electromagnetic fields felt like swooping through a tube at light speed. Her whole body tingled as the network curved back on itself or dropped to another level of the station.

And then she felt it. The heartbeat of Forever Station. The central control room where everything originated.

The competing fields would easily hide her own signature if she could somehow loop it in. It would act like a firewall, protecting her from Gheewala's abilities. Renna found a chink in the field and slipped her own signature inside, hiding it in the code. Her mind raced with numbers and images. She could freaking see everything like a glowing monitor in her head. It made her whole body ache with exhaustion.

"Renna?"

Viktis's voice yanked her out of the connection with the hub, and she blinked.

"Are you all right?" he asked, peering at her with concern.

She nodded. Luckily, she'd already closed the door in the code. She should be hidden for now. "Sorry. Took longer than I expected. I should be safe while we're on the station."

"Good. Then go find your contact and I'll meet you at my safehouse in two hours. Try to stay out of trouble."

The elevator dinged as it stopped on Viktis's floor, but Renna stopped him with a hand on his arm. "Thanks. I know you didn't need to help me."

"Yeah, yeah, knight in shining armor and all that. This is what happens when I let you out of my sight. You need me around just to make sure you don't get into trouble."

Renna smirked back at him. "You know I can't resist you."

Viktis shook his head as he left the elevators. "Get in line, love. You've got competition now."

TWENTY-SIX

Renna stepped off the elevator in the Phoenix sector, the political hub of the station. Amber Ileth and violet Delfine mingled with humans and the four-armed Trezians. Humanity had taken their place with the other species on the station two hundred years ago, when they'd first joined the Coalition. But they'd quickly taken charge of the political scene and now had the biggest embassy on the station. It took up a whole block, the shiny white facade towering over the other buildings. The entrance was an ornate, golden gate that opened into a fountained courtyard filled with apple trees from old Earth. It was quite a sight when they were in bloom.

She'd spent one memorable summer there with an ambassador's aide. He'd been a fantastic tour guide. Among other things. Renna had gotten to know all the secret access ways and hidden rooms in the facility. Her job had gone off without a hitch.

But the embassy wasn't her destination today. She headed toward the Bank of Conyara at the far side of the sector. She had a safe deposit box there with a little nest egg, in case of emergencies.

This certainly qualified as an emergency.

She pushed pashed a group of chattering Delfine dressed in their traditional loose-fitting gowns. Right now, it felt like she was drifting through space in a disabled lifepod, alone and without power. Which was stupid since, until a month ago, she'd done everything on her own.

Bitterness seeped through her. *Everything was going to be different.* Right. She should have known better.

Renna ducked out of the stream of aliens and accents and headed down a narrow alley between two squat buildings. Her bank wasn't one of the fancy ones—the Conyara kept to themselves for the most part—but that made it an excellent hiding place. And the manager owed her a few favors after she'd taken down a con man who'd stolen millions from them in a scam.

Renna pressed a finger to the cool metal pad beside the door. It slid open silently into a dark, shadowy lobby that stunk of sweat and money.

"Well, if it isn't Mae Carson. It's been too long, my girl. Welcome back." The Conyara alien's ridged skull had a several tufts of dark hair that bobbed as he smiled up at her.

Renna stooped slightly to shake his hand. "Nice to see you, Syd. Just passing through to take care of some business."

"Of course. Go on back." He gestured to an arch at the back of the lobby, and Renna ducked through to a long, narrow hallway.

Doors led off both sides to small storage rooms, and Renna counted down to the fourth door on the left.

The room's walls were lined with small boxes, each stamped with a number and boasting another fingerprint scanner. Syd had pretty good security for a second-rate storage operation. And since she never visited more than once a year, there was little chance that anyone knew who she really was.

She pulled out the drawer and set it on the small table in the middle of the space. Inside was a credit chip with a hundred thousand on it, a stack of forged IDs, and a shiny new blaster. Renna took the money and the pistol, then shuffled through the IDs until she found one that would work.

Juley Talley, human engineer working for Taylor Corp, would have to do. She didn't think MYTH would broadcast that they were looking for her by name, but it didn't hurt to be cautious. And if she needed to hire a transport ship, she didn't want her real identity pinging on anyone's radar.

She carefully locked the safe behind her and waved to Syd on the way out. "See you next year," she called.

"Always a pleasure, Mae."

Outside the bank, she carefully blended back in to the mass of people. The Phoenix district cleared out at the end of the day, but right now, it was full of people on their way to their various destinations.

She hadn't been to Forever Station in, well, forever, and she'd forgotten how full of life it was. The Trezians had built it as a monitoring station almost seven hundred years ago, but it had grown until it was some kind of technological monstrosity, expanding outward and upward every few years until it looked more like a floating mountain than a space station.

She'd spent plenty of time here when she was younger. It was easy to lose yourself amongst all the people, a must in her line of work. And since it was both a trading hub and a political hub, she'd found plenty of work stealing secrets as well as credits.

Her stomach growled, and Renna wandered toward the center of the district, a circular hub where vendors set up food carts and people hawked cheap souvenirs. Forever Station was like a carnival, with visitors coming in and out to play, buy, or sell. But the backbone residents never changed—the maintenance people who kept the station running, the security guards, the merchants.

She inhaled a lungful of recycled air and the scent of the food from a hundred different cultures. It smelled like home. She loved the confusion and energy, and hiding in plain sight was the best way to stay off MYTH's radar. Unfortunately, it wasn't going to help her find Samil.

She needed someone else for that.

Carrying a cup of strong coffee and a bowl of noodles, Renna found a table at the edge of the chaos. She sipped the bitter drink, letting it slide down her throat in a burning rush. Real coffee was hard to come by, but this would do the trick. At least it was full of caffeine.

Across the hub, she spotted a woman in a long, dark skirt, her jet-black hair woven into dozens of braids down her back. She carried a briefcase and walked with a purpose toward one of the food vendors.

Kara Dezal.

The woman ordered a plate of noodles and sat down at the table next to Renna's without looking around. She tackled her food like a starving woman, shoveling in great mouthfuls. For someone so tiny, the woman could eat.

Renna pulled out her tablet and scrolled through her news-feed, carefully ignoring the other woman.

"You going to tell me what you need, Renna?" Kara finally asked, still concentrating on her food. "I can't sit here all day."

"Information. But you already knew that."

"Of course I did. That's the only reason you ever contact me." Kara studied Renna's unusually pale face and shadowed eyes. "You look like shit."

"Thanks. That's exactly the look I was going for. You look beautiful, as always." Even back in the tenement, Kara's exotic looks had spared her the worst of the beatings and famine. After her mom died, the pimps all wanted to groom her to take over the business side of handling the prostitutes. Kara's mother had been Japanese, if Renna remembered correctly, and her father had been an Ileth, so her skin had a gorgeous amber tint to it. A stunning combination and one she'd used often to get what she needed from both the politicians and info dealers alike.

"So tell me what you need, Renna. It must be big if you're here on the station again."

"I need information on someone. A Dr. Thana Samil. She works—or worked—for an organization called MYTH."

"I've heard of it. The government's worst-kept secret." She took a bite and chewed deliberately before responding. "What's so special about this woman?"

"She's a traitor. Even worse, she's framed me for something and I want her silenced."

Kara nodded. "Understandable. A thief's honor is her life. For old time's sake, I'll put my other clients on hold and see what I can find. But it'll cost you."

"Of course it will. How much?"

Kara grinned at her. "Straight to business. I always liked that about you, Renna." Her smile was gone as quickly as it had come, her expression turning serious. "When's the last time you were back on Earth?"

Renna froze, fingers curling into her tablet. "It's been a while. Why?"

"I saw your mother the other month. She wasn't looking good."

Dread curled sharp claws into her gut, and Renna shook off the feeling she was walking into another trap. "What was wrong with her?"

"Too much clay. Not enough food. Probably an STD. She was never the same after you left. Didn't take care of herself at all. Took the worst jobs. I'm surprised she's lasted this long."

"Don't fool yourself, Kara, my mother was ecstatic when I left. No more bastard kid holding her back. I haven't talked to her since that day, and I don't plan to, no matter what you say."

Kara shrugged, brushing her long braids back from her shoulder. "Just thought you'd want to know. You know us tenement rats always stick together."

"Tell me what you want for the info, Kara. I need to get moving." Renna watched a station guard patrol the edge of the crowded marketplace. She'd already been sitting here too long.

Kara took another bite of her food before responding. Renna was pretty sure it was to piss her off. Kara had always enjoyed seeing how far she could rattle her clients.

"I need a favor. Something only you can steal," she finally said.

"Kara, I don't have time for that."

"Oh no, I don't want it now. This is a favor to be redeemed in the future. At a time of my choosing."

Renna chewed her lip. In any other situation, she'd turn the woman down flat. Getting involved in Kara's business was...unhealthy. But she was running out of time and options. "Fine. It's a deal."

"Good. I'll get you your information. Usual dropbox?"

"You know the one. I need it tonight."

"It'll be there." Kara pushed the plate away and got to her feet, her long skirt swirling around her ankles. "Watch yourself, Renna. I have a bad feeling about this."

"You're not the only one."

"Maybe you should visit your mom one of these days, too. Before it's too late," she suggested softly as she passed Renna's table.

"Maybe you should mind your own business," Renna snarled.

Kara stopped and put a hand on Renna's shoulder. "We all know you're not that same kid. You don't have to prove anything to anyone. But locking away your past doesn't mean it didn't happen. Visiting your mom might help you come to terms with it." Her gaze dropped lower, to the scar that slashed across Renna's neck from ear to chin.

Renna touched it with a finger. "There's nothing left for me to come to terms with. But thanks for the concern. I'll see you later." She shoved her chair back and jumped to her feet, disappearing into the crowds before Kara could respond.

No matter what the woman thought, there was nothing left for Renna back on Earth but pain. Her mother was an adult—she was responsible for her own choices, just like Renna. And Renna's choice was to track Samil down and prove she wasn't a traitor. Whatever the cost.

TWENTY-SEVEN

Viktis's safe house on Forever Station was a tiny apartment overlooking the casino district. Even behind the closed curtains, lights flashed and danced from the signs and billboards lining the area. But despite the noise and lights, it was a smart location. In the hive of other apartments, his would be difficult to find. Always a plus when trying to stay under the radar.

Renna finished her plate of hastily radiated ramen, then leaned back in the rickety wooden chair. "You going to tell me what the hell is really going on?" she asked, pinning Viktis with a pointed stare.

He paused, fork halfway to his mouth. "What do you mean?"

"Why are you helping me?"

"Why wouldn't I? I don't owe anything to Finn or MYTH. There's no reason for me to help them."

"There's no reason to help me either. You tried to kill me once, remember? You wouldn't help me now unless there's something in it for you."

Viktis pressed a hand to his heart. "Do you really not know me at all, love?"

"I know you far too well," she said with a smirk. "That's the problem."

He chuckled and leaned back in his chair to mirror her pose. "I'll be honest. I'm just happy to get off the *Athena*. If Finn flashed me one more of those smug looks, I was going to shoot him."

"So I'm a convenient excuse?"

"You've never been convenient, love." He grinned around his bite of noodles, and Renna shook her head.

After he swallowed, he pushed the plate away. "MYTH deserves what's coming to them if they actually think you've betrayed them. However, you do not deserve to spend the rest of your life on a prison ship for something you didn't do. So if I can help, I will."

"Very altruistic of you." Renna frowned. "I still don't believe you, but I appreciate the intent."

"Just go with it." He shrugged. "I've got a shiny new ship, a pilot, and a woman who wants vengeance. Life doesn't get much better."

Renna tapped her finger against the worn plastic tabletop. "I don't get it. Why would Finn and Jayla believe I'd betray them? I've done everything that stupid organization has asked and then some. I could have left at any minute, but I'm still here. Why believe Samil over me?"

"Once a thief, always a thief, I guess. Some people can't see past the noses on their faces. Especially those great, honking human noses." Viktis patted her hand. "Finn's not worth another thought, love. Especially since you're here with me."

Finn's betrayal sat like a heavy weight on her chest, making her lungs ache. Even worse, she hadn't stopped caring about the stupid man just because he'd sold her out. Being hurt like this was unacceptable, especially since she'd spent so long guarding her heart against this very thing. What the hell was she supposed to do now?

"What about you and Lieutenant Keva?" she asked, changing the subject. "What's up between the two of you? I saw the looks you were giving each other."

His voice softened and his eyes got a faraway look. "The lieutenant and I became...close while we were here last week. She's an amazing woman."

Renna's eyes widened. "By the gods. Are you in *love* with her?"

Viktis's face flushed dark amber and sat upright. "No! Of course not," he spluttered. But the way his gaze slid away told Renna he wasn't exactly telling the truth.

She chuckled and shook her head. "Look at that. Viktis the pirate's gone and fallen in love finally. The women of the galaxy will weep."

His grin was wicked as he got to his feet. "Have you ever known me to settle down with one woman?"

"Why yes, as a matter of fact." She followed him through the apartment. "I seem to remember a time when it was just me and you. You're not so tough, Viktis. I know you've been in love before."

He opened the door and reset the security system. "And then I tried to kill you. That's usually how all my relationships end."

"Good point," she said with a laugh. "Let's hope Keva's a better shot than you are." She grabbed her bag off the threadbare couch. "Can we stop by my dropbox on the way to the ship? Kara's supposed to get me some intel on Samil."

"Of course. *Fortune's Risk* is waiting on the other side of the station. Luckily, I haven't heard a peep about MYTH searching for you, but we'd still better be careful." He paused and rubbed his chin. "Though I wouldn't mind knocking Captain Finn on his ass just once."

Renna followed him from the apartment. "Wait in line, pirate. I get first shot at him."

Viktis quickly locked the door, setting the security cameras before they headed toward the apartment complex exit.

Renna paused at the door, peering up and down the bustling street. There were way too many places someone could hide.

"Hold on, let me run a scan." She ordered her implant to search for MYTH soldiers, but it returned negative contacts.

They made it to the other end of the district without anyone stopping them, and Renna's pulse finally slowed as they waited for their elevator to arrive. "Are you finally going to tell me about the story behind getting this ship?" she asked, slanting a glance at Viktis.

He smirked. "You heard Finn and I took down mob queen Kitty Cordoza last week? As part of that sting, I just happened to...acquire the *Fortune's Risk* from Kitty, along with a few hundred-thousand credits. She won't need either of them where she's going, and I needed a new ship. Seemed like the perfect solution."

"So you're saying the *Fortune's Risk* is your reward for doing a good deed?" Since when had Viktis turned altruistic?

"You could say that." Viktis sighed lovingly. "She's the prettiest little thing you've ever seen. I've got her stored over with the Ortan port authority."

Renna quirked an eyebrow at him. That was one of the better districts on the station. A lot of diplomats stored their vehicles there, preferring quick access to the station rather than the red tape of the government landing hub. That exclusivity didn't come cheap.

The elevator's arrival interrupted Viktis, and they both stepped into it. Renna entered the code for Kara's district where the dropbox was located, then turned back to the pirate. "Have you ever gotten a ship through normal channels?"

"Have you?"

Renna held up her hands. "Fair enough. No more questions."

The elevator came to a stop, and the pair stepped into a quiet, residential district. She started another scan for MYTH soldiers, but agony sliced through her brain instead.

Air whooshed from her lungs at the red-hot fire shooting through her nerves. *Gods, the pain.* Renna's knees buckled, and she dropped to the floor. The whole station rocked and spun around her as her implant went crazy.

Images burst and faded in her mind—pictures of star charts, images of the tenements where she'd grown up, her first ship. They swirled like abstract art, combining and recombining into different shapes and images. Her tenuous grip on the connection with the hub slipped. She could feel it start to unravel, and she grasped at it, trying to slip back into her hiding place. To cut off communications.

But the harder she struggled, the faster her connection with the station disintegrated. A second later, she felt the communication line she'd turned off earlier reconnect with the *Athena*.

Finn's voice filled her ears. "Renna! Where the hell are you?" he demanded. "Get back to the *Athena* right now!"

"Screw you." Renna shook her head, frantically trying to switch off the line. "Don't come after me, Finn. I don't want to hurt you, but I won't let you take me in."

"I don't have a choice, Renna. It's an order. Come back before we both do something we'll regret." His voice sounded cold, like a stranger's, and an ache started at the back of her throat. How quickly he'd given up on her. Again.

"I've already done plenty of things I regret. I'm talking to one of them right now. But you know what? I have only one more thing to say to you. Fuck you for choosing them over me, and fuck you for believing I'd betray you." She pressed frantically at the comm button below her ear, hoping to turn it off manually, but the line only crackled.

Viktis crouched beside her on the floor. "What's going on?"

Renna shook her head as Finn's voice filled her ears again.

"I don't know why you keep denying it. We all watched you do it. I can't believe I fell for your lies again." Disgust filled his voice, sending a dagger through her heart. That hurt worse than her implant's malfunction, but she forced herself to brush it off.

"Screw you, asshole," she said, slamming her head back on the floor. Her comm let out a burst of static as pain exploded through her.

And then everything was blessedly silent.

"What the hell happened?" Viktis asked, studying her worriedly. "Are you all right?"

Renna blinked up at him, trying not to moan as stars sparked in her vision. "Something went haywire. My implant let Finn's comm through. We need to get the hell off this station."

"Shit." He took Renna's hand and helped her to her feet. "Can they use the implant to track you?"

She nodded. "I lost my firewall in the hub. Gheewala will be able to sense my frequency now. We're out of time." Renna ignored the vertigo that sent her stumbling down the corridor and headed toward Kara's dropbox in the middle of the district.

The small metal mailbox was virtually indistinguishable in the bank of other mailboxes, but Renna found it easily. She input the password for the keypad, and the door slid back.

A small holodisk and packet of information lay inside, and Renna quickly tucked them into her bag. She hoped there was something there that would lead them to Samil, or this escape plan would be dead before they even left the station.

"This is it. Now let's get out of here," she said. Viktis slipped an arm around her to help her walk.

They reached the pressure door that led to next district, and she shrugged him off. The warehouse area wasn't known for its friendliness, and if the residents sensed weakness, they'd be on her in a second, taking her for an easy mark. She ignored the throbbing in her head and shifted her bag on her shoulder to pull it closer.

Viktis's gaze never stopped moving while they walked, searching the alleys that led off the main corridor. Unwary people who came to this area often found themselves on the back of a cargo ship, headed for slave territories.

He nodded toward a group of ragged kids gathered in front of one of the warehouse doors. "Watch yourself," he said.

Renna made eye contact with one of the kids, a girl of about fifteen with messy blonde hair and a firebird tattoo on her neck. She was part of the Cordoza gang. A recent member if the redness around the tattoo was any indication.

The girl met Renna's steady gaze with a nod and said something to the boy next to her. All four pairs of eyes watched Viktis and Renna as they passed, but none of them moved to harass them.

Smart kids.

She glanced back at the girl. Maybe someday she could help girls like that—or, at least, help them get by. Someone sticking up for her when she'd arrived on station would have saved her life more than once.

"Through here." Viktis pointed to an access door hidden in one of the wall panels. "This should be a shortcut through the center of the station. Save us some time."

Renna followed him down the narrow corridor. Dim helo bulbs gave off barely enough light to see a few feet ahead, and she walked with one hand on her blaster. The access corridors were usually locked, but there were always ways to get in. And plenty of black market deals went down there.

Viktis ran down a flight of steps and pushed open the door at the bottom onto a lower level.

"Where the hell are we?" she asked. The smooth white walls and tile floors made it look like a medical wing—or worse yet, Navang's facility. She fought back a shudder.

"A maintenance level between districts. Shouldn't be anyone around, and I happen to have the keycard to the elevator that will take us directly to the Ortan port authority."

"Just so happens, huh? Did you win that in a card game, too?"

"I'll never tell," he said with a sly grin.

The pair rounded the corner, and Renna froze dead in her tracks.

Finn and Lieutenant Blake stood at the other end of the hall-way. The bright light shone on Finn's dark hair, and even from where they stood, she could see the anger blazing in his blue eyes.

Finn aimed his blaster at her. "We're taking you in, Renna. I have my orders."

"Like hell you are." She clutched her own blaster but didn't pull it from the holster yet. That was a step she could never undo.

"Hands up." He moved toward them, gun pointed directly at Renna's breaking heart.

She should have known better. She should have never be-lieved a word he'd said. But part of her couldn't let it go. "You lied to me, Finn. You said you trusted me, that you'd fight with me against MYTH as long as we needed to. What happened to us trying to figure out what we had? What happened to wanting to be with me?"

He slowed, but didn't lower his gun. "I could ask you the same thing. You betrayed me. Again. After promising you wouldn't. I should have known you could never really be reformed." His voice shook, and he cleared his throat. "We're going to bring you in and you're going to fix this. MYTH doesn't tolerate traitors, and neither do I."

"The only traitor here is Samil," she said, letting her fingers tighten almost imperceptibly around her blaster. He'd given her no choice. A shot in the leg should stop him long enough for her to get away. "Samil is the one you should be going after, not me," she argued. "Think about it, Captain. Why would I lie all this time? What's in it for me? It makes no sense."

"It makes perfect sense," he retorted. "Especially if you've been working with Samil for months. It explains how you knew where Myka was, how you escaped Navang's facility, how you were able to control the *Athena*. This has all been one brilliant set-up."

"You're right, it has. I just wish I was the one who'd thought of it. I'd give anything to wipe that smug sneer off your lips, you short-sighted asshole." Anger surged through her, and her vision flashed red as her implant kicked on and off, the heads-up display flickering through Finn's vitals and stats. He was as upset as she was, based on how fast his pulse was racing.

Beside her, Viktis muttered to her under his breath. "Keep it together, Renna. I have a plan to get us out of this," he said softly.

"You and me both." But she took a deep breath and brought herself under control. She ordered the implant off, and shockingly it obeyed. Maybe she was finally getting the hang of this thing.

Finn motioned again with his gun. "Hands up, please. Blake, cuff her. But be careful."

The lieutenant frowned at Renna, then glanced back at Finn. "You sure about this? I still think there's something we're missing here."

Renna smiled at Blake. "Thanks for the vote of confidence, handsome, but you're not going to change his mind. We've got a history, and for some reason he can't see past that. Wish it had been different."

Blake shook his head. "But then I'd never have met you. We'll figure this out, Renna. Just let us take you in and clear it all up."

"Sorry, but that's not going to happen." As Blake closed in, Renna dropped her hands and struck out with her foot. She swiped Blake's legs from beneath him, then side-stepped his attempt to grab her.

Beside her, Viktis launched himself directly at Finn's gun hand. His long amber fingers closed around Finn's wrist, twisting it back. The two men grunted as they struggled for control.

Renna had only a split second before Blake attacked again, but thanks to her earlier sparring with him, she knew exactly where his weaknesses were. And she had no problem using them against him now.

As the lieutenant tried to jump to his feet, she struck again, her boot connecting firmly with his gut. Blake hissed, going down again, and this time he didn't get up. Renna didn't wait to see if he was okay. Instead she turned back to Finn and Viktis.

The two men were locked together, struggling over Finn's gun. Viktis seemed to have the worst of it. Sweat poured down his face, and he gasped for breath as Finn twisted his body, seeming to gather his strength.

Shit. She recognized the move from Bumani, the fighting style he'd taught her so long ago. It was up to her now, and she'd only have one shot at bringing Finn down before he struck. Renna tensed her own body as she readied herself to attack. She'd have to be perfect or Viktis would be directly in the line of fire.

As Finn's leg muscles bunched, she struck out, her hand connecting with the soft flesh of his side. Exactly where his kidney was. Three quick strikes and he'd dropped to the ground, the gun clattering across the floor. He curled into the fetal position with a moan, and Renna grabbed Viktis's arm.

"Run!"

Still panting from his fight, Viktis sprinted down the corridor, Renna following close behind. "Through here," he gasped.

He jammed a fist against the elevator call button, and seconds later it arrived. They rushed inside as shouting filled the hall.

Finn was calling for back up.

TWENTY-EIGHT

Renna and Viktis raced across a narrow bridge and into docking bay 324. A prototype long-range Ultra Explorer sat gleaming under the hololights.

"Prep for takeoff," Viktis shouted into his comm.

Renna and the pirate thundered up the gangplank, and the ship's hatch started closing behind them as soon as they cleared the threshold. The smell of chrome polish and new leather greeted her. Renna inhaled deeply. The ship was gorgeous, but there was no time to admire it now. They needed to get the hell off the station before MYTH scrambled its own ships.

Viktis raced toward the flight deck, a small area at the front of the ship, and Renna followed closely behind.

Another Ileth with dark ochre skin sat at the controls, glancing back as they climbed the deck. "Prepped and ready to go, Viktis."

"Then get us the hell out of here," Viktis ordered.

The warning klaxons screamed throughout the hangar as the alien switched to takeoff mode. The bay door started to rise slowly while the clamps holding the ship in place released as the grav thrusters kicked in. The ship bobbed in place as the door finished rising.

In the port authority command booth, Finn glared down at her. She met his gaze, then flipped him off with a sneer as the Ileth pilot gunned the controls. With a roar from the engines, they shot into space and out of MYTH's clutches.

"Prep for hyperspeed," Viktis said, rubbing a shaking hand over the ridges in his skull.

"Where to?" the pilot asked. "I need a destination to plot our course."

"I don't care. Just get us the hell out of here."

"Very well, I'll head for the Egonne system. It's centrally located, and we should be able to hide out there for a while." The pilot input the coordinates into his nav computer before turning back to Renna.

"Ariz Teray at your service," he said, holding a hand out. "Used to fly for Viktis years ago. I see there are plenty of people out there who still want to kill him."

Renna shook it and smiled at the man. "Until recently, I was included in that list. Nice to meet you."

Viktis shook his head. "Ariz was never one to follow the rules, but then again neither am I. Must be why we get along so well." He clapped a hand on the pilot's shoulder. "We'll give you real coordinates as soon as we have them. Let me know if there's any sign of pursuit."

"You'll be the first to know." Ariz grinned at Renna. "Nice to finally meet you, Miss Carrizal. Back in the day, Viktis talked a lot about you. I can see he wasn't exaggerating." His gaze traveled down Renna's body, and she narrowed her eyes.

"He wasn't exaggerating about how many fights I've won either," she said. "Keep it professional or I'll make sure you learn about my skills firsthand."

Ariz's jaw dropped. "Yes, ma'am. Terribly sorry."

Viktis turned away with a chuckle. "Let's get the tour over with so we can figure out where we go next. As soon as Samil learns we're on the run, I have a feeling she'll be after us faster than light speed."

Renna followed him from the flight deck toward the back of the ship. She was impressed. It was a pretty ship—trim, lithe, and easy to hide in a spaceport. The prototype engine made it possible to use FTL travel several times without refueling, and the stealth systems were cutting-edge.

A pang of envy shot through her. If everything had gone according to plan, she might have retired, sold the Star Sapphire, and bought herself one of these by now. She quickly shoved that thought away. Between the implant in her head turning her into a cyborg and being wanted by MYTH, she really needed to give up on the retirement idea.

"There's a gathering hub, a mess leading off one side, and the sleeping quarters off the opposite side," Viktis said as he continued through the ship. He pressed the button to open the hatch into the central room of the ship, where a round table and several comfortable couches sat, ringing the space.

Another door led to the mess, and Viktis led Renna through

it, pointing out the small kitchen where she could heat up the pre-packaged food he'd stocked. Then it was on to the sleeping quarters.

There were six small berths, more like pods than rooms, just long enough for a bed, which took up the entire space. A button on the wall caused a small shelf to slide out of the wall above the pillow, and another switch turned the pod door opaque, cutting out all light.

"Not quite like my cabin back on the *Eris*," she said ruefully.

"You're so spoiled. Don't you remember the pods back on the *Mikado*? Those things were awful."

Renna chuckled. "I'd forgotten about those. They smelled of sweat and stinky feet." She bumped him with her shoulder. "So you going to show me the captain's quarters? Somehow I can't see you sleeping in one of these."

"Oh, hell no." Viktis led her to the door at the end of the corridor. It slid open to reveal a half-circle of a room. A large bed sat flush against the straight wall, and a pair of soft chairs sat along the left curve.

Renna stepped into the room, taking in the luxurious satin duvet and the fluffy white pillows stacked on the bed. "Nice. It's bigger than my apartment back on Hesperia."

"You haven't seen anything yet." Viktis pressed a button in the wall, and Renna gasped as it went transparent.

The entire wall was a floor-to-ceiling window into space.

"Viktis. That's amazing."

"Want to bunk here with me?" he asked, lips twitching.

Renna gazed out at the inky universe as stars twinkled in the distance hypnotically. She wanted to say yes—not only for the view, but for Viktis's presence. Alone in her pod, she knew her thoughts would spiral into the pain of Finn's betrayal.

But she shook her head. "Are you trying to take advantage of my vulnerability, Viktis?"

He smiled sadly. "Just trying to be a friend. But I understand why you don't trust me, especially after Finn's behavior. I'm sorry it had to happen like that."

"Thanks for getting me out of there." Renna couldn't stand the pity in his eyes and stared out the window instead of looking at him. "You didn't have to help me and you did. That means a lot."

"We're friends. That's what friends do. You don't have to do this alone, Ren."

"I know." Silence hung between them awkwardly until she turned back to him. "How about we figure out what kind of dirt Kara dug up on the evil doctor? Maybe we can figure out where she's going to strike next." She slipped one of the disks from her bag and inserted it into her tablet. Dealing with a clear threat was easier than trying to deal with the emotions swirling around her head right now.

A file, similar to the ones she'd seen at MYTH, loaded onto her device, and Renna scanned through the information.

"Looks like our Dr. Samil grew up on Earth, too. Went to Oxford on a full scholarship. Was recruited into MYTH as soon as she graduated." Renna glanced at the pair of chairs and nodded at them. "Can I sit?"

"Of course." Viktis took the chair closest to the door, while Renna sank into the other.

"Looks like her first assignment for MYTH was helping start

up Titan Industries. That's where she must have gotten the idea for her code name. Due to her promising biochem career, she was pulled into the science team on Banos Prime after an explosion killed a team of MYTH soldiers." Renna paused, feeling her jaw drop. "Dr. Samil's fiancée was a MYTH officer stationed on Banos at the time, and he was caught in the blast, along with Myka. But while the experimental technology saved Myka's life, it looks like it killed the fiancée."

Viktis let out a low whistle.

"I'm guessing that has a lot to do with her hatred of the organization." Renna stared down at the picture of the handsome young man. He had dark skin and eyes and a long, straight nose and strong jaw. He wore the rank of commander on the shoulder of his MYTH uniform, but he couldn't have been more than thirty.

She tried to swallow past the sudden lump in her throat. His stiff pose and serious expression reminded her of Finn. Before this mess, how would she have responded if he'd been killed on a MYTH mission? Would she have blamed them for his death? Would she have tried to destroy them for it?

An uncomfortable pressure ached behind her eyes, and she pinched the bridge of her nose. Of course she would. She'd almost allowed herself to go that route when Blur's compound had been destroyed and she'd thought he'd been killed. She'd wanted vengeance for Hunter's death. Finn, she corrected. And Blur's. They'd been family to her, the only family she'd had, and someone had destroyed it.

Renna cleared her throat, and Viktis glanced at her with a concerned expression. "All right?"

"Yeah. Just putting myself in her shoes."

There was a long moment of silence before Viktis asked, "What's going on in your head, Ren? I know you have to be hurting. Finn's being a royal asshole."

Renna stared down at her hands clutching the tablet. "What do you think? I fell in love with a man who not only betrayed me, but is willing to take me into custody and have me tried for a crime he should I know I didn't commit." She took a shaky breath. "Not to mention the fact that less than two days ago, he promised to trust me." Her voice broke, and she swallowed against the sudden lump in her throat. "I should have been smarter. Look at my past. The last guy I trusted tried to kill me."

Viktis winced. "That's a low blow, love. You know I only did it because of the job. It wasn't personal."

She shook her head. "I knew it was only a matter of time before you turned on me, but I'd hoped it wouldn't happen. How could we trust each other when we were both for sale? It could have as easily been the other way around. You're still the son of the most respected president in Ileth history. You could be the poster child for the next rebellion. Hell, President Viktis has a pretty nice ring to it. I'm surprised someone hasn't taken out a contract on your head yet."

"Who says they haven't?"

"Well, no one asked me. I would have taken the job in a heartbeat a few years ago." She sighed and shook her head. "Doesn't matter. I'm here now. With a job to do. One way or another."

"There are worse places to be," he said with a smile.

Renna reached over and squeezed his hand. "I know. I'm not

sure how I got so lucky." Finn's betrayal had destroyed her chance at having a life, a family. She'd hold on to what she had left with her last breath.

"You haven't yet," he said with a nod toward her tablet. "Now how about you stop getting all sappy on me and get back to that intel. We still have an evil doctor to catch."

"Don't forget about Major Larson. He's just as big a threat. How long has he been working for her? What's his game?"

"Dr. Samil is a beautiful woman. Does he need any other game?" Viktis asked.

"Maybe not, but that feels a little too convenient. I wish Kara had been able to uncover something else on him." Renna grimaced at her tablet, rereading the same info she'd found on the MYTH computers.

"What about this?" Viktis held up another holodisk.

"Let's try it." Renna slipped it into her tablet. "Looks like some sort of audio file." She clicked play and turned the volume up on her speakers.

Dr. Samil's voice filled the room. "Report indicates success with thirty milliliters of solution, along with electrotherapy for the first stage of development. We'll be proceeding as planned."

A deeper man's voice answered her. "Which facility would you like to send the test subjects to?"

"Shalim," Samil answered.

Renna froze. That wasn't possible.

"I'll have them picked up immediately."

"Good. And Larson? Make sure no one sees you this time. We can't afford mistakes."

Renna's hands trembled so badly the tablet clattered on the

table as she tried to set it down.

"What is it?" Viktis asked, half-rising from his chair.

Renna shook her head. "Shalim is on Antibes Prime. That's where I joined Blur's gang. Where I met Finn." The place where she thought he'd been killed.

His eyes widened.

"Impossible," she whispered. "The whole planet was almost abandoned after the Koschei Corporation pulled out five years ago. There's nothing left but a starving population who couldn't afford to leave and mile after mile of empty buildings. As far as I know, Blur's warehouse has been sitting empty since MYTH raided it."

"What better place for Samil to hide then?"

"But why there?" Renna wrapped her arms tightly around her waist. "Why that particular warehouse?

"Do you really need to ask that? Because of you. She knew you'd be unable to stay away."

Renna gazed out into space, her voice flat. "She was right."

TWENTY-NINE

Viktis ordered her to get some sleep before they landed on Antibes Prime, and Renna didn't argue. Her whole body ached, and that strange throbbing in her brain had started up again. Her tiny little pod looked pretty damn good as she slid into it.

She was asleep as soon as she put her head to her pillow, but that didn't mean she dreamed easy.

Images of Blur's warehouse as it used to look filled her mind. Shadowy, rundown, faded paint on the walls and broken windows high up letting in the gray sunlight. The burnt-sugar smell of clay and the constant acrid stench from the dying factories at the edge of the city.

But the screams were different. Screams that echoed through the space and made the hair on her arms rise. Renna tossed and turned, trying to block them out, but they only faded slightly.

She walked slowly through the warehouse, headed for Blur's old office. The high ceilings were bathed in shadows, but the floors bore the rusty stains of torture and pain. Renna tried to breathe through her mouth, but the scent of death still reached her.

Relief flooded through her as she made it through the warehouse gauntlet, but as she rounded the corner, she stopped dead.

Blur, her murdered mentor, barred the way. The lower part of his face had been ripped away, his jaw and part of his skull replaced by shiny new metal and synthetic skin. His eyes glowed red, just like the hybrids back in Navang's facility, and his arms were strong and deadly, the metal glinting in the light. Robot arms now, not human.

"You did this to me, Renna," he whispered. "And now I'm going to do the same to you."

He reached out with one of his robotic hands and closed it around her throat. The cold metal of his fingers burned into her skin as they tightened slowly around her windpipe.

She gasped for breath, thrashing against him helplessly.

With a hoarse scream, she woke up, tangled in the blankets. She stared up at the ceiling of her pod, sucking in air. Dear gods, what the hell was wrong with her? She hadn't had a nightmare like that in years.

Renna wiped the cold sweat from her palms. She'd give anything for a stiff drink right now, but getting up meant Viktis would see her freaking out, and having him hovering over her like a nursemaid wasn't how she wanted to spend the rest of the night.

If she was going to have a long night, she'd rather be back on the *Athena*. In Finn's arms.

She growled low in her throat. Damn her for still wanting him after this. Renna squeezed her eyes shut and tried to block out his face by concentrating on the *Athena*. She tried to focus on how it flew, the way she felt when she'd controlled it. It had felt like coming home. Like she'd always been a part of it.

A hum began to build in her head, but she ignored it. Instead she focused on inhaling and exhaling regularly, trying to get her pulse under control. The meditation technique started to work, and she felt herself finally slipping back into relaxation.

And then she was there. Inside the *Athena*.

It had been so easy this time. She'd just...become the ship instead of struggling with it. And this time she felt different, more controlled somehow. Excitement shivered through her, and with a thought, Renna's view switched between areas, almost like switching between surveillance monitors.

On the flight deck, Kojima monitored the controls alone, glancing at a video on his holoscreen between adjustments.

Switch.

On the bridge, Lieutenant Keva sat stony faced at her console, tracking ship movements and glancing at Captain Finn, who stood at the captain's chair, staring out at the rest of the ship's crew. He looked tired, shadows ringing his eyes and stubble darkening his jaw.

A flutter of happiness danced through Renna at the purple bruise on his cheekbone. Good, Viktis had gotten in a square hit when they'd fought on Forever Station.

A beep sounded from Keva's console. "Captain, comm from the Eris. *Would you like to take it?"*

"In the comm room, please." He strode from the CIC.

Switch.

In the comm room, Finn turned on the holocommunicator and leaned forward, hands on the table. "Commander, tell me you have something. Please." He'd let his rigid posture slump now that the crew wasn't watching him.

Commander Jayla shook her head with a frown. "Nothing. They've vanished. MYTH is insistent that you return immediately for a debriefing. They're sending the Eris *to look for her."*

"If I go back, they'll ground me. We'll never find her." He slammed a fist down on the railing. "Dammit, Jayla. I need more time."

"Time is the one thing we don't have, Captain."

A soft knock came on the comm room door and Finn growled. "Buy me some more time, Jayla. One more day. I need to find her. I was the one that let her into MYTH. This is my fault."

"You know that's not true."

"It's too late to argue about it now. Finn out." He cut the power to the holo and raked a hand through his hair. "I'm coming for you, Renna," he growled. His anger made her skin erupt in goose bumps.

She jerked awake, breaking the connection with the ship. Her fingers trembled as she brushed away the tears streaming down her face. Biting back a sob, she turned on her side and buried her head in the pillow.

THIRTY

T he *Fortune's Risk* landed on Antibes Prime the next day
as the brilliant red sun was setting.

"Are you ready for this?" Viktis asked as they waited
in the hold for the depressurizing unit to finish processing.

"No. But I don't really have a choice." Renna checked her
blaster again, making sure it was fully charged, and then patted
down her pockets and hips for the knives hidden there. "You
don't have to do this with me, Viktis. I'm the one she's after, not
you."

"I'm not going to let you go in there alone. Besides, I still owe
her for blowing up my ship and murdering my last crew. I'll be
happy to bring the bitch down."

She doubted it would be that easy, but Viktis knew what he
was getting himself into. Renna was going to have more than
Samil to deal with. The ghosts of her past hung heavy here. She'd

been such a child when she'd landed on the planet, on the run from a mother who probably hadn't even noticed she was gone. She'd gotten lucky when she'd found the transport ship headed here, and even luckier that one of Blur's gang spotted her when she got off the ship and offered her a place with the gang.

One of the other girls on the same transport hadn't been so lucky.

"Here we go." Viktis pressed a button, and the hatch slid open.

Renna gasped as a wave of bitter smoke hit her. The sun was sinking low in the amber sky over Shalim, its rays streaming between the decaying skyscrapers that dotted the horizon. Smoke plumes darkened the spaces between the bent and jagged fingers of the buildings. Shalim had been dying before she'd left seven years ago, but now it looked like hell itself.

"What happened here?" she asked, staring wide-eyed at the destruction. Her implant whirred to action, pulling up article after article about the chemical spill that decimated the city four years ago.

"Damn," she said. "The Koschei Corporation used their facilities here to manufacture a chemical used for rapid recycling of construction materials, but they didn't follow protocols and there were leaks. When it seeped into the earth, it started to attack the buildings and structures here. They're decaying at a rate of one hundred years for every year."

"What about the people?" Viktis asked.

Renna winced. If the chemical was strong enough to eat buildings, what in the maker's name did it do to humans?

Her implant returned the medical records a moment later.

She stared in horror at the reports. "Only the very poorest were left. Those who couldn't afford transport off-world have...changed." She stepped out onto the soil, her boots kicking up a puff of yellow dust, and tried not to inhale. "Why would Samil build a facility *here?*"

Viktis shook his head, brushing some of the floating dirt from his sleeve. "She attacked whole cities to acquire subjects for her experiments. She probably just had to offer these people a decent meal, and they'd flock to her. Seems like a better return on investment."

Renna's boots crunched on broken rubble as she headed for what had once been the main street through the spaceport. The minefield of destroyed cement and rotting metal stretched around them as far as she could see. Hot air from the decaying buildings clung to her exposed skin like cobwebs, but she shivered at Viktis's words.

Samil was turning these people into hybrids, too. And with the chemical already in their systems, it had to react differently from her other test subjects. Who knew what sort of horrors she'd created here.

Renna's implant flashed up a map of the area, and she turned down a side street. "This way."

"That thing's kind of useful to have."

She shrugged. "It did the map thing before Samil altered it. Now it's trying to take over my brain."

"And steering starships from across the galaxy," he added. "I've never seen Finn so freaked out. He thought MYTH had found us when you took over. But when he realized it was you..." His voice trailed off, and he glanced at her from the corner of his eye. "Sorry. Didn't mean to bring him up again."

Renna wrapped her arms around her waist, constantly scanning the shadows as they walked. She couldn't think about him now. She had to concentrate. Grieving for what might have been could come later.

The smell was unbearable, sharp and acrid, the stench of decay overwhelming. But there were no heat signatures, no sign that anyone was even left on the planet.

"So...what's the plan?" Viktis asked, finally breaking the uncomfortable silence between them. "I can't imagine Samil is going to let us walk in the front door."

"Then we use the back door. You forget, I knew this place like the back of my hand when I was a kid."

Renna rounded the corner and stumbled to a stop, staring at the front of what had once been her home. It didn't look much like the same rundown building she'd expected. Instead, it shone like a shiny new toy in the midst of the half-eaten structures around it. Smooth metallic walls stretched two stories high, completely windowless. The only entry was a high-tech security door with a glowing blue lock.

Viktis whistled. "Impressive. Must be some sort of new metal to withstand this chemical onslaught."

"It is. She developed it on Banos Prime. Maybe specifically for this. I don't know." Renna pulled herself together and gestured to an alley halfway down the block. "Let's head that way. I don't fancy trying to hack that lock." She led him away from the building and around the corner. "If she hasn't changed it, there should be a small ventilation duct we can use to get inside."

The back of the warehouse was built of the same dark material, but the door here was less high-tech, merely made of wood, with a standard lock. She and Viktis crouched behind another building, and Renna studied the facade, searching for the small vent she remembered. It had been a long time since she'd used that escape route. Samil might have even sealed it when she updated the building.

She finally spotted a darker dimple near the bottom of the building. "There!"

Viktis's shook his head. "You want me to fit through *that?*"

"What? Feeling claustrophobic already?" But she studied at it with misgiving, too. It was a hell of a lot smaller than she remembered.

She ordered her implant to do a quick scan of the facility for a vent schematic or another way in, but static just whispered in her ears. Nothing. Something was blocking the signal.

"Damn," she said, shaking her head. "I had this problem back on Banos Prime when Finn and I tried to break into the facility there. It's made from some new material that won't let comms in or out. I can't tell if the vent goes where it used to."

"Lucky us." Viktis squinted at the grate. "You get to go first then."

Renna smirked at him. "You just want to look at my ass."

"Absolutely."

But now that she studied him, Renna wasn't sure he'd fit. It might be a tight squeeze getting those broad shoulders into the hole. "How about this? I use the vent to sneak inside and let you in the door here." She pointed at the heavily locked wooden slab.

Viktis put up a hand. "No heroics, Renna. As soon as you get inside you let me in. We're doing this together. Promise?"

She kept her face expressionless. He knew her far too well. Damn him for guessing that she'd seriously considered leaving him behind to protect him from Samil. "Using my code against me, Viktis?"

"I'm using any advantage I can get with you, love. Promise?"

She sighed. "Promise. See you in a few."

Renna sprinted across the alley and ducked against the building as she used her nanospanner to quickly unscrew the grate cover. She waved cheerfully at Viktis before sliding head first into the dark space. Her elbow slammed against the side of the vent, the vibration echoing through the space. She waited, breath frozen in her throat as she listened for signs of discovery. But when everything remained silent, she slid forward, deeper into the building.

"Schematics," she ordered, but her implant stayed offline. Renna frowned. It was strange how quickly she was getting used to having that extra resource and how helpless she felt when it didn't work. Even if it might take over her whole body, it certainly had its uses.

Good thing it looked like Samil had left the air filtration system alone. If she remembered correctly, there was a junction just ahead.

Renna's knees slid against the slick metal bottom, and she pushed herself along a few more meters. And there it was. The darkness yawned on either side of her. To the left was the exterior door and Viktis. To the right, the interior and, if her hunch was correct, Samil.

If she took that path, she could end all of this. She had the element of surprise, and Samil wouldn't be expecting an attack from inside her own walls. The thought of watching the woman die for all the lives she'd already taken sent a sick sort of joy through Renna. Retribution was a bitch, and Renna was more than happy to be the one to deliver it. Easy decision, then.

She slid toward the right-hand vent but paused, glancing back in the other direction. If she did this, if she went after Samil and failed, they were all lost. And Viktis would never forgive her for breaking her promise.

It was so tempting to do this alone, to not have to worry about anyone else. But after what had happened back on Tartarus, Renna knew Samil was a slippery bitch. She'd need all the help she could get to stop her. Working with Viktis was the smart thing to do. And smart was the only thing that would get her through this.

Slowly, Renna pushed herself backward until she could take the left-hand turn. She counted three sections of vent before she found a grate that opened into what seemed to be an empty room. Renna craned her neck, searching the space for any sign of life, but only silence greeted her.

Shit. With her implant not working, she had no idea if she'd drop down into a room full of guards or set off an alarm.

Silently, she pulled out her nanospanner and unscrewed two of the vent screws. Curling her fingers into the grate, she lowered it, letting it hang open.

This was it. Her heartbeat hammered in her ears as she waited for a reaction, but after a few long seconds of silence, she leaned through the hole to survey the room.

A worn desk, a bank of dead monitors, and an old wooden chair facing the door were the only things there. Didn't look like it had been used in weeks. Renna slid feet first from the hole and landed softly on the ground in a crouch, casting a quick look about the space to make sure she hadn't missed anything.

Her racing pulse slowed when everything stayed nice and quiet. Just how she liked it.

In three steps, she'd crossed the room and switched off the door alarm.

"Get your ass in here, Viktis, I don't have all day," she said, throwing open the door with a grin.

Viktis appeared in the doorway, arms raised. "Renna, we have a little problem."

Major Larson stepped up behind him, blaster aimed directly at Viktis's head.

THIRTY-ONE

S o nice to see you again, Renna." Larson's voice could have frozen lava. "Why don't we all go inside?" He no longer wore the gray-and-gold MYTH uniform. Instead, a black jacket with a green lapel covered his lanky frame. He gestured with his gun. "Don't try anything or your friend is dead."

She glanced at Viktis, trying to keep her expression even and calm. He nodded slightly as if he could read her mind. But she couldn't risk trying to take down Larson with Viktis in the line of fire.

Dammit. When had she lost her nerve?

She raised her hands. "Fine. I'll behave. Leave him alone." Renna backed up into the guardroom until she bumped into the wall.

Larson pushed Viktis into the room, the gun never wavering. "Against the wall, scum."

Viktis stood beside Renna, frowning. "You had a shot at him. You should have taken it."

"Shut up," Larson snapped. He slammed the back door closed and reset the alarm with one hand. The other still pointed the gun at them.

"I didn't think you'd fall for it, but Dr. Samil was sure you wouldn't be able to resist coming here." Larson's lips twisted into a sneer. "You're even more predictable than I thought. She'll be so pleased to know you're here. Just in time to start phase two."

"Just in time to stop you, you mean." Renna leaned casually back against the wall and crossed her arms. "We knew exactly what we were walking into, Major."

"Of course you did." His smirk deepened. "Always have to have the last word, don't you? You really should learn when keeping your mouth shut is the smarter option." He strode to the door on the other side of the room and pressed his index finger to a bioscanner, wincing as a small needle pricked his skin.

Godsdammit. A biolock. Almost impossible to hack, even if you did have a sample of the person's blood. But it wouldn't do to let Larson see her reaction. She kept her face expressionless as the door slid open and he motioned them to start moving.

"So does Dr. Samil pay well?" she asked. "I can't think of any other reason someone like you would join up with an undisciplined mob like this."

Larson let out a low chuckle. "You really are a thief, only concerned with money." He forced them down a narrow hallway. "Do you want to know how well Samil pays?" he asked, pulling up the sleeve of his new uniform coat and pressing a finger to his wrist. The skin on his forearm pulled back, revealing a mess of wires and human nerves. Just like Myka's.

Renna stared at the familiar panel, her whole body going icy.

"I was diagnosed with an incurable disease three years ago," Larson said. "Samil offered to save me in return for my help. It was an easy decision. Even better, I just got an upgrade—state-of-the-art brain and nervous system. Bionic limb, even a shiny new implant, thanks to you."

Renna blinked at him in dismay. Dr. Samil must have started shipping Renna's test results out here as soon as Renna arrived at MYTH HQ. There was no way they could have developed this tech without her DNA.

Which meant that by turning herself in, Renna had actually helped create a whole new level of hybrid.

"I'm so sorry," she whispered. Even Larson shouldn't have to go through something like that.

"Why? I'm alive because of Dr. Samil and better than I could have ever imagined. Of course, I believe in her and her cause. And I'll do whatever it takes to protect her," he added with a growl.

Renna and Viktis exchanged horrified glances. She hadn't thought there could be anything worse than humans being experimented on against their will, but this was it. What kind of insane person would choose that path?

"Enough talking. Inside, both of you." Larson shoved Viktis through the door into a cavernous warehouse.

Renna gazed around the once-familiar space, jaw slack. She recognized it, and yet it was completely different. Back in her day, Blur had set up his desk at one end, out in the open so that everyone could see him. And so he could keep an eye on them.

Finn had had his own office area at the opposite end of the space, but he'd rarely been there, preferring to be down with the rest of the members in the central space. They'd had a dozen long tables scattered about, where gang members could play cards or work through jobs. They'd hung out in low couches in each corner, while a sparring ring was set up at one side for whoever wanted to use it.

Now, Samil had set up an open-air lab area where Blur's desk had been, with machines and medical devices. The sparing ring was gone, along with the couches, but the tables were still there. A whole group of different faces turned to stare at her as she and Viktis entered the space. Renna bit back a gasp. Each one was in some stage of becoming a hybrid—a metal arm or robotic eye or other technological implant clearly visible on each person.

The people standing around the tables in the warehouse space wore neat, nondescript clothing, their skin clean and hair groomed. They were all still obviously human. But how much longer before they turned into the unthinking machines Renna had destroyed at Navang's facility?

Did Samil have a neural network here, too? Once they connected to it and she controlled them, would they even know the difference?

Would Renna?

Viktis risked touching her arm when Larson turned to glance behind them. "You all right?"

She nodded, swallowing away the fear clogging her throat. "I'll get us out of this. I promise."

Before he could respond, a door opened at the back of the hall, and Dr. Samil walked out, dressed in a crisp black suit. The click of her heels against the floor resounded through the space as she approached, and a smile stretched her pretty face.

The hybrids followed her with their gazes, each one wearing the same identical expression of worship.

"Welcome, Renna. It must be strange to come back to your origins after all this time." Samil's tone was friendly, and Renna still had a hard time reconciling the woman who'd helped her back at MYTH with the monster trying to destroy them all.

Renna shrugged, faking boredom. "Not so strange. I escaped from here once. I can do it again."

Samil frowned. "There's no need to be so belligerent. I wish you'd realize that I want to help you."

"By turning me into a robot. Not exactly what I'd call helping." Renna glared at the woman. "I don't care what you do to me, but let Viktis go. He has nothing to do with this."

Samil turned her gaze to the Ileth. "I haven't been able to experiment much on aliens yet. Larson, take him to one of the holding cells. I'll look at him after I'm done with Renna."

Larson grabbed Viktis's arm. The alien tried to struggle, but Larson clapped an exovise around Viktis's wrists before he could move and shoved him to the floor. "Alien scum."

Viktis landed on his hands and knees, wincing as his skin scraped the hard cement. Larson kicked him in the stomach with a thud.

"No!" Renna cried. "Leave him alone."

But Larson smiled at her as he kicked out again with his heavy boot. Viktis collapsed, curling into a fetal position, but he didn't make a sound.

"Major, take him away and do that where the test subjects

won't see," Samil said, wrinkling her nose. "I'll be in my private labs. You won't resist if you know what's good for your friend," she added to Renna.

The fight went out of her. Viktis was here in this mess because of her. She'd do whatever was necessary to ensure he made it out alive. If that meant cooperating with Samil for now, then so be it.

The doctor led her to a large office at the back of the warehouse and held the door open for Renna. A large mahogany desk with two soft chairs in front of it took up one side of the space, while the other side was dominated by a wall full of lab equipment and holomonitors.

"Is this where you destroy lives?" Renna asked sweetly.

"This is where I save them." Samil sank gracefully into the chair behind her desk. "Do have a seat."

Standing would only look petulant at this point, so Renna sat down and crossed her legs. "You call experimenting on people saving them?"

"You've seen these people. They'd be dead or dying without me."

"But at least they wouldn't be monsters."

Samil shook her head sadly. "Now we get to the truth of it. To you, these enhanced people are monsters, things to be destroyed. Is that how you feel about yourself, too? Is that why you came alone? So that I could end all this pain for you?"

"I'm hardly alone," Renna said.

"The alien doesn't count. You've left your MYTH friends to come chasing after me." A knowing smile curved Samil's lips. "Or wasn't that your choice?"

Renna curled her hands into fists in her lap. "You planted that false information. *You* turned them against me."

"And it was so easy. I know you already know how it feels to be all alone, but now you've had something even more important ripped away from you. Love. Trust. A life." Samil leaned back in her chair. "And who did this to you? MYTH. They are a cancer that needs to be purged."

Renna shook her head. "You're completely insane. You're the one who did this, not MYTH."

"No, I just gave them the information. They decided to believe it. To betray you." Samil's expression turned businesslike. "It's nothing personal. I just needed you to understand why I'm doing this. To understand that I'm truly not as bad as you think. That MYTH has its own problems."

"You've killed thousands of people and experimented on thousands more, but you're not evil?" Renna shook her head. "Could have fooled me. Just because some organization hurt your feelings, it's their fault that you've turned into an evil bitch?"

"Oh, I don't blame MYTH." Samil leaned forward to rest her elbows on the desk. "I actually am grateful to them for making me stronger, for showing me what real ruthlessness is. When they greenlighted the experiments on Banos Prime after the explosion, they showed me what was possible, even amidst all that death. I couldn't save my fiancée, but I can save so many more now."

Renna shook her head. "Then what is it you want exactly if it's not revenge on MYTH for killing your fiancée?"

"This has nothing to do with revenge anymore. Perhaps it did once, but I have a bigger goal now." Samil's face took on the glow of a true fanatic. "MYTH has resources beyond your imagining, but beneath their shiny exterior, they've become corrupted. They experiment on children. They've destroyed whole colonies at a senator's whim. MYTH no longer serves the galaxy. They serve themselves. And I plan to change that."

Samil got to her feet, pacing behind her desk. "MYTH is only concerned with how to make more money, how to amass power, how to rule instead of how to serve. I want to create an organization that will become something people can believe in." She nodded to the door. "Those people out there are only the beginning. The poor, the hungry, the crippled. They all want a better life. They want something more. And I plan to give it to them."

"As long as they become your slaves, you mean."

"I don't want slaves, Renna. I want willing soldiers, and there are plenty of people who want what only I can give them."

"And what is that?"

"I can give them a future." Samil's smile was so bright she could have lit the room. "And that's all because of you. Your DNA will fix them, make them stronger. It will help the surgery and the implants and the technology to improve their lives. It will help them connect with each other. You should be proud."

"Proud that someone experimented on me against my will?"

"Sacrifices have to be made," Samil said with a shrug. "I'm sorry you're in this situation, but I thought you, if anyone, would understand. With your history."

Renna's heart kicked with unease, but she remained silent.

"Don't you see how similar we are?" Samil continued. "We both loved someone who betrayed us. We worked for an organization that doesn't care what happens to us, as long as it remains in power. Our skills can save so many people."

"Correction. Your skills, my DNA. There's a bit of a difference there."

Samil rolled her eyes. "If you must be literal. I have a great deal of respect for what you've accomplished and how far you've come from that tenement back on Earth. I know how hard it is to rise above something like that."

"You don't know a damn thing," Renna spat.

"That's where you're wrong." Samil pressed a button on her desk, and before Renna could blink, metal cords snaked from the arms of Renna's chair and wrapped themselves around her wrists.

THIRTY-TWO

Samil pulled a small, clear plastic box from her desk while Renna thrashed and struggled against the ties of her chair.

"What the hell is that? What are you doing?" she demanded.

"A new test. There's a microchip in here that will allow me to use your implant as a transmitter. I want to see exactly how far you've come in your abilities." She held up the small box. "Does this look familiar? I hear you stole several of these from Dr. Aldani before you left his facility."

Renna's blood ran cold. She knew exactly what Samil was talking about. Those devices were meant for long-range communication and infiltration of networks. Gheewala's words came back to her—the implication that Renna's changing implant could help her communicate with someone on the other side of the galaxy.

She pressed her back against the chair, trying to get as far away from Samil as possible as the doctor approached. "What are you going to do?"

"First I'm going to upload the new chip to your implant. If you survive, we'll go from there." She moved behind Renna and pressed a cool finger to the port at the back of Renna's neck.

"This may hurt a bit," she warned. Then she jacked in the microchip connector.

Colors and numbers blazed across Renna's vision in a wash of hazy red pain. It seared her eyes and shot through her brain like a thousand zaps of lightning. Something clicked, and she felt the program start to run through her implant, spinning and whirring in her mind like clockwork. A dark fog grew at the edges of her vision. As the last of the code inserted itself, Renna moaned and slumped back in her chair. She couldn't have moved a muscle if she'd tried.

Samil smiled. "You're still alive. That's a good sign." She pressed a finger to her own communicator. "I need someone to take our guest to the recovery room while I prep for phase two."

Renna tried to open her mouth, to ask what phase two was, but nothing obeyed. Everything was so heavy, her head felt like a boulder on her neck. She lolled back against the back of her chair and let her eyes drift closed. Samil's wicked face was the last thing she saw before the darkness consumed her.

"Wake up, Renna." Dr. Samil's hand squeezed Renna's shoulder, and for a split second, she thought she was back at MYTH

HQ, with the good doctor trying to save her.

Then she remembered. Everything.

Acid burned the back of her throat and her head pounded like she'd had way too much to Draven ice wine, but she forced herself to focus as she searched the space. It was some sort of recovery room, with a hard bed, a wall of monitors, and a long, metal table pushed against the wall.

Samil's silver med-drone floated behind her head, ready to help if the doctor needed it. "Time to see if the chip worked." Samil tapped something into her tablet, and the holovid on the wall flickered to life. "Excellent. Looks like you're back online. Now all I need to do is upload the software."

"Where's Viktis?" Renna croaked. She knew Samil wouldn't tell her, but she had to ask anyway.

"He won't be bothering us. I promise."

Renna struggled to sit up, but she could barely move. "What the hell did you do to me?"

"Like I told you, I've upgraded your implant with a new communications system. Now we get to see how well it worked." She tapped at her tablet again. "There. Program uploaded. How does it feel?"

Didn't feel like anything, if Renna was honest, but it wouldn't do to let Samil know that. Renna glared. "How the hell do you think it feels? You violated my brain. It hurts like a bitch."

"I can't get over how hard your body is fighting this. It's astonishing." Samil shook her head and glanced up at the holoscreen. "I wish I had more time to study you before our final phase."

The ominous words made the skin on Renna's arms turn to

goose flesh. What exactly did the woman plan to do with her?

"Perfect. We're into the system. You are amazing, Renna." Samil smiled up at the holoscreens, and Renna followed her gaze. The screen showed a long, empty hallway, but Samil pressed a button and the image separated into four different panes, each showing a different part of some facility, like a security monitor.

Another press and the cameras zoomed out to show the facade of four different buildings.

The pounding in Renna's head had turned into a high-pitched vibration that made her teeth ache. She clenched her jaw against the pain. "What exactly are we looking at?"

"MYTH headquarters on four different worlds. Including the main headquarters on Titus Beta where you were held. I used the new microchip and your implant's special attributes to jack into their security system."

Renna fought the urge to touch the port in the back of her neck. "How the hell did you do that? Dallas said they locked you out."

Samil preened. "Luckily I already connected you to the neural network installed in their facilities. It was easy, especially since you thought it was just another test. Sorry it hurt so much."

The memory shot through her with a jolt. The metal machine she'd used to scan Renna's eyes had been the first step of Samil's plan. Gods, she'd been so stupid to think she'd ever been a step ahead of this woman.

"Now with this new comm chip," Samil continued, "they won't know we're in their system until it's too late."

"Too late for what?" Renna asked. She glanced down at her legs. She was unbound, but her body wouldn't fucking move.

What the hell had Samil done to her?

"This." Samil typed in a command to her tablet, and a split second later, Renna hissed as a jolt of pain shot through her. Fire sped through her nerves and into her fingers and toes in an angry rush.

"I've just uploaded a virus. Using your implant's connection, it should propagate into the MYTH systems in a few minutes and take down all of their defenses and networks. Then I can pick off each facility at my leisure."

Renna's breath caught in her throat. Finn and Jayla were returning to HQ. They'd be there if Samil struck. She had to do something to stop her.

"Let me guess. You have a platoon of hybrids ready to take down each facility?" she asked sarcastically as her brain spun, searching for a way out.

Samil leaned back and crossed her arms. "I don't need a platoon. I only need one mole inside each command center. And with the virus rampant, MYTH will be blind, unable to communicate with each other. It's the best sort of divide-and-conquer. All I'll have to do is sweep up the pieces when the rest of the universe realizes what MYTH has become."

The images on the holoscreens cycled through different parts of each facility, showing MYTH men and women at their posts or rooms full of servers. There was even footage of the front gate of one of the buildings, with two laser cannons at the ready.

Renna's skin went clammy. Thousands of people would die if Samil went through with this. "These people are smart," she protested. "They'll find a way to stop you and fight back. And when they come for you, I'm going to be leading the charge."

Dr. Samil chuckled. "You won't be going anywhere, my little dove. That virus should also destroy any last resistance between your neural system and the implant. You'll be mine to command in a matter of hours. My ultimate secret weapon."

Renna stared at the woman. She'd expected to feel horror or fear before she turned into a hybrid, but right now she was fucking furious. Her fingers itched to curl around Samil's neck, but she needed to focus on figuring out a way to stop Samil or warn MYTH. Not exactly an easy feat when she wasn't able to move.

But maybe there was another way. Her implant had been behaving lately; maybe she could use it one last time.

Renna let her eyes drift closed.

"Don't you want to watch, dear?" Samil asked. "I think MYTH is about to find out they're no longer the ones in charge."

She shook her head. "I'd rather stab my eyes out with a needle."

"Even if your former lover is on the screen?"

Renna's eyes flew open, despite herself. In one of the panes, Finn and Dallas strode through a hangar. Perhaps the *Athena* had landed or was getting ready to leave again. Maybe they'd be able to escape in time.

She studied his tired face as Finn gestured angrily at something Dallas said and the older man shook his head. Dark shadows ringed Finn's eyes. Even though it had been only less than twenty-four hours since she'd fled from him, he looked like he hadn't slept in days.

"Perfect. Two of my favorite people." Samil pressed a button on her tablet, and a moment later, both men stopped dead in their tracks. Finn's head snapped back and forth as he searched for something.

"That will be the defense warning sirens. The breach is irreparable. I used your implant to take down their shields and render the security systems useless. You, dove, are the best secret weapon in the galaxy. Using you, I can control almost any communication system. Anywhere."

Horror rushed through Renna, making her stomach swoop as though she was jumping to light speed. She couldn't let this woman destroy everything. There had to be a way to stop her.

Renna exhaled as she reached out with her implant to the *Athena*. She needed to feel that connection with the ship, to become one with it again. Maybe she could warn them. They could strike Samil's facility before she hurt anyone else.

Slowly, she felt herself slide into the ship's systems. This time was even easier than before. The footsteps of the crew as they rushed through the ship to their stations vibrated through her. Another deep breath and she went deeper, into the Peron fusion engine and the network that ran through the ship.

Through both of them.

Across the room, Samil chuckled at something on the holoscreen, but Renna concentrated on her connection, on passing her thoughts and feelings to the *Athena*. She needed to send the ship coordinates to this place. Finn would be able to stop Samil, even if Renna couldn't.

She tried to enter the nav systems so she could input the data, but around her, the *Athena* suddenly let out a shrill alarm. The ship threw up a firewall, resisting as Renna tried to take control.

The *Athena* thought she was under attack.

Renna backed out, heart pounding. It had to be the virus inside her making the *Athena* freak out. Unfortunately, she didn't have time to be subtle about it or figure out a way get around the firewall. She'd have to crash through it and hope for the best.

She pushed against the firewall with her mind, using every piece of tech in her implant to bring it down. With a snap, the wall broke and her connection slotted into place. She had control of the ship.

Renna reached out, feeling the connection, feeling the exchange of information.

Her leg twitched.

She ignored it, focusing on trying to input her location into the *Athena's* system. Around her, she could feel the crew scramble to prep for takeoff as the sirens wailed in the facility.

Energy flowed through her like a current as the ship's engine spun up. Her arms twitched, but she ignored it. She was almost there.

"Look at them, running around like ants. Don't they know it's futile?" Samil said, a smile in her voice.

With one last push, a surge of energy rushed through Renna as the floodgates opened. Data flowed freely between her and the *Athena* in a heady rush of power. Her whole body vibrated with it, and she opened her eyes. Had she done it? Had she implanted the data coordinates into the ship's nav computer?

Her right leg twitched again. Must be an electrical impulse from her connection. But maybe…Slowly she curled her toes.

How was that possible? Samil had said…

Screw what Samil had said. If she could move, she could kick the woman's ass. Carefully, Renna flexed each of her muscle groups, making sure it was true. Her heart kicked with excitement.

The virus wasn't working. Samil couldn't control her any more.

THIRTY-THREE

I suppose it's time to show MYTH exactly what kind of power I really have," Samil said, setting her tablet down on the table.

Renna tensed her muscles. She'd have one shot at this. With a huge push, she launched herself off the gurney. Her legs trembled but held as she landed and grabbed Dr. Samil from behind. She jammed her forearm against the doctor's throat, holding her in place.

Samil went perfectly still, pressed against Renna. "Interesting. It looks like my virus calculations were off. I had no idea you could still move."

"Not so smart after all, huh?" Renna squeezed tighter. The woman's labored wheezing vibrated against her forearm. One small movement and she could snap the bitch's neck.

"If you kill me, you'll never get the cure," Samil whispered, as if she could read Renna's thoughts.

"Liar. You don't have a cure."

The woman shook her head. "How else did these people survive the transition? I used a new drug on them, based on your DNA."

Renna loosened her arm slightly. "What do you mean?" She knew better than to believe Samil, but she couldn't help herself. If there was something that could save her...

"These people have all gone through the same process you did. Their implants tried to take over their nervous system. But with help from your DNA, I've developed a formula that helps integrate their implant without it taking over completely. They keep their free will and their minds most of the time. And I'm able to control them when I need to, using my neural network."

"I don't believe you."

"Then you're a fool. Did you think I was trying to build an army of mindless drones? That was step one, of course. I used Navang's early experiments to figure out how to control the integration without destroying their minds. Only a few people survived, but those people were invaluable."

Renna jerked her arm against Samil's throat again, whispering in the woman's ear. "Tell me where the cure is."

"No." Samil chuckled low in her throat. "Poor Renna. Always a step behind. I don't want you dead, dove. You're much too important. But I do want you immobilized, and if I give you the cure, you'll just go right back to being a pain in my ass."

"And yet you're the one seconds from death. A quick jerk and I can snap your neck."

"Did you really think I'd be stupid enough to come in here

unarmed?"

Something small and hard pressed into Renna's side, and she glanced down. Samil had another tranq pistol aimed directly at Renna's midsection.

Before the woman could pull the trigger, Renna shoved her away, using the momentum to duck behind the gurney. She flipped it on its side as Samil's dart hit with a metallic ding.

Fuck, fuck, fuck. She was losing her touch. Why hadn't she restrained the woman before getting all cocky? It was a stupid, rookie mistake. She'd made way too many of those lately.

Renna scanned the room for options. The corner where she was holed up was almost empty, no help there. Just the metal gurney, a dirty white sheet that had fallen to the floor, and a small box of medical supplies. She snatched up the sheet. Pathetic. But it would have to do.

She twisted it into a tight, thick rope. Her heart raced and her limbs still felt leaden, but at least she was able to move. Maybe she could use the sheet to knock the gun away. She just needed to wait for the right moment.

"Come out now and I'll make this painless, Renna," Samil called.

"Really? And why should I believe you?"

"I want you alive and well. Cooperate and maybe we can find some way to end all of this peacefully. No one else has to get hurt."

Renna waved a hand above her makeshift barrier. "Fine. Let's talk. I'm standing up now."

But instead of rising to her feet she darted around the edge of the gurney, striking out with the sheet like it was a whip. It snapped against Samil's arm, and she hissed, dropping the gun.

Renna lunged for it as it clattered to the floor, but Samil was even faster. The two women collided, sending the gun skidding toward the door. Renna shoved an elbow in Samil's stomach and tried to move toward it, but the woman grabbed her, shoving her in the opposite direction.

Renna's body slid across the floor, hitting the edge of the doorframe. She glanced up at the handle, eyes widening.

The door was unlocked.

Screw the gun, she was getting the hell out of here. Renna yanked the handle and shoved the door open, sliding through it into the hall. In one fluid move, she jumped to her feet and slammed it shut. With a loud click she brought home the bolt, locking Samil inside.

But the bitch still had her gun and her tablet. She'd call for reinforcements in seconds.

Renna's body still felt strangely heavy, like it belonged to someone else, and sucked in a deep breath. She needed to find Viktis and get him out of here before her body gave in to the virus. Before Samil's neural network finally connected with her implant.

Before Renna turned into nothing but a mindless hybrid.

She forced her trembling legs to move. First stop, the building's control room. If she could shut everything down, maybe that would stop Samil from calling for help.

She cycled through memories of her time here, when it was Blur's warehouse. Samil had rearranged the interior, but the bones were still the same, which meant one of the control rooms should be at the north end of the building. Knowing the bitch,

Samil would've installed security cameras everywhere. Hopefully Renna could use those security cameras to find Viktis and then figure out a way to get them out of here.

As long as the hybrids didn't find her first.

Renna crept down the corridor, each foot placed carefully so her boots didn't click against the cement floors. Larson had taken her gun when he'd captured her, and its missing weight against her hip made her feel naked. Her Bumani skills were excellent, but she had no idea how Samil's network affected the hybrids. Did it give them extra-strength? Did they know moves gathered from some hivemind? Maybe her own moves had already down-loaded into their brains.

The facility's continued silence pressed heavily against her skin as she tiptoed past each door. Why hadn't Samil sounded the alarms yet?

With each step, she held her breath, heart pounding, expecting the hybrids to burst from each room . At the end of the corridor, Renna paused, glancing back and forth between the junction. Which way? The new walls made the building feel strange, like everything had been turned around.

She tapped her foot against the cement. Moving forward was better than standing still, even if she chose wrong.

"Left. Go left," she muttered, taking that corridor. A few steps down the hall and she knew she'd been right.

She grabbed the handle of the utility room door. It didn't budge. Dammit. She'd give her right arm for her electronic lock-picks right now.

Renna grimaced. Not the best choice of words.

She'd have to make do with the manual pick she always carried hidden in the waistband of her pants. She wiggled it free and inserted it into the lock, but her fingers were trembling so badly she fumbled with it, dropping it to the floor with a clatter.

Samil's presence felt like hot breath on the back of her neck, but she'd waste valuable time if she didn't do this right. She sucked in a deep breath, letting it out in a long measured exhale.

Find your center. Ignore the rest. The words from her first mentor, Jack, wove through her head.

She could do this. Carefully, she slipped the pick into the lock and moved it, searching for each tumbler and clicking it into place. Her concentration calmed her pulse and steadied her hand, and when the lock clicked open, she couldn't help the grin that curved her lips. Damn, she still had it. That was one thing Samil hadn't been able to take away.

Inside the utility room, monitors lined the far wall, while an electrical panel nestled in the corner . First thing's first: finding Viktis. Renna scanned the screens, each showing a different area of the facility. The room where they'd gotten caught. Several views of the main open space. Three small labs and several hallways. She didn't see Samil's private lab on any of the screens. Hardly surprising. Of course the woman wouldn't want her horrific actions recorded.

The last monitor showed a large, windowless room and her stomach dropped to the floor. *Oh, gods. Viktis.*

He was chained to the wall, arms and legs spread-eagled. His shirt was gone, displaying his muscled chest and arms in all their amber glory, and his head hung forward on his chest like it was too heavy to hold up. Larson stood at a table across the room rearranging tools, a shiny silver med-drone hovering nearby. Renna couldn't make out which instruments he was using, but she didn't really need to. She could already see the results marking Viktis's lithe frame.

Bile bit at the back of her throat and she pressed a hand to her lips. Larson was a fucking monster.

A long jagged cut stretched across Viktis's left pectoral, blood seeping down the hard planes of his stomach. His right eye was swollen shut, and blood trickled from it like tears down his face. Perfectly round pockmarks marred the skin on his arms.

Larson had used the gravitic cauterizer in the med-drone to burn Viktis's skin almost down to the bone.

She backed away from the monitors so fast she knocked over a stool with a clatter. Vomit burned her nose and mouth as she heaved and gagged on what was left of her dinner. Viktis was dying, and it was all her fault. She should have left him behind. Should have forced him to stay on the ship.

Renna rocked back and forth, arms around her waist. But what could she do? How could she save him? She whimpered low in her throat. She would never be able to forgive herself if he died on her watch.

Pull it together, Renna, she ordered herself. Having a breakdown now was not part of the plan.

She forced herself to straighten her spine and turn back to the monitors. From what she could tell, the torture room was in what used to be an old storage area not too far from here. She could be there in a matter of minutes, as long as no one stopped her. Which meant she needed to cut the power to the facility.

Before she could take more than a step toward the electrical panel, footsteps thundered outside the room.

"She's in here!" a man's voice called outside the door.

Her whole body tensed, but there was only one thing on her mind right now. Getting to Viktis. Whatever the cost.

The door opened, and a burly man entered, dark hair curling in a halo around his moon-shaped head.

"We've got her!" he called back into the corridor.

"You think so?" Renna asked, crossing her arms.

He held up his robotic right hand and flexed it, the chrome shining in the helolights. "I know so."

Her head pounded like a motherfucker and everything was still slightly blurry from Samil's virus, but she smiled slowly. Show no weakness. "Come and get me then."

Renna gathered her strength, and as he moved toward her, she kicked out, catching him dead in the abdomen. "You might have that fancy arm, but I don't think Samil has created a metal stomach yet."

The man doubled over, and Renna kicked out again, using the Bumani techniques Finn had taught her so long ago in this very building.

Another kick and he dropped to the floor clutching his midsection. He writhed and moaned, oblivious as Renna leapt over him and yanked a handful of wires from the control panel.

The entire facility went black. Panicked shouts echoed through the building as Samil's men searched for the cause.

Renna froze where she was, blinded by the sudden darkness. "Night vision," she ordered, but her implant didn't obey. Around her, the screams and cries of Samil's hybrids filled the blackness, and she closed her eyes. She'd have to do this the hard way.

Fumbling against the wall, she found the door and slipped back into the hallway. Her sense of direction was still all right, and she headed north toward where she'd seen Viktis and Larson. She trailed her fingers against the wall. Her stomach swooped with each painfully slow footfall, as if she expected the ground to disappear from beneath her feet at any moment.

Dammit. She did not have time for this. Viktis did not have time for this.

"Work, damn you," she ordered, shaking her head like a dog after a bath. But still nothing happened.

Her whole body trembled as she moved forward. Her fingers hit the edge of the wall, and she froze. Now which way did she go?

Precious seconds ticked away as she stood, undecided. The scrape of footsteps sounded nearby, and her heart jumped into her throat. Whatever she was going to do, she had to do it now. She turned right, away from the sound of pursuit.

Move it, she ordered herself.

Her fingers trailed against the smooth metal of a door. She fumbled for the handle and pushed it open, listening for Larson or Viktis.

Nothing.

Her own breathing sounded ragged and loud as she crept farther down the corridor. This whole place made her skin crawl. What other horrors would she stumble on here?

The next door was locked, but luckily she could pick it blindfolded. Her fingers trembled as she fit her lockpicks into the slot and she forced herself to steady. The throbbing in her head was getting worse. Maybe the virus was finally taking hold. Maybe Samil was trying to use her network to control Renna.

Stop it. She did not have time to freak out. Viktis needed her.

Steadying her breathing, she made quick work of the lock and pushed the door open, just as the lights in the facility flooded back on.

Renna straightened from her crouch, hand pressed to her mouth to stifle her scream.

It wasn't Viktis. It was worse.

THIRTY-FOUR

Crimson blood streaked the white, tiled floor, pooling around the drain in the center of the room. The stench of death mingled with acrid chemicals, burning Renna's eyes and making her chest ache. She stared, wide eyed, at a dozen stasis trays sitting along the far wall. They were filled with body parts—amputated arms, parts of legs, eyes, even hearts.

All human. All recently removed from their victims. The victims who were still there.

Two men and two women lay on metal gurneys lined up in the middle of the room. Each body was torn open and butchered in a different way. But they had one thing in common. They were all victims of Samil's horrific experiments.

She moaned, putting a hand against the doorframe to keep from sliding to the floor. Their gaping chest cavities and bloody torsos reminded her of Wall's. Of the way he'd been torn apart and dismembered. Evidently he hadn't just been a threat, but an experiment.

But what the hell was Samil doing with these people? Renna tightened her muscles and forced herself to approach the body parts in their stasis trays. They looked like large carry-out boxes made of clear poly-plastic. Each body part was surrounded by bright blue liquid.

The first held a human heart. It lay on its tray, pink and shiny and clean. Perfectly normal. Renna was about to move on to the next tray when it convulsed in a mockery of a heartbeat.

And again.

And a third time.

Renna stumbled backward as the pair of eyes on the next tray swiveled to look at her.

Holy hell. Samil had created living implants.

A sob broke free, and she squeezed her eyes closed until she could pull it together. Her whole body trembled, and every breath she took burned her nose with the scent of blood and chemicals. She had to get the hell out of here. Now.

Renna backed up until her rear hit the door. She couldn't rip her gaze from the motionless bodies and their now-living parts. Who had they been? Had they volunteered for Samil's experiments because she'd promised them a better life?

Obviously she'd lied.

Renna wasn't religious, but she sent up a prayer to whatever gods these people believed in that they hadn't suffered at least. The woman on the end didn't look much older than Renna, with the gaunt cheeks of someone who'd had too much clay and not enough food.

She paused, one foot out the door, then spun to look at the girl again. Her heart jackhammered, sucking the breath from her lungs.

Renna knew her.

Annet Perra had lived in the Izan tenements where Renna grew up. She'd been ten years older, but she'd always been nice to the little kids. When she got a little extra money from the manufacturing job she worked, she'd buy them candy or an extra piece of fruit.

Renna's gaze dropped to the woman's arm—or where it used to be. Her forearm and hand were missing. Industrial accident, most likely. And she knew firsthand what happened to women who could no longer work in the factories. They did what her mother had. They turned to prostitution.

But why would Samil use this girl? Was there a connection or was it merely coincidence?

Renna frowned at the Annet's body. Knowing Samil, there was no way in hell this was coincidence, but she didn't have time to investigate right now. She chewed her lip, glancing between the body and the door. Leaving Annet here in this place felt like a betrayal. Tenement rats stuck together—that was the first law of growing up in that place. But the girl was beyond help now. And Viktis was still alive.

Sending a silent apology to the girl, she slipped back out the door and closed it behind her. She curled her trembling hands into fists. Samil was the monster here, not these poor people.

Shouts echoed through the facility as the men searched for Renna. There was only a matter of minutes before they found her again. She squared her shoulders as she faced the last door.

She couldn't make the same mistake she'd made with Samil. No matter how injured Viktis was or what horrors she found in that room, she needed to stop Larson first. No matter the cost.

Renna tried the door handle. It moved easily, the door swinging open on silent hinges. Clutching her lockpick, the only weapon she had, she stepped into the room. Her gaze darted to Viktis, still chained to the wall. He didn't even raise his head as she took another step.

Was he even still alive?

"Nice to see you again, Renna." Larson leaned a shoulder against the wall, lips twisted in a sneer. "Dr. Samil thought you'd head this way. I'll be more than happy to take you to her. After I've had a little fun with you first." He snapped a finger at the med-drone floating behind him, and it vibrated as its sensors kicked in. "She only needs your mind to work, after all. Perhaps a little pain will make you behave."

One of the drone's spindly arms extended as if it was excited to get started.

"Did you know Dr. Navang?" Renna ignored the needle sticking from the drone's arm and glanced around the room. Larson had pushed the empty metal gurney to the side, and the tray table with his torture tools took up half of the far wall. Viktis's blood streaked the man's hands, speckles of it dusting his face like war paint.

Her whole body shook with anger, but she needed to be smart.

"Of course," he said with a nod. "He was a brilliant man."

"Not so brilliant when I cornered him in his lab. He had lovely, sharp scalpels."

Larson raised an eyebrow. "Why does this matter?"

"Because I slit his throat. And now I'm going to do the same to you."

The major chuckled. "I love that you're still so optimistic. Your files never indicated you had that streak. Give up, thief. You're trapped here, and no matter what you do, Samil will use you to take down MYTH. It will go much easier for everyone involved if you'd cooperate."

"I've never been much of a team player." Renna shrugged. "Then again, neither have you. Getting your men killed in a botched mission, the sexual harassment, all those written reprimands in your files. I'm surprised MYTH didn't court martial you." Larson's lips parted in surprise, and she smiled. "*Your* files indicated you were a fucking asshole."

He growled and launched himself at her. "I've had enough of you."

But Renna side-stepped easily, spinning around so she occupied the space Larson had just left. A few steps back and she'd have a whole tray of weapons at her disposal.

Behind her, the med-drone whirred and spun, but it didn't attack.

"Move another inch and your friend is dead," Larson warned. He strode to the wall and jerked Viktis's head up.

An electric shock collar circled Viktis's neck.

"State-of-the-art torture device," Larson said. "I can program instant death by injection or merely shock my captives. Depends on my mood. And right now I'm not feeling very charitable." He pressed the button on the controller in his right hand and a zap of electricity shot through the collar.

Viktis screamed, a high, unearthly sound as he jerked and spasmed against the wall, head lolling violently from side to side.

"Stop!" Renna screamed. "Stop it right now. I'll do whatever you want."

Larson lowered his hand, and the electricity in the collar shut off. Viktis sagged against his chains, moaning in agony. The metal around his wrists was the only thing supporting him, and they dug in painfully, skin bulging on either side of the bands.

"Good answer." Larson waved a hand at the med drone. "Hold still and we'll make sure you don't escape again."

The metal globe glided through the air toward her, and Renna clenched her fists. She wanted to punch the thing as far away from her as she could, but she couldn't afford to put Viktis in danger again. "If I cooperate, you have to let the alien go."

"Of course," Larson said with a smile.

"Liar. Take his collar off right now."

"Or what?" His smug expression was almost enough to send her over the edge and she gritted her teeth.

"Or I'll kill myself right now and you'll all be shit out of luck." She held up her lockpick. "Don't think I won't. I grew up in the tenements. I know exactly how to kill a person instantly."

A muscle jumped in Larson's jaw, and he glanced between Renna and Viktis. She could see the calculations running through his mind. Was she telling the truth? How could he keep his prisoner and get her under control at the same time?

"I never bluff about death," she said coldly. "How pleased do you think Samil will be when I die on your watch?"

She saw the moment Larson made his decision, heard the instant whirring of the drone as it hurled itself at her, needle extended. She spun around, arm raised to ward it off.

It stopped inches from her throat, the wicked needle glinting in the hololights. A single bead of some clear drug welled at the end of the needle before dripping to the floor.

Renna blinked at the thing and took a step back. It hung motionless in the air, nudging a memory at the back of her mind.

The punching ball back on the *Eris*.

Across the room, Larson cursed, struggling with the drone's controller. She turned around almost leisurely and sent the drone careening toward him. Before he could even throw an arm up, the needle embedded itself in his throat, and Larson's eyes widened as the vial of liquid emptied into his veins.

"What have you done?" he cried, dropping the controller and shoving the drone away with both hands. He clapped a hand to his neck, eyes bulging as he gasped for breath.

Renna released her control on the machine and it backed away from Larson. His skin had turned milky, and he swayed on his feet. With a moan, his knees gave out and he slid down the wall, landing on the floor with a thud.

She approached the trembling man, her smile growing with each step. Seeing him powerless and cowering made the adrenaline rush hot and rich through her veins. "You would know. You're the one who stocked the drone." She tilted her head to study him. "I'm guessing it was just a tranquilizer. I should be flattered. You guys really don't want me to get hurt."

"I'll kill you myself, no matter what Samil wants." Larson's voice had dropped to a croak and his hands lay limply in his lap.

"Right. I'm shaking." She urged the med-drone closer, using her implant to run through the list of attachments it carried until she found the one she wanted. She was going to enjoy this.

The round attachment slid from the drone's body, sparks dancing at the tip of the sliver spike. If Larson could have moved, he would have crawled up the wall to get away from it.

"No," he whispered. He'd gone even paler, if that was possible, all the blood draining from his face.

"Yes." Renna ordered the machine forward.

It hummed as the spike touched Larson's cheek and the spark arced into his skin. The gravitic cauterizer seared into the flesh on his cheekbone. The reek of burning flesh filled the room and a scream ripped from Larson's throat.

"Please," he begged. "Make it stop. I'll do whatever you want."

"Make it stop?" she asked. "And did you stop the hundreds of times other people begged you to do the very same thing?"

"It's different. Please."

"It's only different because you're on the receiving end now."

Across the room, Viktis groaned.

Renna snapped around. Gods, what was she doing? She snatched up Larson's controller from the floor and switched off the collar. Gently she lifted it from Viktis's neck, then tackled the shackles, slipping a shoulder under his arm so he wouldn't fall to the floor as they released. Gently, she let him slide until he was sitting with his back propped against the wall.

Viktis blinked up at her, eyes unfocused and full of pain. "Is that really you, Ren?"

"It's me, handsome. And I'm going to get you out of here. Can you walk?"

He shook his head. "I don't think so. The asshole broke my ankle and my whole body hurts like hell. I don't know if I can even move."

Shit. Renna chewed her lip and glanced at the door. The hybrids could show up at any moment, and she wouldn't be able to do a damn thing about it.

"Go on without me," he said. "Get out of here before Samil catches you again." He squeezed her hand weakly. "Just put me out of my misery first, eh?"

"Don't you dare talk like that, you washed-up old pirate. We're both getting out of here." The med-drone floated toward them. "I'm giving you a painkiller. It'll help you get through the next couple of minutes so we can get out of here."

"Better triple the dose." Viktis tried to chuckle, then winced. "Damn. Hurts to laugh."

"Then don't laugh." Her gaze shifted to the metal gurney. "All right. We need to get you up there. This isn't going to be fun."

"Just do it. I can feel the meds kicking in already." Viktis clenched his jaw as Renna hauled him to his feet. Her finger slid against one of the cauterized holes, and he hissed.

"Gods! I'm so sorry!"

"Get moving before I pass out again. You can apologize later."

Together, they limped toward the table. Renna got him to the edge and pressed the controls to lower the height enough that he could slide back onto it. She picked up his legs and swung them onto the gurney, then covered him with a sheet.

"We're going to hope they don't ask too many questions and assume you're dead."

"I'm close enough. I'll barely be acting." Dried amber blood streaked his face, and she carefully kept her gaze from lingering on the holes dotting his arms. If she let herself look, she'd be destroyed. Useless for anything except screaming.

Or killing.

"Renna? You okay?" he asked. "Samil is probably on her way."

"One last thing to take care of." Renna grabbed one of the long, thin knives from the tray and stalked back toward Larson's motionless body. The drug had knocked him out, and his head was slumped on his chest, mimicking Viktis's earlier pose. She curled her fingers around the knife. The man had tortured her friend and enjoyed it. He'd betrayed MYTH and caused thousands more deaths. He deserved to die. And she'd be more than happy to oblige.

Too bad he wasn't awake to watch her do it.

"Renna! What are you doing?" Viktis asked.

"Killing the bastard."

"Let it go. We don't have time for this."

Renna glanced back at Viktis's destroyed face, then down at Larson. Anger licked beneath her skin, and she crouched in front of the man.

"I'll always have time for this."

With one fluid motion she jammed the knife up and through his diaphragm, directly into his heart.

THIRTY-FIVE

Viktis gasped as Larson's body slid sideways. Renna rose from her crouch, wiping her hands on her trousers. "Now doesn't that make you feel better?" she asked Viktis.

Viktis stared. His amber skin had turned gray and deep lines framed his narrowed lips. "When did you get so ruthless, Renna?"

She blinked. Why was he looking at her like she was a monster? He should be glad the man was dead.

When she didn't answer, he shook his head. "It doesn't matter now. Let's get out of here. I'm not feeling so well." As he spoke a bubble of blood formed at the corner of his lip, bursting in a fine spray across his skin.

Fuck. Internal bleeding? Punctured lung? Something worse? Renna threw open the door, grabbed another knife from the table, and wheeled the gurney out into the hallway. Whatever it was, Viktis needed medical attention immediately.

The drone followed like a dog, hovering several paces behind. It had been even easier to control than the punching ball. Had Samil's virus changed something? Or was her implant progressing faster than she'd thought?

Either way, she was running out of time.

Renna cautiously peeked down the next corridor. Empty. Where the hell was everyone? Not that she wanted a welcoming committee, but the silence made her nervous. She much preferred to keep Samil and her army where she could see them.

The gurney's tires squeaked against the cement floor as she maneuvered it down the hallway and through a back passage. If she could skip the main area, maybe they'd make it out of here without being caught. The drone struggled to keep up, its engine wheezing and spluttering.

Strange, but she didn't have time to worry about it now. Viktis had passed out again, and his chest wound still bled sluggishly. He'd lost a lot of blood, and he'd lose even more if she didn't get him back to his ship.

She entered the hall, freezing as every muscle clenched. The room was full of Samil's men. Standing perfectly still.

Had the doctor activated the neural network? Was she controlling them now? But why weren't they attacking?

Renna stared at the blinking red lights deep in the hybrids' eyes. The lights she'd seen in her own eyes. Were hers blinking now, too, and she just didn't know it?

She pushed the thought away and tried to focus. If these hybrids were connected to Samil's network, maybe she could do the same thing they'd done in Navang's facility. If she could input a virus, she could destroy this place and these monsters for good. She could stop them from attacking MYTH and destroying the people she cared about. She could protect Finn, Myka, Viktis.

She could stop Samil.

Renna swallowed back the sudden lump in her throat. Even though Finn had betrayed her, maybe even hated her, she was still in love with him. And she had no idea if that would ever change, now that she'd let him in.

On the gurney, Viktis coughed, more amber blood trickling from the corner of his mouth. His skin had started to turn green, a sure sign of internal hemorrhaging.

Renna glanced back toward the lab area. A few more minutes and she could end this.

And end Viktis while she was at it.

A surge of realization flowed through her as she stared down at her old friend. The old Renna would have taken any chance to win, despite the odds. She would have left Viktis there to die if it meant stopping Samil. But somehow, in the last few weeks, she'd changed. That Renna—the one who worked alone, who didn't need anyone—was gone. She needed Viktis alive. And that meant moving her ass.

Clenching her fingers around the gurney handle, she pushed it down the hallway and into the back area where Larson had captured them a few hours ago. The drone followed, but instead of gliding, it jerked and bobbed along as if it was running out of energy. The motor hissed and spluttered loudly.

If she didn't know better, she'd think it was malfunctioning, but those things lasted for years and this was a brand-new model.

Renna unlocked the back door and pushed it open onto the watery light of Shalim. "We're almost there, Vik," she said, turning back to him.

Behind her, a zap sparked from the drone's body. Light flashed in an electric arc from the motor, and the thing dropped to the floor.

Metal pieces scattered across the cement, bent and broken. She peered closer, frowning. The insides of the thing had melted together, the wires corroded and twisted. Like it had somehow overheated or malfunctioned.

But it had been working perfectly for Larson. It had worked perfectly until she'd taken control of it. Had she infected it with Samil's virus? Renna stared at the twisted metal. By the gods, had she infected the *Athena*, too?

She took a steadying breath. It didn't matter now. She had to get Viktis out of here. Without a glance back, she headed for the *Fortune's Risk*. There was only one place that could save him now.

THIRTY-SIX

Renna paced the halls of the Ileth hospital on Viktis's home world, waiting for some news of his condition. They'd taken him to surgery three hours ago, and she hadn't heard a word since, despite stopping every nurse that walked by. Her whole body twitched and hummed. She didn't know if it was from stress or from Samil's virus, but it didn't really matter. She had two goals now. Make sure Viktis survived and make sure she warned MYTH about Samil's plans of attack.

After her sixth cup of bitter coffee, one of the nurses finally took pity on her. "He's out of surgery and in the recovery room. You can see him for five minutes."

"Bless you." Renna took the woman's cheeks in her hands and kissed her on the forehead. She followed the nurse back into the recovery room and stopped dead inside the door.

Viktis lay pale and still against the white sheets. The bruise around his eye had darkened to an angry green and a jagged cut stretched across his cheekbone, but at least the holes burned into his skin had been tended to, and his other wounds cleaned.

Renna sank into the chair beside his bed. Gods, she was so tired. Her whole body ached. But she wasn't done yet. Not until he was out of the woods. She slipped her hand into his and squeezed gently. "Don't you dare die on me, Viktis. You're the only one I have left. I can't lose you, too."

"Good thing I'm not going anywhere, then," he said weakly. The one eye that wasn't swollen shut fluttered open.

Relief surged through Renna like a dam breaking. "You're awake."

"And you look like shit. What the hell have you been doing?" He coughed violently, and Renna cringed as she waited for the fit to subside. He grimaced. "Guess I probably don't look so great either."

"You look handsome as always. You'd better watch out or you'll have every nurse in this place eating from your hand by the time they spring you."

He nodded. "A man can hope. So are you going to tell me what happened?"

Renna had been wondering that herself as she paced the halls, but since she only had five minutes with him, it was time for the abbreviated version. "Samil infected my implant with a virus so she could use me to disable the defenses and communication systems at all MYTH facilities. They're cut off and alone. She's going to pick them off one by one. Starting with HQ."

"You have to warn them."

"That's my next stop, but I need a favor. I need to borrow

your pilot and your ship."

Viktis closed his eyes. "Dammit, Renna. I just got her."

"I'll be careful with her, I promise. Please? She's the fastest ship in the sector. She's the only way I can get there in time to save everyone."

He nodded, not lifting his head from the pillow. He looked exhausted and pale, and another pang of guilt twisted in her gut like a knife. He'd been tortured because of her. He'd cared about her enough to put himself in that kind of danger. It was an unfamiliar feeling, this new openness, this feeling of connection. Even if she had to do this alone, she knew he'd always have her back.

"Fine. Take her. But if there's a scratch on her when I get her back..."

"I'll owe you more than the Star Sapphire. I got it." She got to her feet, pressing a gentle kiss to his uninjured cheek. "Focus on getting yourself better, my friend."

"Renna. Don't do anything stupid. Remember you're not in this alone." He squeezed her hand. "Help is out there, just wait for it."

"It's been a fun ride, Viktis. Take care of yourself." She pulled away and forced herself to stride from the room without looking back. He'd never let her live it down if he saw the tears streaming down her face.

Ariz Teray typed a command into the *Fortune's Risk* navigation system, then turned to Renna. "Entering the Mishi system.

We'll be in Titus Beta space momentarily."

She stood from her perch on the co-pilot's chair to get a better view of the planet's green surface. It grew larger by the second as they headed for the MYTH base near the jagged mountain range in the northern hemisphere. The planet was considered Earth-like, but it was far enough away from central coalition space that it was lightly settled. Perfect for a clandestine MYTH headquarters. Those bastards knew their stuff. Too bad they hadn't gotten their heads out of their asses long enough to believe her warning.

Renna rested her hip against the arm of the chair. "Thanks for the ride, Ariz. I'm going to have to face the firing squad one way or another, so as soon as we have clearance to land and I'm off the ship, get the hell out of here. Viktis will catch up with you on Forever Station when he's recovered."

"My pleasure, Renna. Glad I could help." The pilot tapped another command into his system and brought up communications.

"MYTH Base Alpha. This is the *Fortune's Risk* requesting permission to land." Static filled the comm channel for several seconds before he tried again. Finally he shook his head. "They're not answering."

"Shit. Comms must still be down." Renna chewed her lip. "We're going to have to risk landing and hope they don't shoot us out of the air."

"Do you really think that's a good idea?" Ariz asked with a frown.

"We don't have any other choice. Bring us down." She needed to warn them about Samil, and if that meant putting herself at risk, then so be it. In her head, warning them had become her number one priority. Once that was done, everything else was their problem to solve.

Ariz started their descent. They were still forty-thousand kilometers away when the mountain exploded.

A wall of flame burst into the air, followed by the roar of detonation. The whole side of the mountain was gone in an instant, consumed by fire.

The pressure of the explosion slammed into the ship, making it stutter and pitch like a drunken sailor as Ariz tried to regain control

A wordless scream echoed through Renna's mind, and she gripped the back of the pilot's chair to keep from falling. Finn. She clawed at her throat, unable to breathe. Beside her, Ariz's eyes went wide at the destruction.

"Gods," he breathed. "No one could have survived that." He ran a shaking hand across his face before turning to Renna.

But she was frozen. She couldn't rip her gaze from the burning, smoking crater where MYTH HQ used to be. Her whole body felt numb, like she was watching this outside of herself. Was he really gone? Were they all gone?

Black smoke billowed into the air as they circled the space that had once housed thousands of people. The air shimmered with heat, and Ariz ordered the ship to higher, away from ground zero.

"We can't risk landing. The whole area is unstable," he said.

Renna's hands curled into claws, digging harder into the leather of the seat. Her death grip was the only thing keeping her on her feet.

A great gust of wind blew through the central strike area,

clearing the smoke for a few seconds. Fire engulfed everything that could burn—trees, cement, twisted and melted girders. Saltani iron, the strongest metal in the galaxy, dripped like melted plastic.

Ariz was right. No one could have survived that.

A sob tore from Renna's throat, and she felt tears stream down her cheeks. She closed her eyes and tried to reach out to the *Athena*, to feel that connection again, but there was nothing. No tingle, no hum.

Dead.

Finn was gone. Gheewala was gone. Alistair and Jayla. Everyone who'd helped her, who'd been part of her life.

She sank down into the empty seat and curled her arms around her waist. What did she do now? Everything she'd cared about had been ripped from her. There was nothing left.

Except Pallas. Dr. Samil. Whatever the woman called herself, she was a murderer, and she was going to pay for this.

THIRTY-SEVEN

Renna lay curled into a ball on Viktis's bed. Ariz had ordered her to try to get some rest while they flew back to Illia and the hospital. Rest was the last thing she'd be able to do, but the pilot's silent sympathy made her skin crawl. Being alone with her grief was the only way she knew how to deal with this.

She stared out into the blackness of space, unseeing, and angrily wiped away the tear trickling down her cheek. Grief could come later, when she'd stopped Samil once and for all. But how? She needed a better plan than marching in and shooting the bitch in the head. That kind of recklessness would only get Renna killed. And after all this, she couldn't afford to fail now. She owed it to everyone who'd died in that explosion. Finn, Alistair, Commander Jayla, Keva...

Oh gods, someone had to tell Viktis she was gone. She didn't know what had been between the two of them, but she had a feeling it was stronger than he'd let on. Viktis was a lot like her when it came to relationships—letting people in was difficult, but when it happened, he was a vulnerable mess.

Wrapping her arms around her legs, she rested her head on her knees and let her brain churn through options.

Going back to Shalim wasn't really an option. Renna couldn't take the whole facility on by herself, no matter how good a thief she was. She needed to figure out a way to draw the doctor out, to face her one on one. But Samil was the one with all the power now.

She had been from the very beginning, always a step ahead. But how? How did she always seem to know where Renna was going to be before she did?

The click of the intercom echoed through the room, jerking her out of her spinning head. Ariz's voice filled the cabin. "Renna, there's a comm coming through for you."

"Fine. I'll take it in here." The last thing she wanted to do was talk to anyone, but she got to her feet and switched on the holo device on Viktis's desk. It flickered to life, bringing up the image of Dr. Thana Samil.

Pallas.

Hatred flooded through Renna in a blazing rush. She gritted her teeth to keep from screaming, but she knew her loathing was written all over her face.

Samil shook her head sadly. "I'm sorry it had to come to this But MYTH had to be purged. Now it can rise like a phoenix from the ashes to become something better. To actually protect humanity."

"Right. Because creating a cyborg army out of the poor and needy is protecting them," Renna said. "You can lie to yourself all you want, Doctor, but I know you're the biggest monster of us all."

"You misunderstand me, dove. I want to use my new organization to heal instead of hurt, to protect instead of attack. We'll make a difference in this galaxy."

Samil's smug face made every atom in Renna's body twitch with revulsion. "You're definitely making a difference, what with all the murder and experimentation you're doing. Just stop this, Doctor. Face me one on one. Let's end this."

Samil smiled. "That's exactly my plan. You are my key, Renna. I want your altered implant as the hub of my neural network. Your unique physiology will allow me to connect with my teams across the galaxy. I can respond instantly to threats or danger. Think of how much you'll be helping humanity."

"You're fucking insane."

"Insane. Visionary. Whatever you call me, I plan on changing the world. And I've already started. You'll be pleased at the difference I've made in the Izan Tenements."

Ice formed a solid ball in the pit of her stomach. Annet Parra. That's why she'd been in Samil's lab.

"What have you done?" Renna demanded.

"Nothing the residents didn't ask me to do." Samil paused and pulled a vial out of her pocket. "This is the drug Navang injected you with. I've refined it, based on the changes to your DNA. It should allow the transition to occur in a matter of hours once the implants are installed. These new hybrids will be transformed and added to my neural network and completely under my control within twenty-four hours."

Renna shot to her feet. "Leave them alone! They have nothing to do with this."

"But they do. They asked for my help. They want better lives, and my implants will give it to them. They'll be part of my organization—healthy, well-fed, taken care of." She smiled. "Those who survive the transition at least."

Renna remembered all the kids she'd grown up with, the prostitutes who'd helped raise her, the shopkeepers and laundresses who'd worked so hard to get ahead. Samil wanted to change them all. Control them. She couldn't let the woman succeed.

"Come to me, Renna. You have my word. I'll stop building my army. I'm done experimenting on people. I have what I need to make a difference now."

"Your word is worth less than a penis on a Russka," she spat.

Samil ignored her comment. "I know what it is like to be alone. Your lover is dead, and so are most of your friends. There's no one left to save but yourself. I'll be waiting in the tenements for you, Renna. I hope you make the right choice."

The holo flickered off, leaving Renna staring at the blank wall behind it. It was obviously another trap. Samil had given up all pretense of subtlety at this point. She already knew what buttons to push to get Renna to jump through her hoops.

But at this point, what else did Renna have to lose?

If there was a possibility of stopping Samil once and for all, she had to take it. If the woman unleashed this army on the rest of the galaxy... Renna shook her head. It didn't bear even thinking about.

Wrapping her arms around her waist, Renna paced Viktis's cabin. Samil had made it obvious she'd go to any lengths to get Renna. Meeting her on Earth might be a trap, but Renna was dead either way. And the woman was right. Finn and Jayla and Alistair and the rest of the crews of the *Athena* and *Eris* were dead because of Renna. She'd destroyed MYTH HQ just with her presence. She couldn't live with the souls of all those tenement people on her conscience, too.

The only thing left for her was to make it right. And kill the bitch.

THIRTY-EIGHT

Renna pointed at the crumbling landing pad at the edge of the tenements. "You can set her down there, Ariz."

He glanced at her from the corner of his eye. "You sure about this? Viktis is going to kill me when he hears what you've done."

"Tell him I held a gun to your head. He'll believe it." She smiled at the pilot. "Make sure you get his ship back to him without a scratch. I don't want that on my conscience, too." Renna patted down her weapons, verifying she still had her two blasters, three knives, and a pair of small throwing stars tucked into her sleeve. Her lockpicks were hidden in a back pocket, just in case she needed them.

The *Fortune's Risk* touched down with barely a bump, and Renna held out her hand. "It's been a pleasure, Ariz. Fly well."

The Ileth shook it, squeezing her hand at the end. "Good luck, Renna."

She slipped out the open hatch, stepping away from the landing area as Ariz took off. The *Fortune's Risk* was out of sight moments later, and the sudden silence pressed down on her like a heavy hand.

She was alone. Poetic, really. She'd left this place on her own ten years ago; it made sense she'd come back to it the same way.

Renna inhaled deeply. It even smelled like she remembered—dying grass, rusting metal, and the peculiar scent of decay from the river. The shiny skyscrapers of New York were visible across the sluggish black water, kept exclusive by the carefully guarded bridges onto the island.

But here in the tenements, weeds struggled through the cracked cement, and rusting speeders gathered dust where people had abandoned them when they stopped working. At the edge of New York, the people who couldn't afford to live in the floating palaces and glass-windowed buildings crowded against the river, watching as the rich and wealthy lived in ways they could only dream of.

Renna had spent more than a few hours on a bench near the river herself, dreaming of the day when she'd have her own apartment in the city. When she'd own a shiny new speeder and be able to fly to the upper reaches of the place. But now she could see the wear and tear on the once-modern buildings. The steel wasn't quite so shiny; the speeders, not as fast; the perfect lives, nothing more than a mirage.

Renna picked her way across the debris field surrounding the landing pad. Her body went stiff as she spotted a ragged backpack someone had abandoned beneath a well-worn bench. The brown canvas was ripped and ragged. A faded red patch had been sewn to the front flap.

The Rats.

Instantly, she was thirteen again.

She'd been running with the Rats to make some money. She'd done odd jobs for the gang—stealing, gathering secrets, just being a lackey—but she'd carefully hidden every cent of her earnings in a crack in her mother's wall. She needed enough to buy a transport off this world. Anywhere she might be able to find a job—she wasn't picky.

It had been just another day when she'd finally decided to go. Nothing special had happened to send her running, nothing bad was on the horizon. She was just finally ready.

She'd gotten dressed, packed her ratty backpack with three changes of clothes and a holo of her friends, grabbed her credits from the stash in the wall, then shut her bedroom door behind her.

She'd paused outside her mother's darkened room for almost a minute, wondering if she should bother saying goodbye. Her mother wouldn't remember; she was sleeping off her latest over-dose. But Renna had needed to say goodbye for herself.

Taking a deep breath, she'd entered the stuffy bedroom, the burnt-sugar scent of clay still clinging to the bedclothes. Renna had stared down at the woman who'd raised her, who'd tried to kill her, who'd been her best friend and biggest enemy. A thir-teen-year-old hadn't known how to deal with those types of feel-ings. She'd only known mothers weren't supposed to act like that. They were supposed to protect you.

And her mother had failed at that long ago.

Renna had turned and left the apartment without even leaving a note, knowing her mom wouldn't notice she was gone for two days at least. As her ship left the earth's atmosphere, she'd promised herself she'd die before coming back here.

Guess that promise was about to happen.

The skunky smell of cheap coffee jerked her out of her memory. She wrinkled her nose as she walked past a crowded coffee shop. The battery acid she used to buy from there had given her stomachaches for days, but it had been the only thing she could afford, beside the day-old rolls the barista kept for her in back. Just beyond the shop, a towering tenement building shadowed the block.

Her building.

She crossed the street and approached it through the alley, stopping as she entered the open space in front of the building. At one time, someone had called it a park, but the grass was long dead and a rickety swing-set sat at one edge with two broken swings. The tenement kids had used it for pick-up soccer games when she was growing up.

Now she'd be playing a much different game.

THIRTY-NINE

Completely out of place in the decay of the tenement, a gleaming ship sat at the end of the street. Samil's ship. Top of the line Dimensional Striker, if she wasn't mistaken.

But where was Samil?

Renna took a step forward. Her implant port sparked, the skin on the back of her neck starting to burn.

"Shit!" She clutched at it, rubbing against the pain. A high-pitched buzzing filled her ears, worse than the usual hum from her implant. She took another step, and it grew sharper. Was it coming from the ship? She wouldn't put it past Samil to have rigged the whole area with some sort of torture device.

"I'm so disappointed you weren't here waiting for me," Renna called out. "I thought we were friends."

Her sarcasm echoed off the walls and reverberated in her

head. She wanted to press her hands against her ears and shut it out, but Renna forced herself to stand still. Calm. Unconcerned.

"I was gathering the welcome party." Samil's voice had a tinny quality to it, like she was broadcasting over a speaker, and Renna shook her head, trying to clear it.

The doors to the tenement building opened, and a stream of people flowed out. Men, women, even a few children—all with the same gaunt, hungry look Renna remembered from her childhood. Thank the gods she didn't recognize any of them. There were at least a hundred, walking in single file until they reached the far edge of the park. Then the group broke into columns to stand stiffly, like soldiers.

More hybrids.

Samil had already turned them, probably using Renna's DNA. She studied the girl closest to her, barely sixteen, with long, dark hair. She wore a mechanic's coveralls, and her fingers were streaked with grease. A red light flashed deep in her pupils.

A moment later, Samil stepped through the same doors . Her hair was pulled back neatly in a bun, and she wore a tight, white jumpsuit with a white, knee-length coat over it. She practically glowed.

The perfect foil for Renna's own black clothing. Good vs. evil. Except at this point, with the things Renna had done, it was closer to Evil vs. More Evil.

Samil opened her arms. "Renna. So glad you decided to take me up on my offer."

"Me, too." She yanked the pistol from her belt and fired a blast at Samil, aiming for the woman's heart. If she even had one.

The shot went right through her, shattering the glass window behind her. Samil's image wavered for a split second.

"Fuck," Renna spat. Trust the sneaky bitch to be hiding out on her ship. Samil's chuckle filled the space. That would explain the tinny tone. "You forget, my little dove. I know you well enough to guess your plans. I thought a hologram was a wise choice until we were able to come to an agreement."

"And what agreement would that be?" Renna tried not to glance behind her at the shuffle of more feet. Another platoon of tenement residents took up their place with the others. "I don't see that we have much to talk about since you already broke your promise to leave these people alone."

"You don't understand, Renna. They *wanted* this. They were all given a choice, and every single one of them took it. They know what the future will look like. They want to be part of the solution. You should want the same thing."

"You'll forgive me if I don't know what problem you're trying to solve. Free will? Independent thinking?"

"Pain. Poverty. Despair. What good is free will when you're starving to death on the street with no hope for your next meal? Or your neighborhood is being taken over by aliens when an organization like MYTH was supposed to protect you?"

Renna shook her head. "I don't think you give these people enough credit They'd kick any alien's ass if they tried to move in here. But you have this grudge against MYTH that blinds you to everything."

"You still don't get it," Samil said sadly, the hologram shaking its head. "I'm the *solution.* My breakthroughs will change everything. No human will need to die senselessly again. You are the last piece of that puzzle. Your unique physiology will make it possible to reach millions of people. To protect them. Don't you want that, Renna?"

"I want to stop you from hurting anyone else. You've killed thousands of innocent people in your misguided vendetta against MYTH. How do you live with yourself?"

"I know it's for the greater good."

There was no sign of the woman. Dammit. How could she attack if she didn't know where Samil was?

Maybe she could use her implant to try to find her... But would that open her up to Samil's neural network? Would she be strong enough to keep control of her own mind this time?

Dangerous or not, she didn't have much choice. Renna reached out with her implant. The familiar surge of power shot through her brain, making her shudder as she felt the connections opening.

She pushed deeper, letting the feeling of machine and metal become part of her. She could feel the prickle of the electrons and radiation from the nearby buildings. From speeders. Even from Samil's ship itself. The connection wasn't there like it had been with the *Athena*, but she could feel the ship's essence flowing through her.

And something else. A strong, underlying command ordering her to obey Samil. It curled like tendrils around her implant, whispering in her ear. It was dark and insidious, and somehow it had affected every electronic device in the area. Anything that came within range would be infected. Samil would be able to control it.

Renna pushed it away. It didn't matter. She already was infected, and right now she needed to find the doctor.

"I didn't want to have to do this," Samil said. Her voice had lost the tinny sound of the holo, and Renna opened her eyes to find the real Samil standing on the steps of the building across from her. A thin, haggard woman stood beside her.

A bottomless pit of guilt, hatred, and fear opened in Renna's chest.

Samil had her mother.

FORTY

Ryla Carrizal looked exactly the same as Renna remembered—wispy brown hair, sunken blue eyes, hollow cheeks, angry scar stretching from cheek to eyebrow. Renna even thought she recognized her dress. The years hadn't been kind to her mother, and neither had the drugs. It was shocking she was even still alive.

Samil stepped forward, bringing Ryla with her. "I find it so very interesting my best test subjects come from the slums. Drug addicts, dealers, anyone who's dabbled in clay. Somehow the drug works brilliantly with my neural implants. Ryla was almost as good a test subject as you."

Half of Renna's mother's head was shaved, replaced with a shiny metal plate. The skin was still red and raw where the two had been fused together.

Acid burned the back of Renna's throat, but she steadied her voice. "What did you do to her?"

"I wanted to see if it ran in the family. I gave your mother a cranial implant, as well as upgrading some of her nervous system. It's taken beautifully. Though she doesn't have your communication abilities, unfortunately."

"Renna? Is that you, baby?" The woman's voice was like gravel, wavering weakly as Ryla peered out at her. "I can't tell if it's her, Doctor," Renna's mother said, looking back at Samil. "She looks so different."

"It's her," Samil said. "Renna, aren't you going to say hello to you mother?"

Renna blinked at the woman she'd been running from most of her life. The woman she'd never been able to escape. Her whole body twisted with tension, her limbs trembling and weak. She couldn't do this. Dealing with her mother was not part of the plan.

Samil continued. "Your mom happily agreed to help me with my latest round of experiments. I've promised she'll be clean and healthy in six months."

"That's what you've always wanted, right, baby?" Ryla twisted her fingers in the front of her dirty dress.

Black spots appeared in Renna's vision as the world spun. "Leave her alone, Samil."

"Or what? Your mother wants what's best for you, and she knows this is the only way to get her life back together. I can give her a future."

"You've already taken away her future."

"Please, baby. She said once I'm clean you'll forgive me. We can start over." Ryla's hollow eyes bored into Renna's. There was remorse there, but something else as well. Love, perhaps?

It was far too late for that. "Starting over isn't an option. But trusting Samil will only get you killed. Just walk away, Mom."

"To what?" Ryla's calm shattered as her voice rose to a warbling screech. "I'm living on the streets now, Renna. I can barely scrape enough money together for a hit of clay. Before the doctor found me, I hadn't eaten in days. And it's not like *you've* taken care of me. I hear you're better off than the president. Is it too much to ask you to help support your poor old mother?"

Renna's fists clenched, but she forced herself to stay silent.

When she didn't respond, Renna's mother continued. "Dr. Samil promised she'd take care of me. She says it's not too late for me." Ryla's eyes narrowed. "That's more than you ever did. You gave up on me a long time ago."

Hurt surged through Renna like a punch to the gut, and her words erupted in a volcano of hate and anger before she could pull herself together. "I gave up on you when you tried to slit my throat in a drug-fueled rage. Did you forget about that? Or the times you were too high to even remember you had a child? Or is it still somehow my fault you're in this situation?"

She glared at the woman who'd become a stranger. She'd wanted to confront her mother for so long, to tell her how she'd ruined Renna's life, but this woman was beyond that now. She'd never take responsibility for what had happened. It was up to Renna to finally let it go.

Her anger drained away as quickly as it had come. She felt lighter almost. It didn't matter anymore. She wasn't the same child who'd left this place. She'd created a new life for herself. After searching for years, she'd found a new family. And right now the only hatred she should feel should be toward Samil for taking them away.

Renna stepped forward, glaring at the doctor. "Samil, release these people. Release my mother. You promised."

She shrugged. "I promised to not perform any more experiments. This is my final group of hybrids, and the most powerful, thanks to your DNA." She raised her arm, and another line of people exited the building and took up their spots with the others.

"You know I'm going to stop you, right?"

Samil smiled. "You won't because, with one command, I could have your own mother shoot you where you stand. I could have my army swarm you."

"But what's the fun in that?" Renna asked. "Don't you want to face me yourself?"

"I'm afraid your taunts won't work on me, Renna. Now let's move this conversation to my ship. Unless you'd like me to kill your mother while you watch."

Renna's hand slipped to her waist to unsnap her holster. If only she were as good a shot as she was a thief.

But before she could twitch a finger, the roar of a ship filled the air. Pain burst through her as Renna's implant short circuited, and she gasped, locking her knees so she didn't tumble to the ground.

Every hybrid turned to watch the ship land beside Samil's at the end of the block.

The static in her brain slowly cleared, and her eyes could focus again. Her heart skipped a beat. "The *Athena*," she breathed. But how was that possible?

She held perfectly still, her gaze never leaving the ship as she tried to connect with it again.

There! A tiny sliver of the old *Athena* greeted her, the familiar electromagnetic pulse wrapping around her like a friend's hug.

Something hot prickled behind her eyes, and she brushed away a tear. They were alive.

The gangplank slowly lowered, and three people strode out, guns at the ready.

"Nick," she whispered. He was dressed in MYTH gray again, his uniform pressed and clean. He walked with a purpose, and as their gazes met across the park, there was that jolt she'd felt the first time she'd seen him again. Like he was the only one who knew her. Lieutenant Keva and Major Dallas flanked him on either side, their faces grim as they surveyed the scene.

Anger surged though her like a sun flare. At her relief to see him, at his betrayal, at the confusion that flooded through her. Godsdammit. The man was still alive, and he hadn't bothered to tell her. Again.

His eyes met hers hesitantly, and he gave her a half-smile. Instead of smiling back, she could only glare. If she hadn't been so fucking upset at his death, she'd kill him herself right now. But that familiar expression sent her skin tingling, despite her anger. She wanted to strangle him and kiss him at the same time.

"Hey, Ren," he said softly as he approached. "You all right?"

"No thanks to you," she snapped, but her heart still hitched at hearing her name on his lips.

Samil cleared her throat, drawing their gazes back to her. "Welcome, Major. Captain. I thought I'd taken care of you with your other comrades. I see you escaped."

Dallas aimed his gun at Samil. "As a matter of fact we did. Luckily, the *Athena* got a warning message before the attack began. We were able to evacuate quite a few of our facilities before your drones struck."

Relief flooded through Renna. It had worked. Her connection with the *Athena* had saved lives. She turned back to Samil. "For someone so smart, you sure do make a lot of mistakes."

For the first time in days, she truly believed they were going to beat this woman. They were going to win. And then she was going to have a serious discussion with Captain Nick Finn.

Samil shook her head. "I prefer to think of it as an experiment, not a mistake. Because each time I fail, I learn something new. For example, after you escaped my warehouse, I realized the virus had indeed connected you to my neural network, but you'd resisted a full upload. Which allowed me to alter the frequency and gain more control over my followers. It also allowed me to create a failsafe. If you came in contact with the network again, I laid a trap that would allow me to connect to your implant."

"Doesn't seem to be working," Renna said with a shrug. "Give yourself up, doctor. There's nowhere else for you to run."

"I don't need to run." Samil pulled a small tablet from the pocket of her white coat.

Renna rolled her eyes and reached for her gun. Her hand stopped halfway to her hip. She blinked at her non-responding limb, trying to flex her fingers, but her arm wouldn't move. Like it was made entirely of cement.

Her gaze flew to Finn's. "Run!"

FORTY-ONE

"N obody move," Samil barked. Whatever the woman planned to do with Renna wasn't going to be good. She needed to get Finn and the *Athena* out of here. "Finn. You need to run!"

"I'm not going anywhere, Ren," he said softly. "I let MYTH convince me that pretending to betray you would be the best way to get Samil out in the open. I'm not turning my back on you again."

Gods, how she wanted to believe him, but she was still so hurt, so angry at his betrayal that she could barely speak. She stared at him, trying to read the expression in his eyes and finding nothing but regret.

"So touching, this little reunion." Samil pressed a finger to the tablet, and Renna's arm jerked again.

Beside Samil, Renna's mother had pressed her hands to her

lips, her frail body trembling as she watched the scene unfold. Tears welled in Ryla's eyes, but she still stood at the doctor's side, a mute servant.

Screw her. Renna tried to clench her muscles, to stop the movement of her body, but she had no control over anything. Her arm straightened, and she tried to struggle as Samil made her grab the gun at her waist.

"Please, Finn. Get out of here now," she begged. "I can't control this."

He shook his head. "Fight it, Ren. You can't let her win."

Even furious at him, she couldn't face the prospect of losing him again. It had felt like someone had ripped out her heart and left it beating on the ground. If nothing else, she could make sure they were all safe. "I'm the only one who can stop this. Let me go, Finn."

Finn's lips thinned. "I'm not letting you do this alone, Ren."

The gun was heavy in her hand as she raised it. Tears streamed down her face. "Please." She didn't know if she was begging Finn or Samil or some unknown god. She just needed it all to stop before Samil made her shoot someone she loved.

"I don't want to hurt anyone else," Dr. Samil called. "Come with me now, and I'll let your mother and your friends live."

Renna glanced at Major Dallas, still pointing his gun at Samil. At Keva, who wore a grim expression and carried a shiny new rifle. At Finn. She couldn't live with their deaths. It might be too late to save the tenement residents, but it wasn't too late to save her friends.

"Let them go," she called to Samil. "I'll come with you."

"Renna! What are you doing?" Finn demanded, grabbing her

other arm.

She shook her head. "We have to stop her. This is the only way I know how."

"No!"

She smiled sadly at him. "I'm glad you're alive, Finn. I could barely live with myself thinking you were gone. Please do this for me."

"No. Renna, we can stop her together."

"We can't. She'll make me kill you. Get out of here while you can. I have a plan. Trust me. You owe me that at least."

Finn's gaze flicked to Samil and then back to Renna. "I do. But I don't trust her."

"Go."

He frowned at her, pain seeping into his blue eyes. "But it's not supposed to end like this."

"It's not supposed to end at all, but sometimes life has other plans. Despite your recent lapse in judgment, you've turned into a good man, Nicholas Finn. I'm proud to have known you." *To have loved you*, she almost added.

He traced a finger down her cheek and pulled her into his arms, kissing her gently. "Don't make me do this, Renna," he whispered.

"You don't have a choice. You have to get as far away from the *Athena* as possible. As soon as you landed, she took control of the ship with her network, and I don't know what she's planning." Renna's muscles tightened, and her brain throbbed as Samil ordered her other arm to move. "Go," she said.

Finn spun on his heel, barking commands into his comm with one last long look at Renna. The *Athena's* crew sprinted from the ship, and the platoon quick-marched away from the tenements.

"Now that your touching goodbye is over, I have my own goodbyes to take care of," Samil said. "Did you really think I'd let them leave? Poor Renna."

The hybrids surrounding the park suddenly snapped to attention, eyes flashing red.

"No! I'm coming with you. You don't need them," Renna protested, feeling the tug of the neural network surge through her as well.

"You should know by now that I hate loose ends." The hybrids marched like a well-oiled army platoon after Finn's team.

But Renna's mother hadn't moved, hadn't obeyed the command to follow the *Athena's* crew. Ryla watched them go with a frown, then her gaze fell to Samil. Renna wished she knew what was going through her mother's mind. Was she happy with her choice? Was she truly Samil's slave? Or was there something else left inside?

Ryla smiled sadly at her daughter. "I wish things could have been different, Renna. I wish I'd been the mother you deserved. I'm sorry for everything, but I'm so proud of the woman you've become."

Before Renna could react, Ryla launched herself at Samil, knocking the tablet from the woman's hand. It went spinning away from them, kicking up a trail of dust.

Instantly, the painful pressure in her brain cut off, and Renna's arm dropped to her side. She was free.

Across the park, Samil and her mom struggled together on the ground. Gray dust streaked Samil's once-white coat and her neat bun hung in scraggles down her back as she flipped Renna's mother onto her back. Ryla's worn dress was torn and her face battered, but she was holding her own.

Until Samil dug her fingers into the fresh scar's on Ryla's head.

Renna's mother let out a bloodcurdling scream as she flailed beneath the doctor. Ryla's fingers clawed at Samil's face, but years of drug use and starvation had made her weak, and Samil easily overpowered her.

Renna's body unfroze, and she dashed toward the tablet, toward the two women. She had no idea what she was going to do, but she had a few tricks up her sleeve, along with a knife or two.

Four steps later, she knew she was too late. "No!" Renna screamed, stretching out a hand.

Samil had snatched up the tablet from where it lay on the ground. Her fingers tapped frantically at the screen.

The world slowed to a crawl. Renna slipped the throwing star from her sleeve and pulled her arm back. As she released it, Samil smiled down at Renna's mother.

Ryla screamed again as the implant in her head exploded.

FORTY-TWO

N o!" Renna screamed again. Her knees gave out, and she dropped to the ground as the plate in her mother's head disintegrated. Smoke poured from the wound, and Ryla went still.

Samil struggled to her feet. Dirt smudged her face as she studied Ryla's crumpled form. "Don't cry, dove. She wasn't much of a loss. Besides, she was mostly machine. I'm sure she didn't feel a thing."

"Bitch." Renna clawed upright on trembling legs. "I am going to kill you."

Samil shook her head. "I don't think so."

In the distance, a volley of gunshots echoed through the alley, and Renna's head snapped toward the noise. *Finn.*

"Looks like my army is tying up those loose ends. Time to finish this."

A moment later, Renna's whole body jerked forward as Samil controlled her again. It felt inevitable somehow. Like everything had been leading to this moment. She didn't even try to fight it this time.

Renna glanced back at her mother's lifeless form as she followed the doctor up the stairs to Samil's ship. From here she could see only part of her mother's face, eyes closed, lines softened. For the first time in Ryla's life, she finally looked at peace. Renna had mourned the loss of her mother years ago, but today she'd seen another side of her. A side she wished she'd known.

Renna tore her gaze away as Samil ordered her through the hatch and down a narrow corridor lit with bright hololights. Her footsteps rang on the metal floors as they marched through the ship, and she tried to get a sense of where she was. Dimensional Striker models were short-distance transports and ran with minimal crew. Only a pilot and a helmsman, but she didn't see either as she followed the doctor to a small med lab at the back of the ship.

Still under Samil's control, Renna's knees bent, forcing her to sit in one of the stiff metal chairs. Her right arm lifted on its own accord to rest on the small table in front of her.

"You haven't tortured me enough by now?" Renna asked.

"I know how much you enjoy it. Just wanted to make you feel at home." Samil's smile was sweet as she slid an IV into Renna's arm and slapped some kind of sensor to her forehead.

Renna's skin stung and burned as the drug seeped into her veins, but she couldn't move her arm. The panic started deep in her gut, growing stronger until she gasped for air. Squeezing her eyes shut, she forced herself to take a deep breath as the pounding in her head grew louder. She hadn't felt like this since she was a kid, since she'd been unable to fight back when her mother had attacked her.

She'd trained in three different forms of self-defense to make sure she'd never feel that way again. Except here she was, back where it had all started.

"Not much longer now and you'll be completely integrated. I'll be able to use you to control my entire army. From anywhere in the galaxy. We'll be able to do so much good together, dove."

Samil sounded practically gleeful, but Renna didn't break her concentration. Nothing mattered any more besides stopping this woman. Samil's ship shuddered as they prepped for takeoff. It was now or never.

Renna reached out with her mind, searching for the *Athena* again. The virus running through her had damaged Renna's connection with the ship, but she could still feel it there, at the edge of her consciousness. Tendrils of electromagnetic waves curled into her, weaving into the implant and the neural network that hummed through Renna. She might be part of Samil's plan, but she still had enough control to use that to her advantage.

She found the cracks in Samil's network, the places where she could feel the *Athena* even more strongly, and focused on widening them until she could feel the ship's controls, the familiar sense of belonging.

But there was something else there now. Something dark and monstrous. The virus had already populated through the *Athena's* systems. Guilt twisted through her. She knew now that she'd infected it earlier, when she'd tried to send the coordinates from Samil's warehouse. The *Athena* was dying.

She couldn't focus on that. She needed to control the *Athena's* weapon systems before they took off. Renna slipped further into the ship, becoming part of the system. Fear clogged her throat and set her pulse racing. She didn't want to die, but she was out of options.

With only an order to her implant, she rewired one of the ship's missiles to fire.

She thought of Finn's heart-twisting smile. Of Myka's unconditional belief in her goodness. Of Viktis's sexy laugh. She was doing this for them, but gods, she wasn't ready to leave yet.

But a good thief always knew when a job was up, and with one last command, she entered the firing codes.

The sirens in Samil's ship screamed as the proximity sensors felt the *Athena's* targeting system locking on.

Samil jerked her head up from her tablet, eyes widening. "What did you do?"

Renna smiled. "I won."

The explosion sent the ship careening across the landing pad. A whole section of the roof blew off, sending cargo and goods flying into the sky. Renna flew across the med bay, landing in a tangle on the far side of the room. Her leg cracked under her as she fell, and she screamed at the white-hot pain shooting through her.

The metal side of the ship shrieked, shearing off as it scraped against the cement. She gasped for air as smoke filled the med compartment, thick and heavy with the scent of star fuel and burnt plastic. Something warm trickled down her face, and she touched a finger to the blood on her cheek. Somehow she was still alive.

She forced her gaze to focus on the dark, smoky interior of the med bay. Across the room, Samil moaned, shifting from beneath a tray of tools. Even worse, *she* was alive.

Renna felt her muscles clench and unclench as Samil lost control of her and the neural network disconnected. Every cell ached like she'd been beaten to a bloody pulp by a Trezian, but she forced herself to sit up, inch by inch, using every last bit of her strength to keep from vomiting as pain rolled through her in waves.

As she tried to drag herself across the floor, the ship suddenly tilted as it settled against one of the tenement buildings. Renna slid across the slick tiles, landing with a thud against the wall. She panted shallowly, trying to avoid sucking in any of the smoke rolling into the cabin.

Evidently, she should have used two missiles. Who would have thought MYTH would cheap out on their ballistics? She giggled hysterically.

Pull it together, Renna.

Ignoring the pain shooting through her, she continued forward. As she scrabbled through the debris, she spotted a shiny scalpel from Samil's tray. Her hand curled around the handle, the cool metal lending her strength.

The doctor lay near the door. Less than eight feet away. She could do this.

Inch by inch, Renna crawled closer to the doctor, dragging her injured leg behind her.

Six feet.

Four feet.

Each inch was a victory in itself.

Samil bolted upright, eyes wild as she squinted through the smoke. She met Renna's gaze, a flicker of pain shooting across her face as she scrambled to her feet.

Renna tensed, gripping the scalpel tightly, ready for the doctor's next move. But instead of attacking, Samil stumbled from the bay, away from Renna.

Dammit. She was going to escape.

Renna tried to climb to her feet, but agonizing pain shot through her leg as soon as she tried to put pressure on it. She gasped and collapsed back to the floor with a hiss. Broken.

She had to finish this. Dragging herself across the floor, she made it to the med bay door as another smaller explosion shook the ship. One of the small fuel cells must have caught fire.

Heat seared the side of Renna's face as a fireball shot through the space. Her cheek throbbed angrily, but she forced herself to move again toward the gaping hole in the side of the ship. The metal had been torn away like tinfoil, the edges ragged, but outside, sunlight streamed through the smoke billowing from the ship.

Hand over hand, she clawed her way out. With a great push, she tumbled through the hole to land in the dirt beneath the ship. Renna screamed as her leg twisted beneath her. Bone ripped through skin as her broken shin shifted.

Pain. So much pain. If she didn't do something, she was going to pass out. A command to her implant turned off her neural receptors, and the agony stopped like someone had cut power to her brain. She knew it hurt, could see how bad it looked, but luckily she couldn't feel a blessed thing.

Across the park, Samil limped toward the *Athena*, clutching her side. Her white coat was streaked with blood, her hair hanging in lank strands around her pale face. The bitch was going to get away.

Even worse, Samil still had her tablet. With a quick tap, she locked onto the *Athena's* controls, brought down the hatch, and climbed in. A few seconds later, six hybrids ran toward the ship at full speed, thundering up the gangplank as they boarded. Enough crew to get the *Athena* off the ground.

The door slid shut behind them, and the ship's engines roared to life.

Fuck.

Renna watched helplessly as the *Athena* started to rise. On the bottom of the ship, the missile bay doors opened. The ship cleared the top of the tallest building, and Renna realized what Samil was planning. Dear gods, she was going to attack the tenements.

An arc of fire shot from the bottom of the ship as one of the bombs burst from the bay. She watched in horror as it hit a nearby building, erupting in a surge of flame and heat. The explosion thundered through the neighborhood.

As smoke rose from the destroyed upper level, Renna watched another missile descend from the belly of the ship.

What was left for Samil to target?

Renna stilled. The missile was for her. If Samil couldn't use Renna for her evil plans, she didn't want anyone else to either. And with Renna out of the way, she'd be able to escape and regroup with her new data.

Then no one would be able to stop her.

The *Athena* picked up speed, shooting toward the Earth's atmosphere as the missile locked into position.

"I'm so sorry," Renna whispered as she closed her eyes. She slipped back into her connection with the *Athena*, saying her goodbyes to the ship before she found the switch in the command systems. Every MYTH ship had one.

Self-destruct.

As if it could feel Renna's intent, the *Athena* bucked and shuddered against her mind. It might have only been the ship clearing the atmosphere, but it felt like panic beating against Renna's implant.

Samil's neural network felt like cold tendrils in her mind as it reached out to capture her again. It had already infiltrated the ship, using the comm field to broadcast its signal to Samil's army. The doctor could still control them. Which meant Finn and the others were still in danger.

Using the ship's electromagnetic field, she found Samil standing beside the pilot's chair. The woman's blood-streaked face was gleeful.

"Fire at will, then head for Centa IV," she ordered the hybrid pilot. "We'll regroup there and figure out our next strategy."

The hybrid pilot started typing Samil's command into the console.

If only there was another option. But somehow it felt like this was meant to be the end. The *Athena* had saved all of their lives more than once. If she was already dying from Samil's virus, perhaps her last sacrifice wouldn't be in vain.

Renna's heart broke as she slipped the last piece of code into place.

Sirens screamed throughout the ship. *"Warning. Warning. Self-destruct in twenty seconds."*

Samil's eyes went wide as the blinking timer counted down on the console. "What the hell is going on? Shut it off!"

The hybrid pounded at the controls, but nothing worked. The *Athena* shot closer to space.

Thirteen.

Twelve.

Eleven.

"Do something!" Samil screamed. She slammed her fist down on the control panel, but the numbers ticked closer to zero.

"Goodbye, Doctor," Renna said, leaning back against the ground and closing her eyes. She caressed the ship one last time and shut off the connection. "Goodbye, my friend."

Above her, the *Athena* burst into a searing fireball, the boom echoing through the air a moment later.

The gunfire in the distance ceased as every hybrid went offline.

The *Athena* had sacrificed itself to save them all.

She glanced upward, at the remains of the *Athena* drifting in ashes through the afternoon sky. It was so pretty. Like snow in spring.

And then the pain flooded back through Renna in a blinding wave.

Everything went dark.

FORTY-THREE

Whe Renna woke, the first thing she noticed was the silence. For the first time in weeks, the strange electric humming in her head was gone. She blinked at the warm, afternoon sunlight streaming through the windows, a soft breeze ruffling the gauzy curtains.

Had she died?

Renna shifted on the bed and hissed as pain burned through her leg. Not dead then. In a hospital. She focused on taking in the rest of the room—the soft bed, the pale yellow walls and muted artwork that could grace a museum, the state-of-the-art holo-monitor tracking her vitals.

Not exactly the usual hospital room.

The soft snick of a door opening drew her gaze, and Finn poked his head in. His smile was as bright as the sun.

"Can I come in?" he asked.

She nodded, feeling strangely tongue-tied as emotions swirled through her. He was still alive. But he'd lied to her and betrayed her. And she still loved him. Renna had no idea how to handle any of those feelings. Maybe she didn't need to right now. Maybe just seeing him was enough.

Finn pulled up a chair beside her bed and cupped her cheek, looking deep into her eyes. "I thought we'd lost you."

"You should know by now I'm tougher than I look."

He smiled. "Thank the stars for that. When we found you in the wreckage, you weren't moving, your leg was broken in three places, and you'd lost a lot of blood. Luckily the *Eris* swooped in just in time, and we were able to get you here to the MYTH hospital. I've never seen Alistair bark orders like that before."

"Is everyone else all right? What happened?" She studied him closely, looking for signs of pain, but Finn looked handsome as always. Clean-shaven, dressed in his captain's uniform, and completely unharmed.

He nodded. "The *Athena's* crew took up a stand at the edge of the river, but we were quickly overwhelmed by the hybrids. One of them shot Keva and one of the mechanics died, but the rest of us were still fighting when we saw the *Athena* take off. I was sure that was it—sure we were going to die and you were already gone. And then it exploded." Finn gazed out the window. "She was the best ship I've ever flown."

"I'm sorry. It was the only way."

Finn sniffed and turned back to her. "I know. She'd be proud that she saved all of us. As soon as she burst into flames, the hybrids froze, like someone had cut their puppet strings. Then they collapsed. Whatever happened killed them all instantly."

Renna closed her eyes against the pain. More deaths on her tab.

"Hey," Finn said, touching her arm. "It's not your fault."

"I know. But they were family once. They didn't deserve to die like that."

"But we stopped Samil and put an end to all of this. It's not perfect, but maybe it's enough." He stroked a piece of hair back from her forehead. "How do you feel?" His gaze dropped to her neck, and she knew he was talking about her mom.

"Conflicted. She was never there for me growing up. I hated her for so long because of that, because of this." Renna ran a finger along the scar stretching from her ear and down her neck. "But in the end, she sacrificed herself for me. She knew what would happen if she attacked Samil, but she did it anyway. For that moment, she was my mom again."

Tears welled in her eyes, and she brushed them away.

"It's okay to grieve, Renna," Finn said gently. "It's okay to feel conflicted. She was a complicated woman. But she loved you in her own way. Hold on to that."

She smiled at him through watery eyes. "Dammit, I wasn't going to cry today."

"I won't tell." He squeezed her hand. "I have some good news if you want it. Maybe that'll help."

"Of course."

"Aldani examined you and your implant."

Her heart jumped. "Yes?"

"He doesn't know how, but the integration with your nervous system is complete. And it looks like it's developed in a way that has created a symbiotic relationship. You're still you—just enhanced."

She furrowed her eyebrows. She should feel relieved, but instead she just felt confused. "I don't understand."

"You know how vaccines work, right? You inject a small part of the disease you're trying to prevent into the person, and it allows you to develop antibodies. Well, somehow Samil's virus did the same thing. Instead of fighting your implant, your body has started working with it. Accepting it."

Renna shook her head. "Maybe that'll make more sense when I've had a few days to think about it."

"Whatever you need. I'm just happy you're still you." He traced circles across the top of her hand with his thumb, and happiness shot through her in a wave so strong it took her breath away.

"Me too," she said, smiling at him.

A soft knock sounded at the door, and Major Dallas pushed it open. "Up for another visitor, my dear?"

Renna's gaze snapped to him, her contentment draining away. He was the last person she wanted to see right now, and based on the sheepish expression on his face, Dallas knew it.

He didn't wait for her answer, but strode into the room, taking up a position at the foot of her bed. "I owe you an apology, Renna."

"You owe me more than that." She knew she should be furious at him and at Finn, but right now she was too exhausted to summon the energy.

Dallas nodded. "I know. But let me say my piece. Commander Jayla told me what was going on after your first stop at Titan Industries. I was skeptical, but then came the attack on headquarters and it all made sense. I wasn't expecting it to be Dr. Samil, but eventually that made sense, too. The commander kept me posted on what happened after finding Wall, and we came up with a plan we hoped would give us an advantage over Samil. The doctor obviously had spies within MYTH, and sending you out on your own seemed like the best way to draw her out."

He ran a hand through his salt-and-pepper hair. "Finn protested violently. He thought we could do it another way. But Admiral Usamov and I decided this plan was our best shot. You are smart, resilient, and tough. We knew you could get it done. We made a mistake."

Renna glowered at him. "Damn right you did. If I'd had back up, we probably could have ended this back at Blur's warehouse, and Viktis would never have been tortured."

"I know. We underestimated her at every move." Dallas raised his gaze from the foot of the bed to meet her gaze. "Which is why we'd like to offer you a special position within MYTH. We need someone like you on our team, someone who can think outside the box and keep us all honest."

She let out a bark of laughter, then winced as pain shot through her mid-section. "Are you saying you need a thief to keep you honest?"

"Yes. If nothing else, this fiasco has shown us that MYTH needs to change. It needs to refocus and find its way again. And I think you can help."

"What if I don't want to? I seem to remember you promising me a full pardon and a fancy house on Paradisio Prime when this was all over."

Dallas seemed to deflate, but he nodded. "Of course. We've already wired the credits to your account. If you choose to retire, we'll honor our agreement."

Beside her, Finn sat stiffly, his gaze focused on the floor, but she could tell every word put him further on edge. What the hell was going on?

"I'll need to think about it, Major. I'm in no shape to be making those kinds of decisions right now."

"Of course. Just know that we'll do everything in our power to make our mistake right. You'll have your own crew, your own ship, your own missions to run as you see fit. We need you, Renna."

Dallas saluted her and strode from the room, shutting the door softly behind him.

Silence stretched awkwardly between Finn and Renna, and she picked at the edge of her blanket. What the hell did she say to him? What did she even want?

"I need you too, Renna," he finally said, still not looking at her. "I can't lose you again. Lying to you was the hardest thing I've ever done. I thought I was protecting you, but I know I made a mistake. I am a MYTH captain, through and through, but you are more important to me than anything else, even MYTH. I should have stopped this plan as soon as Dallas suggested it."

"And how exactly would you have done that without ending up in the brig for treason again?" She let out a low sigh. "I'm still hurt and angry about it, but I get it. I might have done the same thing. But Finn, I'm not MYTH material. I'm a thief. It's what I do."

"That's why you'd be heading up part of the MYTH Intelligence Agency. Who better to catch a thief than another thief?"

His crooked grin made her heart clench. If she accepted, if she truly became part of MYTH, everything would change.

Except everything had already changed.

She'd fallen in love with this man. Could she really leave him and go back to her old life? Did she even want that life anymore? When Dallas had first recruited her, all she'd wanted was to get the hell out of accepting contracts and retrieving difficult items. Becoming a part of MYTH would certainly slam the door on her past.

She had no idea what the future might look like. Except she wanted to be with Finn.

"What happens to us if I join?" she asked, slanting a glance at him. "Doesn't MYTH have fraternization rules?"

"I think Dallas will make an exception. I've already made him promise I'll be part of your crew if you decide to accept his offer."

"Really?" Her voice went higher than she would have liked, and she cleared her throat to cover it.

"Do you really think I'd let you go off and have all the fun by yourself? I know the kinds of trouble you get up to. Trouble that's sorely missing in my own life." He grinned again. "I know it's a big change. I know it's not what you ever planned for or wanted, but I love you, Renna. And I'll take you however I can get you, even if it's only temporary, even if I'm just your ship's captain."

"Nick, you can captain my ship any time."

He groaned. "That was awful."

A smirk twisted her lips. "Hey, just getting you back." She sobered quickly and touched his hand where it lay beside her on the bed. "You're right. I never saw this coming. For fuck's sake, a month ago I thought you were dead. Now I've gone and fallen in love with you and I don't know how to handle it." She paused as his expression lightened and added softly, "But I'm willing to try to figure it out."

"That's enough for me." Finn stood, letting his fingers caress the scar on her neck before moving to her jaw. For the first time in her life, she didn't flinch or feel embarrassed.

He turned her face so she had to look at him. "I never doubted you for a moment."

"Well, I promised I'd kill her. And you know how I feel about promises."

"I do indeed." A wicked smile curved his lips as he brought them to hers. Heat shot through her at his touch.

He pulled away slightly. "And I promise whatever you decide about joining MYTH, I'm going to take you to that beach on Paradisio Prime for a very long, very private vacation once you're better."

"I'm going to hold you to that," she said with a grin, pulling him back down to seal the promise with a kiss.

EPILOGUE

A warm breeze rustled through the palm fronds above them, and Renna snuggled her head against Finn's bare chest. The sunlight felt like cashmere against her skin, and her whole body was more relaxed than she'd ever been. Two weeks in paradise with a handsome captain would do that to a girl.

Finn's fingers traced circles along her lower back, and she arched her naked body against him. "Keep doing that and we're going to have to start all over again, Nick," she said with a smile. "Your record from yesterday still stands. I think we may need to try to break it."

He chuckled, his laugh sounding warm and rich in her ear. "You're insatiable, woman. I need to recover before we try that again."

His hand moved higher until he could play with her long hair.

He stroked it gently and gazed off at the sparkling blue ocean just feet away.

They'd been on Paradisio Prime for almost two weeks and had spent most of it in their private bungalow on the beach, only leaving to pick up their food deliveries at the end of the road. Not another human in sight.

The perfect vacation.

But Renna recognized that tiny furrow between Finn's eyebrows. He was worried about something.

"What are you thinking?" she asked, stroking her fingers through the dark hair that dusted his chest.

He shrugged. "Our time here is almost up, and you still haven't made a decision about joining MYTH."

She let out her breath in a low sigh. She'd been putting off thinking about it. Focusing on the present was good enough for her, especially after the month she'd just had.

"Finn, I just don't know. If I do this, it'll change everything between us. We'll be working together. Living together. Can we handle that?"

She loved being with him, loved the way his scent wrapped around her when they spent time together, and how safe he made her feel. But joining MYTH would be a huge step in their relationship. They'd be assigned to the same ship, the same missions. There was bound to be conflict between them on how to handle each assignment. Would it bring them closer together or drive them apart?

"Nothing will change, Renna," he said softly. "I already know I love you. I already know I want to be with you. And this is the best of all options. I'm usually gone for six months out of the year on missions. It would kill me to be away from you that much. This way we don't have to."

Her whole body tensed. She stared at the waves crashing against the golden sand as she forced herself to relax. "I love you, too, Finn, but I'm not sure I'm ready for that kind of relationship. I'm still the same person, Finn. With the same hang-ups. Falling in love with you hasn't changed that." Renna untangled herself from him and sat up, drawing her knees to her chest so she could face him. The breeze off the water gently blew her hair across her face, and she pushed it behind her ears.

He propped himself up on an elbow. The sun highlighted the chiseled planes of his chest, the scars from his many missions that marred his skin. "I'll give you all the space you need, Renna. You know that. But we promised to see this through."

She sighed and rubbed the bridge of her nose. She felt herself wavering. "Why do you have to be so damned reasonable all the time?"

His grin took her breath away. "Because you know I'm right."

A chirp came from inside the bungalow, both of them turning to gaze into the dark interior.

"Dammit. That's my comm. MYTH frequency," Finn said. "I should take this."

"Is that going to be your answer every time we're in the middle of something and MYTH calls?" she asked with a raised eyebrow.

"Renna..."

She waved a hand. "Fine, go answer it."

He got to his feet and pressed a kiss to her forehead. She enjoyed the view of his naked ass as he wandered into the bungalow. The man had the muscles of a god.

But was that enough to risk everything? Was she being a coward by turning down MYTH's offer? If nothing else, the mess with Samil had taught her to grab life by both hands because you never knew when it was going to end. She'd thought Finn was dead, and it had broken her heart. That had to mean something. Maybe it was enough to stay with him for a mission or two. See what happened. She could always hop a transport ship if things got too weird.

Finn poked his head out of the bungalow. He'd thrown on a loose, linen shirt and a pair of shorts. "Renna. It's Dallas. You need to get in here."

"Dallas had better know exactly how far I'm going to kick his ass for interrupting our vacation," she muttered as she got to her feet. "What does he want?" she asked as she slipped into the robe Finn held out for her.

"He has our first mission." Finn searched her face, something unreadable behind his eyes. "If you choose to accept it."

His emotionless words sent an icy shiver through her, despite the warm sunshine. "And?"

"Someone found out the truth about the Star Thief."

THE END

Thanks for reading ATHENA'S ASHES. I hope you enjoyed it!

- Would you like to know when my next book is available? You can sign up for my new release e-mail list at http://eepurl.com/DDYhj,.

- Reviews help other readers find books. I appreciate all reviews, whether positive or negative.

- You've just read the second full-length book in the Star Thief Chronicles series. The other books in the series are The Star Thief, and a bridge novella, Fortune's Risk. I hope you enjoy them all!

If you'd like to read an excerpt from the novella, Fortune's Risk, please turn the page.

ABOUT THE AUTHOR

Jamie Grey writes sci-fi and futuristic romance about smart women and the men who fall in love with them.

She spent most of her childhood writing stories about princesses who saved the day and pretending to be a daring explorer. It wasn't until much later that she realized she should combine the two. Now, as a tech-obsessed gamer geek, her novels mix amazing scientific developments, future worlds, and the remarkable characters that live in them.

Jamie lives in Michigan with her significant other and their pets, who luckily tolerate her overspending on tea, books, and video games.

You can learn more about her at www.jamiegreybooks.com

ALSO AVAILABLE FROM JAMIE GREY

THE STAR THIEF
(STAR THIEF CHRONICLES #1)

Stealing another galactic secret will get her arrested, but playing by the rules might just get her killed.

At twenty-three, Renna Carrizal is the most notorious thief in the galaxy. There's just one problem - all she wants is to get out of the business.

But after Renna rescues an injured boy on her final job, she finds herself on the run from the mob instead of enjoying retirement. She unwittingly becomes ensnared by MYTH, a top-secret galactic protection agency who offer her a choice - either help them on their latest mission, or spend the rest of her life on a prison ship.

Forced to work under the watchful eye of handsome but arrogant Captain Finn, Renna learns the former mercenary-turned-hero has a few dirty secrets himself. As Renna works to discover the truth about Finn's past and keep the tantalizing man at arm's length, she unearths a plot to create an unstoppable army. The target? The human star fleet.

Now Renna must pull off the biggest job of her career - saving the galaxy. And maybe even herself.

FORTUNE'S RISK – A STAR THIEF NOVELLA (STAR THIEF CHRONICLES #1.5)

Captain Nick Finn has spent the last seven years trying to escape his drug-running past and become the perfect MYTH soldier. At the peak of his military career, he should be leading missions to capture the galaxy's most wanted criminals. Instead, he's stranded on a stolen MYTH ship with Viktis, a notorious pirate and an unlikely ally.

Being on the run from MYTH and trying to keep a low profile is nothing new for Viktis, so he's happy to set course for bustling Forever Station - the perfect place to restock supplies and squeeze in a little entertainment on the side. But for Viktis, this visit is less about fun and games and more about revenge. Kitty Cordoza, a notorious mob boss and his sister's killer, has gone all-in on a high-stakes poker game.

Only Finn can help him plant the evidence that the Station's security needs to put her away for life. But the Queen of Crime has a few tricks up her sleeve, and as they're about to find out, she's not going to show her hand until it may be too late to fold.

ULTRAVIOLET CATASTROPHE

A mind is a terrible thing to waste.

When sixteen-year-old Lexie discovers her parents have been using drugs to suppress her outrageous IQ, she understands why the advanced theories in her physics books have suddenly started making sense. But they're not done dropping bombshells. Branston Academy, a school run by the world's most powerful scientists, is searching for her so she can join them – as a research subject.

Her only safe haven is Quantum Technologies, a secret scientific community where her father works as a lead scientist. Now Lexie must prove herself at QT's school-for-geniuses, where competition is cutthroat and the other student prodigies make Albert Einstein look like an amateur. Including the infuriatingly hot Asher, QT's resident boy wonder.

But after a series of suspicious accidents in the restricted labs, Lexie discovers that Branston plans to unleash an ultraviolet catastrophe that will destroy everyone she loves. With the enemy closing in, Lexie must find the strength to face her past, or risk losing her future forever.

FORTUNE'S RISK

C aptain Nick Finn raised an eyebrow at the Ileth pirate lounging in the captain's chair. "You want me to do what?"

"Help me win a poker game," Viktis said, lowering his voice and glancing around the Athena's command center.

Finn pushed himself off the railing and shook his head. "Why the hell would I do that?" They'd been on the run two weeks. Somehow, in Viktis's head, that made the two men friends. He was sorely mistaken. "We don't have time for games. MYTH's after us. We have to keep moving."

"We're going to be on Forever Station for at least two days, Cap. That's more than enough time for you to win the tournament. Take a look." Viktis passed over his tablet.

The red, flashing font demanded Finn's attention as he scanned the garish advertisement. "The Point Blue Casino Charity Poker Tournament," he read aloud. "Five hundred thousand credit payout. Win a prototype Long-Range Ultra-explorer. Drink your weight in champagne with the most beautiful waitresses on the station."

Finn shoved the tablet back at Viktis. If the pirate thought

Finn was going to help him rig a poker game, he clearly needed professional medical attention. "Oh, hell no. This is not going to happen while I'm in charge."

Viktis tucked the tablet into the inside pocket of his coat. He then got to his feet, coming to stand beside Finn at the CIC railing. His long, leather jacket, similar to the one Renna favored, flared out behind him as he walked. Maybe it was some kind of thief uniform he wasn't aware of. Things had changed a bit since he'd been in the business.

"Listen, Cap. I know you want me off your ship and out of your life. I know you want to live happily ever after with our girl, Renna. I know you hate my Ileth guts. But did you know that the fastest way to get me out of your hair is to help me get my own ship?" Viktis grinned, rubbing his hands together. "That beauty is calling my name. She's meant for me—I can feel it in my bones."

"You sure that's not just the STDs spreading?" Finn leaned back against the railing and crossed his arms. "Why not steal it? You're a pirate."

Viktis scoffed. "Did you catch that this tournament is for charity? I'm not going to steal something that could help a bunch of kids."

"Well isn't that sweet? Maybe you do have a heart after all. But I'm still not helping you."

Viktis glanced at him from the corner of his amber eyes. "Poor little orphans don't move you? You're a hard man, Captain. Think about this for a minute. That mob family back on Hesperia? The ones who kept Myka in that crate for weeks?"

"The Cordozas." How could he forget? The kid had been filthy, nothing but skin and bones when Renna had rescued him.

The mob had moved him between five cities in four weeks. He didn't know how Myka had survived.

"Kitty Cordoza, the head of the family, will be on the station for the tournament. And to sell some recently acquired tech to the highest bidder."

"And exactly why should I care?" Finn had heard more than a few stories about the dangerous Cordoza family, including chilling tales about the woman who'd taken over for her husband after he'd been assassinated. Rumors had circulated for years, suggesting she was behind it, but no one could prove it. Her ruthless nature had earned her a host of nicknames – mostly so people didn't have to use her name in public. Whatever the truth, she'd made the Cordozas one of the most powerful mob families in the sector.

Finn had no intention of tangling with the Black Widow, especially not with MYTH breathing down their necks.

Viktis arched an eyebrow ridge, tsking. "Why, Captain. I thought your halo was shinier than that. This is the perfect opportunity to take down the whole Cordoza organization. You'd be a fucking hero. Renna wouldn't be able to keep her hands off you."

Finn started to shake his head, but Viktis threw up a hand. "Very well, if that's not enough to convince you, I'll agree to split the pot with you – fifty/fifty. I get the ship, you get the credits. It'll be a good start for keeping up with Renna. We both know she's an expensive girl to love."

Finn glared and leaned toward the pirate. "How many times do I need to say this? I am not helping you cheat at poker. We need to keep a low profile. Besides, what makes you think you're going to be the one to take Kitty down? She's got a dozen dirty lawyers ready at a moment's notice if any law enforcement agency so much as sniffs the air around her. And half a dozen senators who'd spring her if it ever got that far."

"Ah, that would be telling, wouldn't it?" Viktis shrugged. "I'm going to do this, with or without your help. I just thought you'd want to iron another badge on your MYTH uniform as the person who helped rid the galaxy of the evil Cordozas. It's kind of your thing."

"Yeah, but cheating isn't."

"It's more like a set-up, Cap. The only person getting hurt is Kitty. The kids still get their money, I still get my ship, and you get your credits to build a love nest with Renna. Everyone wins. Not to mention it'll be fun. Or have you forgotten what that is? You'd better hope Renna's gotten a lot less adventurous since I knew her. You're going to bore the girl to tears." Viktis shook his head and stalked away.

Finn clenched his hands around the cool metal railing until his knuckles turned white. Godsdammit! He wished the slim, metal pipe was the alien's fucking neck. Viktis would be lucky to get off this ship in one piece—unless Finn decided to blast him out of the airlock.

"Everything all right, sir?" Lieutenant Keva asked from her station, tilting her head in concern.

Finn carefully wound his flaring temper into a tight coil, schooling his features into a mask of impassivity. His XO saw right through his Zen bullshit most of the time, but it didn't hurt to try to keep himself in check. He was the captain of this ship, after all. He had an example to set. Even if the shithead alien threatened to launch Finn's hair-trigger temper every time he opened his mouth.

"That damned pirate better be blessing the stars that Renna made me promise to behave. Otherwise, I'd be happily teaching him religion, by offering him up to one of the gods," he added ominously.

The Delfine's grin made a dimple flash in her cheek. "He's…interesting. I found him waiting for me outside the showers this morning. Asked if I needed some help washing my back."

Finn gritted his teeth until his jaw ached before he spoke again. "Anyone who bothers my crew isn't welcome on this ship, friend of Renna's or not."

"It's fine, Captain. I can take care of myself. Viktis won't be hanging outside the showers ever again." She smiled sweetly and Finn shook his head.

"I should have known you'd put him in his place." If only Finn could do the same. But that man got under his skin in ways he didn't think possible. Finn had been through basic training with the nastiest officer in MYTH. He'd been a part of Blur's gang of miscreants. He'd even killed some of the most dangerous criminals in the galaxy, but none of those men had gotten to him like Viktis.

None of those other men had slept with Renna, either.

Finn shoved away the thought of the two of them together. It was a different point in both their lives. Renna had thought Finn was dead. Finn thought Renna was a slaver. There were so many reasons why it shouldn't matter. But every time he saw the Ileth, he couldn't help but picture the man's long fingers against Renna's sun-kissed skin.

It made him crazy.

He knew Renna had carved out her own life without him. He should be able to get past this.

The fact that Finn hadn't been able to let go of his animosity toward the roguish alien was shoved aside. He didn't even want to consider the feelings and emotions tied to his behavior.

The snick of the intercom came a second before Lieutenant Kojima's voice sounded in the CIC. "Captain, we've docked at the station."

Finn sighed and straightened. "Thank you, Flight Lieutenant." He turned on his own intercom. "We've docked at Forever Station to refuel and restock. I grant you all a forty-eight hour shore leave. Do whatever you'd like, but keep your comms on at all times. We need to be able to leave instantly if we're discovered. Dismissed."

Almost immediately, the ship filled with the sound of the crew scrambling for their gear. Forever Station was one of the biggest entertainment hubs in the Costa system. Every weird fetish, exotic food, or black market item was available there. And if it wasn't, you weren't looking hard enough.

Finn had spent entirely too much time there when he was younger, after his parents had been killed. He wasn't exactly looking forward to going back.

"Sir, do you want me to stick around? Help you with the pirate? Or the Aldanis?" Keva glanced back toward the corridor where Viktis had disappeared.

"No, go on." Finn forced a smile to his lips and nodded encouragingly. He'd been a monster these last few days, and Keva had borne the brunt of it. "You deserve shore leave more than anyone here. I'll let you know if I need your help."

He'd lucked out when Dallas had assigned her as his XO; she'd been the perfect person to help him run this ship. Now he'd forced her to go on the run from MYTH and become a traitor. Guilt surged through him, turning his stomach like he'd eaten a bad eel from Vesper Nine.

Keva nodded, oblivious to his discomfort. "Very good, sir. Comm me if you need anything." She saluted as she left the bridge, leaving Finn alone with the quiet ship and his not so quiet thoughts.

AVAILABLE NOW AT ALL MAJOR EBOOK RETAILERS